Neon Elegies

The Wolves of Woodbine Hollow
Book 2

L.B. Benson

EMERALD MOON
PRESS

If you're trying to find your shine, remember you make your own light.
xo, LB

Also by L.B. Benson

ANDROMEDA'S ACCOUNT

The Bartered Soul
The City of New Aphros
Andromeda's Vengeance
The Northman's Lullaby

———

THE WOLVES OF WOODBINE HOLLOW

Sunset Daydreams
Neon Elegies

Neon Elegies

By L.B. Benson

Wolves of Woodbine Hollow
Book Two

First print edition July 2025
EBook ISBN 979-8-9896350-4-7
Paperback ISBN 979-8-9896350-3-0

Cover design by Tyler Evelyn Rood
Illustrations by Marta García Navarro

Edited by Kelly Hammond
Pickles Literary, LLC

Content Warning & Author's Note

Neon Elegies is an adult paranormal romance that contains mature content. It is intended for readers over the age of 18.

To view detailed content/trigger warnings, please visit the author's website: https://lbtheauthor.com or scan the QR code below.

Chapter 1
Lana

Familial tension looms large in the small, wood paneled meeting room. The pine is designed to mimic the logs of the cabin above us and make the space feel homier than the concrete walls underneath. To make the pack feel like we're with nature even when business forces us indoors. Unfortunately, feeling like I'm trapped inside a tree does little to ease my nerves.

I've never liked basements. I don't like the feeling of being trapped underground, of being trapped at all. I need to see the sky and feel the wind whisper over me. But today, I tamp down my displeasure to support my brother. He sits next to our father at the carved table used for pack business in Alpha Cameron's home. I stand behind Shane's chair, just enough to the side where I can see his expression. I'm between him and the door, keeping watch and worrying at my fingernails while I hold my hands behind my back. Watching his back like I promised. We are the only ones present besides Alpha Cameron, and while I don't expect anyone to cause trouble, I'm still alert. Apparently, that's my only setting now.

After lunch, Shane insisted that our mom help Kaycia settle in at home while we find out what consequences our actions at his cabin have reaped. I had hoped Aubrey would come with us, someone else from our family who wasn't involved directly in the conflict to lend support, but when I searched for him, he was already out running in the woods. He's been distant since Shane returned, but I haven't asked him about it, too preoccupied with my own problems, and with what happens next for Shane. For me. For our family.

Now, the conversation has taken a turn I didn't expect.

It seems I'm not the only one unprepared for what Alpha Cameron has proposed.

"What are you talking about?" Shane asks incredulously, looking between our father and Jon Cameron, the alpha of the pack we were born into. The only alpha we've known. The man who handed down Shane's exile ten years ago.

"Exactly what I said." Alpha Cameron's tone is softer than I'm used to. Relieved even. His eyes seem tired, and from where I'm standing, I notice how worn he looks. "Your win over Colton Ross has changed everything. It's offered the opportunity for our communities to finally merge peacefully."

"No. Not that. The part about your plan to name *me* heir to *your* pack."

It's been a decade since I've been around my brother, but that doesn't mean I can't read the tension coiled in his shoulders when he catches my eye. I give a tight-lipped look in return, hoping it says, *"I had no idea about this either."*

If I'm reeling from the announcement, I can only imagine how my brother—a wolf who up until last week had been unable to set foot in our home territory or have any contact with his family—is processing the information that our alpha planned on making *him* his heir despite the exile agreement with the neighboring pack.

The rival pack which Shane is, for all intents and purposes, the leader of now.

"Since you defeated Colton, your alpha status will negate the exile. You'll be announced as my heir and the acting alpha for the Galax Ridge pack at the next gathering," Alpha Cameron states.

He's around our father's age but looks older. The stress of losing his son and heir a decade ago, and the pressures of navigating pack politics, have etched deep lines in his tanned, weather-beaten skin. His beard is completely silver and thick streaks of gray run through his dark hair. He smiles gently at Shane, the way he used to when we were pups and he would have dinner at our house before talking for hours with our father, his second.

"You and Ethan were like brothers, Shane. You're the closest thing I still have to a son."

Is that regret I hear in his tone?

But Shane isn't as sentimental as I must be. A sneer curls his lip when he asks coldly, "And what if I don't want that? I didn't want to challenge Colton in the first place. I didn't want to be alpha of *one* pack, let alone two."

I cut my eyes toward Shane at the same time as our father. Our dad's eyes widen in surprise, but I expected this. I just hope it doesn't drag Shane into more shit. My older brother has insisted he didn't want to take over from the moment Colton Ross' wolves dragged me, hooded and drugged, from the back of their SUV. I don't think Shane would have ever challenged Colton if Kaycia hadn't been at risk that night.

I feel sorry for Shane, even if I resent the years he's been absent. Years I've spent trying to fill the void he left in our family and pack. He's spent his entire adulthood building a life alone, and now that he has a girlfriend and a successful business hundreds of miles away, he's dragged back home and burdened with a responsibility he never asked for.

This isn't good news to him.

I'll give it to him though, he has balls to question Jon Cameron outright.

Alpha Cameron's jaw flinches, and his eyes sharpen when he meets my brother's gaze, but he gives Shane a sad smile. "A wolf needs a pack, son. A family. I'm glad to have you back." He reaches across the scarred wood of the table to pat the back of Shane's hand.

"I have a family. I had to make my own when *you* exiled me." Shane's expression remains neutral, but I tense at the ice in his tone.

He flexes the hand still beneath Cameron's, making the awful, shiny scar on his forearm reflect the overhead light. I glance down at my own forearm where the Cameron pack mark stands out, the design etched in black ink. The same mark that was carved from Shane's flesh the night they sent him away for killing Logan Ross.

Jon Cameron exhales, dropping his gaze in a rare look of defeat and pulls his hand back.

"Maybe we should table this discussion," our father, Sean McKinley, offers. "Shane's only been home for a day, Jon. He's going to need time to reacquaint himself. We still have to determine how the transition should be handled with the remaining Rosses."

"We've given them seven days to bury their dead and mourn their losses. The gathering will be at the end of that time. Shane, you'll need to consider what you'd like to do. I won't pressure you to stay. I understand this is sudden. Your hand was forced when Colton threatened your family and involved a human." Cameron stands, the motion triggering my father to rise and Shane to follow.

I remain at attention at the head of the table, still standing as my brother's second, whether he wishes to be alpha or not. Whether I wish to bear that responsibility.

"We can merge the packs under my and your father's leadership if you wish, Shane," Cameron reassures. "To give you time to decide how you'll proceed. But I hope you'll return and take the place I'm offering you."

Alpha Cameron extends his hand to Shane, meeting my eyes over my brother's shoulder before they shake. As if I have any influence on this male who's returned like a prodigal son. We may have been thick as thieves as children, but all I really know about my brother now is that he's grown to be a good man and a strong wolf. But that doesn't mean he's going to uproot his life to come back here for one pack that ruined his life and the other that didn't defend him.

My father and I both dip our heads in respect when Shane steps away from our alpha. Shane maintains eye contact though. He's an alpha now, too. At least until he chooses otherwise.

"I'll think about it. And talk it over with Kaycia. But no promises." With that Shane turns and leads the way out the heavy door.

My father walks at my side while we trail behind. When I catch his eye he gives a smile, but he can't hide the worry that radiates from him as he watches Shane prowl to the big black truck he borrowed from his friend Max for the trip to Woodbine Hollow.

"Go run with him tonight," Dad mutters when the driver's side door slams, shutting Shane off from us.

"I don't think a run is going to make him change his mind right now," I reply, rounding to the back passenger door while my father places his hand on the front handle. "He has a whole life away from here."

"I know. But it might help remind him of what he's missed. What he could have again."

I swallow and nod. I can't explain to our father what I witnessed at Shane's cabin. Despite the chill of the rain and the fear and blood, I saw exactly what Shane would be leaving behind. The friends who came to his aid without a thought for themselves. The love that's kept him afloat when ours was too far away.

I never envied my brother's exile, but at that moment I envied his life.

———

The sun dips below the trees, the sky turning pretty shades of pink and orange, but Shane doesn't pause to admire the Woodbine Hollow skies. He parks next to Mom's beat-up truck, cuts the engine, and hops out of the driver's seat without a word. The ten-minute drive home was silent except for the soft music on the radio and the crunch of gravel as we crawled up the driveway. Shane caught my eyes in the rearview mirror a couple of times, but I kept my mouth shut to let him process.

I can't help but smile when I see his dark expression transform at the sight of Kaycia waiting for him on the porch swing. She leaves her sketchbook and blanket on the cushion and hurries to throw her arms around his neck when he reaches the stairs. Shane buries his face in her wild blonde mane, and I have to look away from their happiness.

If I watch for too long, I'll think about Taryn.

And if I think about her, I might not be able to keep up the collected front I've maintained since I moved back home. I might give in to the urge to go through the old photos on my phone or think about texting her.

Dad claps me on the shoulder, making me gasp at the unexpected jolt. "You okay, Honeybee?" he asks, still calling me by my childhood nickname.

"Yeah." I blink, hoping the dust from the driveway can be blamed for any water in my eyes. My dad just narrows his gaze, disbelieving. I've never been good at lying, but I can smile and hide how bad I really feel if he doesn't look too closely. He drops it, thankfully, smiling and gripping my shoulder before giving me an affectionate shake and patting my back once before he goes around back to his workshop.

Everyone in the McKinley family has a place where they retreat when they need to forget their troubles. My dad to his workshop, my mother to her garden, Aubrey to the woods. It seems Shane's place is Kaycia. And since I was a kid, my place has been music, especially my fiddle. A place Taryn has broken, too, even though she was never truly a part of it.

My hands itch for my bow, for a pen and notebook to expunge the sadness in ink and the shape of musical notes so I don't have to admit any of the feelings out loud. I don't say anything to either of them, now speaking quietly on the porch swing, as I rush through the front door and up the stairs to my room. Neither Shane nor I seem in the mood for a run right now.

Chapter 2
Max

"So, when are you getting back in town?" I ask, holding my phone between my cheek and shoulder while loading my guitar case into the back of Ryan's car. "I don't mind you having my truck, but it would be nice to have it before our next gig."

"I know. We're heading back this weekend. I had to go with my dad to meet with his alpha and some of the representatives from the Ross pack to discuss the new hierarchy," Shane explains. In the background, the sounds of a full house surround my friend—pots and pans banging, ice hitting glasses from a refrigerator's ice maker, and women's voices chattering. "It's all working out smoother than I expected. I'll explain more when we get back. I'll send a message with an ETA when we're on the road."

"Sounds good," I reply, getting into the front seat where Ryan sits behind the wheel. With a nod hello, I add, "Is that Lana I hear? She doing okay?"

"Seems to be. She's a tough one. That hasn't changed since she was a kid."

"Tell her I say 'hi'." I buckle my seatbelt, ignoring Ryan's curious look. He pulls away from the curb and taps his fingers on the wheel while we wait for a light to turn green.

Shane snorts a laugh in that sarcastic way that I know is accompanied by an eye roll. "Tell her yourself." After a moment, he says, clearly on speakerphone, "Hey, Lana! Max is on the phone."

"How's that pretty bird doing cooped up in the big city?" Lana's honey-warm voice coos from somewhere near Shane, but it's obvious that she's not speaking directly into the phone as the sounds of cooking continue.

I remember the woman well. Hell, I've thought about her regularly since I woke to find her staring down at me soaking wet in her ragged tee and jeans that night in front of Shane's cabin. I thought an angel had come down to carry me off. Turns out it was just my best friend's little sister.

No wings—just claws and a wicked smile.

That was right before she saved her brother by shooting a guy. She's a different kind of angel altogether.

I should probably be less focused on how she looked at me that night, and more concerned about how easily she pulled the trigger, but shifters are a different breed, wolves especially. They take care of their own.

"Hey, darlin'. You remember that any time you want to check out this big city you have someone who knows all the best places."

"Ha!" Lana laughs. "Kaycia has told me all about you, buddy. I guarantee that you tell all the girls that. And the boys, too."

"Kaycia! What lies have you been telling about me?"

"I would never!" Kaycia giggles, feigned shock reflected in her voice, then asks more seriously, "Are my plants alive?"

"Yes, your two sad little plants are fine. You both just bring my truck back or I'll hold Shane's bike for ransom."

"Someone help me get these dishes to the table, please!" another woman's voice cuts through the conversation before Shane, no longer on speakerphone, says, "Gotta go, man. I'll be in touch."

"Yeah, all right. Bye." I end the call as Ryan pulls onto the main street heading into the city.

"McKinley bringing your truck back soon? I'm sick of having to lug all your shit with me for gigs," Ryan says, turning the radio up now that the call is over.

I scowl, but there's no real malice behind it. "I'm not even going to answer that. I've driven you and Jet around for years, you can return the favor for a couple weeks. You ready for tonight?"

"Yeah, Aces Wild is always a good time. They like to get rowdy, and we can find someone to keep us warm when we're done too." Ryan grins, looking at me over his sunglasses before merging into traffic and picking up speed.

"Yeah, it is warm tonight." I reply, distracted. I realize too late that he wasn't talking about the weather.

"You good, man?"

"Yeah." I make an excuse rather than admit that, for some reason, the idea of a random hook-up has lost its appeal in the last few weeks. "Thinking about some new songs I've been working on. I've got a couple projects lined up for work, too. Just busy."

"Sounds good." Ryan side eyes me, but brushes off my mood by keeping the beat on the steering wheel before we exit toward the city proper.

———

Shot glasses clink together as the guys and I toast with three women at the bar. I'm not really in the mood to party tonight, but I'll be a good sport for the band. The trio of tourists caught Ryan's eye from stage when we were packing up and he dragged me over to meet them shortly after. Jet is the shyest of us, giving a sideways smile to the brunette in a short skirt who's got herself propped on his lap. Ladies love drummers almost as much as they love lead singers, whether they can hold a conversation or not, and this one seems to be no exception, encouraging Jet to put his hand high on her bare thigh while she talks.

Ryan's happy to flirt with either of the other two, always down to be a wingman for me. But tonight, I can't seem to hit my stride, missing questions and only half-heartedly flirting as I sip a longneck.

The show was a good one, even if Aces Wild wasn't as busy as Lucy's usually is, and the crowd looked like they were having a good time. It's always a rush when they sing along with your original music and not just cover songs.

It's an equal rush finding someone in the crowd to connect with for the night. But when the blonde standing closest to me strokes her manicured fingers down my forearm and looks up at me through her lashes, the same way she'd been eyeing me while I was on stage, I can only think of the blonde she isn't. The one who ribbed me on speakerphone a few hours ago. The one I may never see again.

I don't even know this woman's name, but she presses closer to me, wrapping her arms around my neck to pull me in. I lean down, thinking that if I go along with her train of thought, I might be pleasantly surprised. She smiles, biting her lip and looking between my eyes and mouth, clearly wanting me to make the first move. When our lips meet, she tastes like cheap tequila.

I kiss her half-heartedly, but she's not deterred, letting out a little moan before she pulls away and whispers, "Wanna go back to our hotel room?" She runs one palm down my chest and toward my belt, but I catch her hand with mine before it descends below my stomach.

"Sorry," I reply, stepping away from her and releasing her hand. "I've got an early day tomorrow. A project to present to a client."

"What are you talking about?" Ryan asks. He has the other woman's lipstick smeared on his mouth and his arm around her waist. He and Jet exchange a look of confusion.

"I'll just grab a cab, but you guys have fun." I distance myself from them, leaving the blonde with a frown on her pouty lips. "It was nice to meet you," I tell the woman, then turn to grab my guitar case.

"I'll be right back," Jet says behind me. My hearing is acute enough that I can tell when he scoots the barstool back and sets the girl on her feet. Then, I track his footsteps hurrying to catch up with me as I near the door.

"Max! Hey, man. Wait up!" Jet jogs so he walks out the door right behind me. The air is cool tonight, ruffling my hair and drying any of the sweat still dampening my scalp after the show. I close my eyes for a moment before looking at Jet.

"What's wrong? She not your type?" Jet looks back toward the door, indicating the woman I left behind.

"Not tonight." I'm not sure why Lana McKinley has such a hold over me, but it doesn't feel right to have spoken to her earlier and to be fucking someone else tonight.

"All right," Jet mumbles, looking unsure of what to do next. "You want to talk or anything?"

"Nah, man. Go have a good time. I've just got some shit on my mind." I run a hand through my hair, looking at the passing cars instead of meeting his eyes.

"Okay. Let me know if you need anything." Jet gives me a solid pat to the back, then slips back into the door of the slowly emptying bar.

I flag down the next cab, sighing before I shake my head with a soft laugh. If only Jet, or anyone in this city, could help me with what I need.

Chapter 3
Lana

"So, Shane. You're leaving the day after tomorrow?" our father asks, passing a basket of rolls around the dining table.

"Yeah," Shane answers, his hand not as surreptitiously stroking Kaycia's thigh under the table as he thinks it is. They are so clearly in love that it would make me want to gag a little if I didn't like them so much. "Kaycia needs to get back to her paintings and I have bikes that have to be worked on. Raquel has held down the shop as well as she can, but she can't do it alone much longer." He looks up with a tight jaw, adding, "I'll have to figure out a schedule if I'm going to be coming back to check-in with the pack more."

"I still can't believe that boy got so lost," Mama mutters shaking her head.

"It all worked out in the end," Dad replies, scooping green beans onto his plate.

I catch Kaycia's eye and give her a little smile. Meeting

your new boyfriend's family is stressful enough. Being the only human in a room full of wolves casually discussing the man you shot to defend that boyfriend can't be easy for her. Even if her bullet wasn't the fatal one.

In any other household, my shooting and killing the neighbor would *not* be considered things "working out". But since Colton Ross broke numerous pack rules, kidnapped me to try to lure Shane back from his exile, and then attempted to kill Shane when he had won a challenge fair and square, my defense of my brother was looked upon as justice by both packs.

Thankfully, they managed to side-step the topic of whether or not I should have been a contender for alpha since my bullet ended Colton Ross. My interest in leadership is even less than Shane's.

The meetings between Shane, Cameron, and the representatives from the former Ross pack went smoothly. The decision to merge leadership wasn't as dramatic as Shane had feared, owing to the fact that no one living in Galax Ridge was particularly happy with Colton's ruthless leadership, and that Jon Cameron posed it as a temporary decision while Shane reacquaints himself with pack life after his exile.

With Alpha Cameron and our father agreeing to manage both packs temporarily, Shane is free to return to his life in the city. For now.

Shane agreed to weigh in on decisions and to return for major events. With the exile lifted, he can come home whenever he wants, and this solution allows him more than a few weeks to decide whether returning as alpha permanently is the future he wants. He won't be given forever though.

I've been present in the talks about the changes, but I've tried to downplay my involvement in the whole fiasco, and have managed to avoid mentioning the nightmare of wearing a burlap hood crammed in the back of that SUV to anyone. No one knows about the flashbacks of shallow breaths and blurred vision from the rough fabric. I don't want them to know that my mind and memories are hazy and untrustworthy from the drugs they forced into me to keep me subdued while they hunted my brother. Or that I've been waking each night since the challenge haunted by the fear of being taken again and the vision of Colton's blank stare hovering in front of me. Somehow neither Aubrey nor Shane have heard me when I wake from my dreams, despite sharing a wall on either side in our childhood home. If they have heard anything, they've kept it to themselves.

I did what was necessary, but it's getting harder to mask the way that choice makes me feel. My emotions were already raw over my move home before Colton's men grabbed me. Now, it's like they've been run through a meat grinder. Like I'm a sausage without its casing—falling apart. Fear and guilt and rage and relief all vie for the top spot depending on the moment.

The conversation carries on, discussing everything from the weather to who gets the last roll, but I remain quiet, focused on the idea that's been swirling in my mind. I want to talk to Shane alone before he gets packed up. If I wait too long, it will be too late.

He and Kaycia whisper to one another, leaning close and stealing little touches, each one like a paper cut to my wounded heart. I need to get away from this town. This pack. All the things that remind me of my losses. And I think my big brother is the way to do it.

Even if I have to ride back suffering through their cuteness.

Loading the dishwasher, I scent Shane before he passes by the kitchen on his way up to his old room. He's been sharing the space with Kaycia since they've been here, and I can't be the only one who's noticed that their scents are entwined almost as tightly as our parents'. She may be a human, but he's bonded to her. Their relationship is as serious as if they were married in the eyes of the wolves.

"Hey, Shane! Hold up a sec?"

He pops his sandy head around the wall with a curious expression as I towel off my hands and turn the dishwasher on.

"Come outside with me? I need to ask you something."

"This can't be good," he jokes before realizing I'm serious. He cocks his head, his smile fading as he studies me more closely. "Everything all right?"

I brush his concern off with a sarcastic smile and eye roll. "Yep, just come on."

The air is cool on the porch, autumn is inching forward and the open skies of the countryside make it feel colder, even tucked in the cradle of the tree covered mountains. I pull on an oversized sweatshirt and pull my legs into it on the porch swing while Shane leans against the railing, arms crossed with wary eyes.

"What's going on, Lana?"

"I want to come back with you."

"Elaborate." His brow is furrowed, but the tilt of his head is encouraging.

"To Argent. I want to ride back with you and Kaycia. Can I do that? Do you think I could stay with one of you for a little bit? Just until I can find a job and my own apartment?"

"What brought this on? Seems sudden for you to just pack up." Shane is hard to read. He doesn't seem upset at the idea, but it's been so long since I spent time with him that I can't tell what he's thinking anymore. He's colder and quieter now than he was when he lived at home. Exile and being hunted will do that to someone, I guess.

"It's not sudden. My girlfriend and I split up a few months ago. It's why I'm living with Mom and Dad again," I explain, pulling my arms into the sleeves of my sweatshirt so I'm just a ball of fleece with a head and sock-covered feet.

"Oh," he says, rubbing a hand across the back of his neck. "I guess that makes sense. When I heard you on the phone the day I called Mom, I figured you hadn't left home. But when I walked past your room the other day I noticed the stuff overflowing from your bags. I thought maybe—"

"That I was a horrific slob?" I cut him off with a frown.

"I mean... I've been gone ten years, but some shit doesn't change."

"Oh, fuck you!" I laugh, sticking one arm out of my sleeve to throw one of the little decorative pillows from the porch swing at him.

"I'm sure Kaycia will let me shack up with her. You can stay at my apartment if you want. Neither of us has had time to replace our stuff that got trashed by Colton's boys, but we can make do."

"Ugh, will I have to share a wall with you two? My ears might bleed." Shane looks confused for a moment, brows drawing together before I add, "I know y'all haven't been sneaking out for hikes, brother."

Shane blushes so hard his ears turn red, but he rolls his eyes.

"Gods damn it, Lana. You're the one who wants to come back with us. Beggars can't be choosers, little sister." He pauses with a resigned sigh, then gives a sideways smile, glancing up toward the window of his old room, where Kaycia is probably waiting for him right now. "You and Raquel are going to be an absolute nightmare, aren't you?"

I chuckle, remembering the fierce little raccoon shifter threatening Colton Ross with a shotgun.

"When we get back to the city, we can find you somewhere to live and figure out a job. What have you been doing for work?"

"Waiting tables at the diner, but they'll be fine without me. I can get another serving job in the city."

"My friend Jamila may be able to help. I'll send her a message and see. Be ready to go Friday morning."

I give him a nod. "Thanks, Shane."

"Sure thing." He pushes off the railing as I stand up, pulling me into a bear hug, and rocking me roughly from side to side until I laugh and push him away. Some things haven't changed. "If you need to talk, I'm here now. I'm sorry I wasn't before."

"I know." I swallow, hiding my real feelings with a false smile and cold shoulder as I go back inside. He doesn't need to know all the shit that plagues me.

Maybe I'll tell him once we are back in the city he calls home now. Maybe I won't.

But either way, I need a change of scenery.

Chapter 4
Lana

"You gonna say bye?" I ask, kicking Aubrey's foot where it sticks out from his blankets. He scowls, but his eyes are bright, no trace of sleep clouding them even though it's just shy of six in the morning.

"You're the one running away." Aubrey pouts just like he did when he was still a pup and I wouldn't let him come with me somewhere.

"I'm *not* running away. I just need some time." I lean against the door frame, my arms crossed over my chest, but I can't seem to meet his eyes. "I just need some space to figure shit out."

"I know," he whispers, looking down at his hands. His knuckles are scarred, some look freshly healed. But I don't get a chance to ask what happened before he adds, "I'm sorry it all went down this way, Lana. I should have done something. Should have known."

"For the last time, stop apologizing. You couldn't have known. It's no one's fault. Certainly not yours."

Aubrey still doesn't meet my eye, so I plop down on the edge of the mattress and give a little pinch to his arm to force him to snap out of it. None of this is his fault. Hell, it isn't even Shane's fault. And I won't have anyone feeling sorry for themselves on my behalf.

He squirms and elbows me, finally smiling. His hair is the same color as mine and Shane's, mussed and sticking up from tossing and turning, but his eyes are blue instead of hazel. I always joked that he was the prettiest of us.

"Brother?" I draw out the word, suspicious of his reticence this morning.

"Yeah?"

"You need to tell me something?" I study him, giving a pointed look at his hands and trying to sense what he's hiding.

"No." At the sight of my quirked lip and raised eyebrow he insists, "I told you it's over." Emotions war in his expression, his eyes are sad, but his mouth is tight with anger and he rubs a palm across his knuckles.

I narrow my eyes at him, not sure I believe him or those fresh marks. Before I can give him any more shit though, Aubrey sits up and I give in, wrapping him in a hug, just like I used to when he was a little kid. He squeezes me once and I remember when he used to come running to me just as often as he did to Mama when he was upset. A part of me feels guilty for leaving him here. The last of the McKinley kids in Woodbine Hollow. But nothing says Shane and I both won't come back for good soon. And I keep reminding myself that I can't be there for anyone as fucked up as I feel right now.

"Look, I'll keep in touch. You can call or text me anytime you need something. And I'm sure Shane and I will come back pretty often for pack stuff."

Aubrey huffs a little, pushing me gently to get me to stand, then follows me toward the open doorway. "I'm used to him being gone. I'll miss *you* though."

"Hey—" I stop before we leave his room, grabbing his arm. "You can't be mad at him for being hesitant to come back after all he's dealt with. Alone."

Aubrey looks chastened for a moment. He greeted Shane warmly when he and Kaycia arrived, but I think it disappointed him that Shane wasn't the same big brother who left ten years ago. I've been focused on keeping track of shit with this alpha transition and trying to get a few hours of sleep. I couldn't worry about repairing the sibling bond this week. Aubrey's troubles will have to wait.

Kaycia and Shane are already outside with our parents. Our bags are stored in the truck and the doors stand open, waiting for us to load up. Kaycia smiles, hugging Mama like she's been part of the family for years. She fit in well during her visit, adapting to the routine and exploring the forest and countryside, snapping pictures and sketching things that caught her attention. Even though she's human, she got along with my parents better than Taryn ever did. I try not to think about that particular ache right now.

Shane walks up to the porch and holds his hand out to Aubrey, and I sigh a relieved exhale when Aubrey walks past it and wraps him in a hug. They pat each other's backs for a few seconds before pulling apart. Then it's my turn to say goodbye. I hold Aubrey tight, hoping whatever he's keeping close isn't going to get him hurt.

Saying goodbye to my parents is filled with conflicting emotions; restlessness tingles under my skin and I'm ready to get on the road, but I'm going to miss this place. The sun is just coming up, bathing the mountains and trees surrounding our cabin with muted light and casting my parents in a warm glow. I don't know how the hell Shane did this by himself.

"You be sure to call me and let me know how you're doing. You can come home anytime you want to if you don't like it there," Mama says, brushing away tears before they can fall.

"I'm twenty-five, Mama. I'll be fine," I whisper with a half-hearted laugh. I don't cry. I'll save that for when I'm alone. "I love you."

"Be good, Honeybee." My father holds himself together better than Mama, but his tight embrace tells me things will be somber at the dinner table tonight.

"Love you, Daddy."

"Love you, too."

I wasn't sure what to expect from Argent. The city is almost mythical, a place where no one knows you, where you can escape and live out your wildest dreams. But riding in the backseat while Shane and Kaycia chat about plans and people I don't know, or point out sights to me like tour guides, I don't see anything all that magical.

People mill about on the sidewalk, so many more than I'm used to seeing at once, avoiding one another instinctively like they're performing a dance I don't know the steps to. Traffic stops and goes at the whim of lights and honking horns. The buildings reflect the bright sunlight off broad sheets of reflective glass and connecting steel—shining silver like the city's namesake. I suddenly feel like a poor country girl as my eyes shift from building to building, car to car, person to person. The lack of wilderness chafes already. I understand now why Shane has his cabin. He can't possibly be content in this anthill.

What have I done?

I thought running away from Woodbine Hollow to new surroundings would be what I needed to get my mind off Taryn leaving me and the mess with Colton. But now I wonder if I've just asked to be inserted into a different kind of nightmare.

"How can you stand it?" I ask, blurting out the question over the radio.

"What?" Shane asks, glancing at me in the rearview mirror.

"How can you stand this place? It's... too much."

"You get used to it," Shane answers, watching both me and the road in intervals, as though he fears I might open the back door and throw myself into the street.

"You do after a little while. I was so homesick, well, until I started hanging out with Shane," Kaycia confides, her pretty face turning pink when she glances over at him. His soft smile reminds me of how Taryn used to look at me and a pit settles in my stomach. "I basically stayed in my apartment, doing nothing but working until Shane brought me into his little group. We can introduce you to Jamila—she's Raquel's partner—and you already know Quel and Max. We'll all help you get used to it!"

Kaycia has turned in her seat so she's looking at me, beaming a smile so sweet I can't help but return it. The thought of Max makes the smile feel more genuine. He was something else.

I don't think I'll ever forget him transforming from his broken falcon form into the shape of a handsome human man. He wasn't what I expected when he started talking either, that deep voice like whiskey and honey. The bravery he showed in attacking a wolf on his own, just to free me and buy Shane some time, secured him a place on my good side. And seeing him walk around with nothing but Raquel's jacket tied around his waist lightened the mood enough to keep me from losing my mind.

For a little while at least.

I sobbed almost the entire lonely drive back to Woodbine Hollow, gripping the steering wheel so hard my fingers ached. But hearing his soft drawl on speakerphone when he does his regular check in with Shane has been diverting.

A little harmless flirting between friends never hurt anyone.

Shane parks at the curb in front of a three-story building that looks like an old house from a storybook. Trees line the street, but everything is crammed together—stores, apartments, offices—it's hard for me to focus on any one thing without something else catching my eye, my shifter senses on overdrive as I breathe in the different scents and try to sort through all the noise.

"This is it," he announces, killing the engine.

"Thank the gods," Kaycia whines, stretching as she slides out of the passenger seat to stand on the sidewalk. "I'm so sick of sitting in the truck."

"Would you have rather been on the bike?" Shane teases, wrapping his arms around her when he gets to the sidewalk.

"Absolutely not. My ass hurt bad enough on the long route to the cabin." She grins up at him and he slides his hands over her back pockets to sneak a squeeze.

Why did I think coming back to a strange city with two people who are newly in love would get my mind off things?

Groaning inwardly, I jump out of the backseat to join them on the sidewalk. My presence drags Shane away from Kaycia. "Come on, let me help you get some of this stuff and I'll show you to my place."

He takes my suitcase, while I grab a duffle and my fiddle case. Shane had raised his eyebrows when I packed our grandfather's fiddle but he still hasn't asked me about the instrument. When he left home, I was still practicing, my skills far from proficient. He carries Kaycia's bag in his other hand while she unlocks the front door and they both lead me up three flights of stairs.

"No wonder you two ended up together," I joke when we make it to the small, shared landing between their two apartments. "Was the landlord a matchmaker? How could you not run into each other all the time?"

"You'd be surprised," Kaycia laughs. "It took me nearly knocking him down the stairs to get him to notice me." She slides a key into the door on the right and swings it open. When I follow them inside, I run my fingertips over the deeply gouged claw marks on the door and shudder. The other door sporting new locks and hinges must be Kaycia's because the open loft I'm standing in is as uptight and minimal as my older brother.

Inside the apartment, the strong scent of wolf mingles with aftershave and oil, the familiar smells of my brother making me feel secure in the strange city. Kaycia's perfume is there too, along with that of a raccoon, the soothing feminine fragrance of another woman, and the same masculine scent of cologne and falcon that lingered in the truck. Max has been here recently, and the thought of him makes my heart flutter a little against my better judgment. I wonder how long it will be until I get to see him.

Chapter 5
Max

"Max, this is really good!" Jamila croons, skimming the lyrics I've jotted down in the little notebook I keep on me almost all the time. "It's different than your usual stuff."

"Is that good or bad?" I ask, grinning at her. Our styles are different but I don't think she's bullshitting me.

"It's just raw and emotional. You're usually more of the 'fun guy'. The last moody piece was something Jet wrote, right?" She hums a melody to herself, toying with the words of the song I've shown her.

"Yeah. I guess I'm growing, huh? I have a couple others that I'm working on with the guys."

"Anything to do with a pretty wolf that crossed your path recently?" Raquel asks, plopping onto the sofa next to Jamila as she rips open a bag of chips.

Shane and Kaycia are supposed to be back in town this afternoon, so I'm killing time until they get home. Raquel and Jamila's place is closer to Shane and Kaycia's than my condo, and I won't have to fly out again since I finished up my work in the city.

"Aren't you supposed to be at the shop, you pest?" I return. I won't confirm or deny whether I was inspired by a certain blonde wolf.

"Well, I took the afternoon off to spend with my girl-friend, but *someone* needed to come discuss their art." Raquel purses her lips with a pointed look, narrowing her eyes while Jamila laughs and waves her off.

"We have plenty of time for dinner and drinks, my love," Jamila says. "Sometimes art can't wait. Now that we have Kaycia in the group, you and Shane are just going to have to learn to love our creative mania."

"Whatever." Raquel shoves a handful of chips in her mouth, brushing the crumbs off as she shakes her head with an indulgent smile, turning her head to me. "Have you talked to Lana since they left? Or were you just being you?"

"What the hell is that supposed to mean? What does 'being me' mean?"

"That you'll flirt with, and fuck, anything with legs?" Raquel offers.

"That's not fair."

"I'm not slut shaming you, Max. I'm just being honest. You're known to be quite successful in your conquests. I just wasn't sure how you were going to try to storm the castle that is our best friend's sister."

"Raquel! Lana isn't some fortress to be breached!" Jamila acts shocked but turns her attention back to me with a somber expression. "Shane will probably murder you if you hurt his sister. Or she'll take care of you herself."

"You two are way ahead of yourselves. I was just being friendly. It's not like I'm going to see her again. She lives days away and I've only said a handful of words to her since she left."

Jamila gives me a look that tells me she can tell I'm lying, then holds up the notebook with raised eyebrows. "Mmm hmm. Okay, Mister Delusional."

I'm saved by the chime of a text message.

KAYCIA

Ten minutes out if you want to meet us at the apartment.

Sounds good. I'm at Quel and J's. Be there in a bit.

She replies with a thumbs up emoji and I tuck my phone back in my back pocket.

"Well, that's my cue. I'm heading over to Shane's to get my truck. You want to hang onto that, J? I'd welcome suggestions."

"Sure, let me just take a picture of it and I'll see what I can do. Did you have a melody or anything in mind? I was just playing around but you know I don't know music as well as you."

"I have the beginnings of something," I answer, then sing a few of the lines a capella for her to get the idea.

"Okay, kind of rough and folksy then?" She nods approvingly. "I'll see what I can do." Jamila snaps a picture on her phone, then hands the beat-up notebook back to me. "It's good, Max. I really like it."

"Thanks, J. See ya, Quel. Y'all have fun tonight." I let myself out of their apartment, heading toward Shane and Kaycia's building. It's only a few blocks away, and I don't feel like stashing my clothes to shift. Since it's a nice, early autumn day, the walk won't hurt a bit.

Waiting at the crosswalk a block from Shane's I can't help but hum the melody I've been working on, the lyrics for a second verse escaping me. I sigh, pushing my hair from my eyes as I continue across the road and around the corner by the little market.

My timing is excellent.

My truck is already parked in front of their building, doors open to be unloaded. Shane is striding down the steps of the building to take a bag from Kaycia. They smile unguardedly at one another, the emotions between them written in every motion and line of their bodies. A little pang of—*is that envy?*—stabs at my chest.

Jamila and Raquel weren't wrong. I do find myself in the arms of lovers easily, but none have ever stuck. I'm beginning to realize as all my friends pair up that I'm getting a little lonesome. My falcon vision hones in on movement at the door of the building, pulling my attention to the figure in the doorway. I know my vision is excellent, but I have to push my sunglasses up and narrow my eyes to focus on the last person I expected to see.

What the fuck is Lana doing in Argent?

I'm not the least bit upset to see her, especially when she slings a backpack over her shoulder, slams the truck door, and locks eyes with me, raising a brow and flashing a playful grin that steals my breath.

———

"Well, well, fine seeing you fully clothed in the daylight," Lana greets me with a laugh.

When she smiles again, I can see the little gap between her front teeth that I found so endearing the night we met, despite the circumstances. I've seen that smile in my dreams, even if I keep telling myself nothing can happen with Shane's sister.

"Didn't expect to see you, darlin'. Couldn't resist coming back to me?" I tease.

"Don't flatter yourself, pretty bird," she retorts.

"Here are your keys," Shane interrupts, a crease between his brows as he looks between Lana and me, holding my truck keys out. Perhaps he's just as protective of her as he is of Kaycia. "Thanks for letting me borrow it. I filled it up on the way back into town."

"Thanks," I reply, catching the tossed keys. "How was the trip?"

"Better than expected," he replies.

"I'm going to go up to help get Lana settled in," Kaycia says to Shane. Smiling at me, she asks, "You want to come up?"

"Nah," I answer. I suspect she's just being polite. I'm not sure if Kaycia is capable of being anything else. They've been on the road for a while and are probably ready to figure out what they have left in their respective places after they got trashed. Raquel, Jamila, and I managed to help clean up the messiest parts for them while they hid at Shane's cabin, but there's still a lot to sort through. "But you two owe me dinner for cleaning and watching your places. Let's all plan to grill at my place this weekend. Bring steaks." I wink at Lana. "You come, too."

"I'll check my busy schedule," Lana replies with a sarcastic huff.

"Sounds good," Shane answers, shaking my hand as Kaycia and Lana head up the stairs and into the building. I watch, hoping Lana might look back, but she just lets the entry door slam behind her. "Thanks again for letting me use the truck."

"What's your sister doing in Argent?"

"Long story, but she asked if she could come stay with me for a while. She's getting over a breakup and was sick of living with our parents, I guess."

"She doing okay?"

"Don't seduce my sister, Max."

"Shit, Shane. I'm just asking how she's doing," I reply, holding my hands up. "I'm not trying to sleep with her." I lower my voice before adding, "I watched her shoot a man after being tied up by kidnappers. I think asking after her wellbeing is the decent thing to do."

"Sorry," Shane answers, rubbing his palm across the back of his neck. "Sorry, you're right. I'm tired, it's been a long drive and a longer few weeks. She says she's okay, but I'm sure she could use a friend."

"Yeah, I'm sure. I bet J and Quel would take her out or

something. And Kaycia. Them and the city can keep her mind off things."

"Yeah. All right," he says, hoisting the last bag off the ground. When he looks toward the building, I note the lines of worry around his eyes and mouth. He's more concerned about his sister than he's letting on. "I'm going to head in. You sure you don't want to come up?"

"Nah, I have songs to work on. I'll text you about getting together this weekend."

"Sounds good, see ya." He claps his hand on my shoulder before following his women into the building.

Sitting in my truck I adjust the seat and mirrors, but I'm distracted by the new scent lingering on the interior. Shane and Kaycia are familiar, but the new smell takes me back to that rain-soaked night outside Shane's cabin—the wolf and wildness I recognize as Lana. Now, it's not just a memory washed away by mist and time.

I feel a little bad knowing that I lied to Shane.

I'll try my damnedest, but even if I don't seduce her, I won't be able to resist if Lana decides to seduce me first.

Chapter 6
Lana

I spent my first night in Argent curled under the blankets of Shane's bed wondering what I'd gotten myself into. I was used to the natural night sounds of Woodbine Hollow: my parents' house creaking and settling, insects and frogs singing their songs, or the sound of Taryn's soft breathing when we shared a bed.

Argent is bright and noisy no matter the hour. Street sweepers passed at 3:00 AM, drunk guys laughed and jeered as they stumbled down the block, and a car alarm startled me just before dawn. It's been one of the few nights I haven't lost sleep from nightmares, though. Can't lose something you didn't have in the first place.

A white noise machine is top priority when Kaycia takes me shopping later.

I can hear Shane and Kaycia talking through the wall. The ebb and flow of their voices mingling with pots and pans and low music. Half an hour after they wake, a tap at the door drags me from the covers.

"Good mor—" Shane begins as I open the door. He's holding out a cup of coffee, but scowls when he gets a full look at me. "*Damn.* You look rough."

"Well, fuck you, too," I reply, snatching the cup and walking away with the door left open so he can enter his apartment. I sit cross-legged on the sofa, clutching the cup between both hands, ignoring the ugly rip in the leather that will be nearly impossible to repair. The Rosses really did a number on this place.

Shane frowns at the damage. "Were you uncomfortable? You look like you haven't slept at all."

"I was fine. It's just noisy."

He nods with a knowing look. Had he felt the same way when he moved here? Had *his* actions haunted him in his sleep then, too?

"Come next door for breakfast." Shane pats my head, and I nearly spill my coffee swatting him away. He just chuckles at me, then leaves me in peace to go back to Kaycia before I can answer.

Sighing, I unfold myself from the couch, pull a change of clothes from my duffle, and swallow a few more sips of the bitter black liquid before turning on the shower. Today will be day one of my fresh start.

I keep close to Kaycia's side on the subway ride, fighting the urge to snarl at the stranger who stared too long at her and the oblivious woman who smacked me in the shoulder while she carelessly removed her monstrous backpack. When a man wearing an expensive suit smiled at me, I met his eyes with a glare, causing him to avert his gaze quickly. It's all I can do to not rush up the stairs to fresh air when we step off the train, but I force myself to slow my steps to match Kaycia's. The stink of rats and spoiled food mix with the metallic scent of the tracks as we wind our way through the benches and trash cans. I wrinkle my nose, breathing shallowly through my mouth to avoid the worst of it.

"You get used to it," she assures me with a sweet smile when she sees me grimace at the back of someone who abruptly stepped in front of me at the turnstile. "People don't mean to be rude, they're just..."

"Assholes?" I offer.

She barks a laugh. "I was going to say 'focused on their own problems', but yeah, some are just assholes."

Once we exit onto the sidewalk, I take a deep breath. Even with the cars and press of humanity the scent is better than it was underground, and the sharp whine of the subway is replaced by the din of horns and people talking to one another. I'd never realized that my wolf senses would make living in a city so... distracting.

Kaycia leads me to the shopping district. Stores selling everything from clothing and shoes, to home décor and novelties line both sides of the busy street. Kaycia waves animatedly when we reach our destination, and a pretty Black woman with a megawatt smile returns the gesture. I assume she's Jamila when I see Raquel holding her hand and being dragged from the storefront she's staring into.

"Hey there!" Kaycia greets Jamila with a hug while

Raquel pouts. When they part, Kaycia holds her hand out toward me like I'm a surprise on a game show saying, "Jamila, this is Lana."

"Nice to meet you." I reach out to shake Jamila's hand.

I'm surprised when she scoffs and opens her arms to wrap me in a hug like she did with Kaycia. Like we've known one another forever. She smells like essential oils and whatever gum she's chewing, laced with Raquel's distinct scent. Inhaling deeply, I'm instantly more relaxed.

"You're practically family," Jamila says when she releases me. "Sorry, I'm a hugger."

I smile at her warmth, surprisingly not bothered by the close contact. Then I ask Raquel with a smirk, "What's got you in a mood?"

"Nothing." She sighs, side-eyeing her partner, before grumbling, "J wouldn't let me look."

"She can't help herself. If there's something shiny in the window, I'll never get her to leave," Jamila teases while Raquel purses her lips. "Don't be mad." She presses a quick peck on Raquel's cheek.

I chuckle at the idea of Raquel, looking tough with her tattooed sleeves and throat, dressed in all black, struggling with shiny objects because of her raccoon nature. "Good to know she has a weakness." I wink at Raquel.

Raquel scoffs, then changes the subject, "How you holding up?"

"I'm fine." I don't want to talk about how I'm doing today. The whole point is to forget. "Where to first?"

Kaycia and Jamila walk side by side, arms intertwined, window shopping and laughing as they weave through the crowded sidewalk on the way to our lunch destination. Raquel and I stroll a few paces behind, catching snippets of their conversation but remaining mostly in a content silence as I scope out this part of town.

"Do you two live near here?" I ask Raquel, noticing the apartments that tower above the stores.

"Not too far away. We're between here and Shane's place." Raquel cuts her eyes toward me. "Max lives farther north."

"Good to know." I can't help the slight upturn of my lips at the mention of Max. Raquel offers a similarly coy smile but rushes forward to grab the door of the little restaurant and holds it for all of us to enter.

By the end of lunch, I've figured out that Jamila is as equally sunshiny as Kaycia and that Raquel fucking adores her.

"So, tell me this, Quel. How did a smart-mouthed little thing like you land a babe like Jamila?" I ask, sipping an iced tea while we wait on the check.

"I'm very good with my smart mouth," Raquel retorts. I think Kaycia may have snorted ice water out her nose. Raquel just waggles her eyebrows and waves her fingers at me with a grin. "And with these."

"Raquel!" Jamila squeaks, her cheeks darkening as she leans toward her partner to bump her shoulder with affection. "Hush!"

I can't help but cackle with delight at Raquel's joyful irreverence.

"Anyway," Kaycia interrupts, eyes sparkling with

amusement. "Are you going to come to Max's this weekend?"

"You have to! Nothing says 'welcome to the city' like drinks on the patio with barbecue and my special slaw," Jamila insists.

Before I can answer or make an excuse, the server drops the check off. It saves me from having to confess that, even though I'd like to see Max, I'm exhausted from pretending everything is fine and don't want to ruin the party.

———

Kaycia's bummed by my response the morning of the get together at Max's, but Shane looks unsurprised.

"You're sure you don't want to come?" Kaycia asks one last time. She'd knocked on my door on their way out, and I almost give in to her. I can see why Shane is wrapped around her pretty paint spattered fingers with those big, blue puppy dog eyes.

"I'm sure. I think I just need a little down time."

"Leave her alone," Shane says, his tone gentle as he engulfs Kaycia's hand in his. Her long ponytail sways as she looks up at him with a little frown. He's carrying two bags, one a tote with some kind of dessert packed in it, the other a grocery bag with different cuts of meat for the grill. I inhale deeply and my mouth salivates at the scent of the sugar and steaks. When my stomach growls, Shane says, "There are take-out menus in the drawer in the kitchen. Order food."

His narrowed eyes and tilted head tell me he senses I need some time alone. And that I haven't been doing a very good job taking care of myself.

"I'll be fine. Y'all have a good time."

I step back to close the door and just barely hear Kaycia add, "We'll tell Max hello for you."

I want to see Max, but I'm not sure what it means that he's been on my mind more and more since I saw him outside the building that first day. My emotions are still raw from Taryn leaving and I don't want to rebound with someone who's so important in my brother's life. I can't deny my attraction, but I'm not sure if it's mutual or if he's just a flirt. I'm not willing to embarrass myself trying to find out this weekend.

Taking a sip of the soda I'd opened before Kaycia knocked, I make my way to the sliding door and watch as Shane and Kaycia get on his motorcycle. The sound of the engine rumbling lasts until they turn the corner and are out of sight.

Once they're gone, I open my fiddle case, running my fingers along the polished wood. I pick up my bow and cradle the instrument between my chin and shoulder. Now, with no one to eavesdrop, I can finally seek solace in its strings.

Chapter 7
Max

It's been a little over a week since I picked my truck up from Shane, but Lana's scent still lingers in the cab. I toss my laptop in the passenger seat, determined to work on a project that's due next week before our set this evening at Lovely Lucy's. Shane told me Kaycia is insistent that they come to the bar tonight to watch. I'm not sure if Lana is coming with them, I danced around the topic but refused to ask him directly, and he didn't volunteer any hints. But I really hope she is.

It's only three o'clock, so the bar is empty except for a few locals drowning their weekly sorrows. Jamila won't be in until five or six, so I grab a seat at one of the tall tables and open my laptop while I slowly sip my pint. I've been struggling to get the graphics exactly the way the clients want, distracted by the unfinished lyrics consuming my mind. I've always written songs, but for some reason they're more insistent now, like a well of inspiration has been tapped.

By the time I've adjusted the branding in several color-ways and sent the email to my client, Lucy's is getting busy. The happy hour crowd is ready for the weekend, and several regulars tap my shoulder to say hello. Just before six o'clock, Raquel strolls in with Jamila. J waves and rounds the bar to get ready for the night, but Raquel snags the stool across from me.

"How's it going?" she asks, stealing a sip from my fresh beer.

"Can't complain. Ready to play." Marina, one of the waitresses that's worked here forever, sashays by wearing a warm smile and carrying a basket of chicken wings. My stomach rumbles and my mouth waters at the scent. "Let's get some of those!"

Raquel chuckles, stealing another long sip of my beer. "Poor birdie, I'll go get you some sustenance before you keel over from hunger." She pats me on my shoulder with a faux pout.

"Get me another beer too, you little thief!" I call after her. She replies with a good-natured flip of the bird over her shoulder.

I shake my head and close my laptop, storing it away before she makes it back carrying two beers and a metal table tent with a number from the bar.

"You seen Lana?" Raquel asks, sliding back onto the stool. She takes a swig of her pint, the foam from the beer lingering on her upper lip as she smiles.

"No, you?"

"We had the girls' lunch with her and Kaycia, and then I saw her when I stopped by Shane's a couple of days ago."

She watches me over the rim of her glass as she takes another sip.

"How's she settling in?" My nonchalance is impressive.

I missed her at the get together at my place, but I thought I hid my disappointment from everyone. The way Quel's looking at me with a playful smirk makes me rethink that.

"Seems to be okay, but I get the sense she doesn't like the bustle of the city much. She's still on edge. One of the downstairs neighbors dropped a pan or something and she acted like someone was going to jump out and grab her."

"You'd probably feel that way too if someone had fucking kidnapped you, Quel. Have a little empathy." I feel my cheeks heat and try to hide them behind my pint glass.

So much for that nonchalance.

Raquel narrows her eyes, studying me with a tilt to her head. "Fair point."

"She coming tonight?"

Raquel shrugs, but her dark eyes sparkle with mirth again. "I have a feeling Kaycia is going to drag her with them whether she wants to or not. She has *got* to get out of that apartment and live a little, and Kaycia has made it her mission to make her love the city. Plus, Jamila mentioned she'd try to get her a job, so I bet she'll come check the place out."

I try to fight the smile, casually rubbing my palm over my beard to cover it, but Raquel sees as soon as my lips quirk up. Any remarks she may wish to make are halted when Marina delivers our wings and fries and the scent of fried chicken and hot sauce fills the air, stealing her attention.

I've never been so thankful for hot wings in my life.

———

Jet and Ryan join Raquel and me at the bar to keep Jamila company during a lull before our set. We take a shot of tequila, slamming the shot glasses on the bar with grimaces. As I suck on the lime wedge to cut the burn, my eyes are drawn to the door. Shane and Kaycia stroll in hand in hand, but they're not who I'm looking at.

Lana stands framed in the doorway, illuminated by the neon beer signs. Her honey-blonde hair is loose, hanging straight to just below her shoulders. I hope I'm not drooling as I take in her long legs in cut-off denim shorts and cowboy boots, my eyes drifting over them before I can stop myself. She's completed her outfit with a plain tee and a red bomber jacket with a wolf's head over the heart. Only a fellow shifter would recognize it as a symbol of her pack, anyone else would think she'd scored it from a vintage shop.

I'm not the only one who's noticed Lana. Heads turn to check her out as she walks past, and a little flare of jealousy runs through me as I glare at the regulars who stare for a beat too long.

For a moment I wonder what Shane and Lana's parents look like. I've always thought Shane was damn good-looking, and Lana is just a more feminine version of her brother. Is it a wolf thing, or a McKinley thing, that makes them so alluring? Lana's eyes rake over the crowd, studying the patrons with a mix of curiosity and wariness. When she spies me, she smirks. That's when I realize I still have the lime in my mouth as I grin.

Lana strolls through the crowd, avoiding a pool cue and a spilled beer, while I spit out the lime and toss it in the trash can behind the bar. Sidling up to me, she throws an arm over my shoulder in greeting. "How's it going, pretty bird?"

"Just fine, darlin'. Glad you could make it."

"You must be Shane's sister," Ryan says, holding up his beer as if he's toasting her. "Heard there was another McKinley in town."

Lana rakes her eyes over the bassist's lean frame. He's taller than me, wearing his usual cap, pearl snap button up, worn jeans, and boots. He's a little rough around the edges with his scruffy beard and light brown hair that curls around the edge of his hat, but I've never seen a woman turn him down. When she runs her gaze back up to his face I want to growl.

Is she checking him out?

"Yeah, I'm Lana." She's not overly friendly in her response, which wilts Ryan a little and makes me want to ruffle my feathers.

I run a hand through my hair, pointing to Jet. "This is our drummer, Jet."

"Hey," Lana says with a small wave.

Jet smiles and waves back with a soft, "Nice to meet you."

She looks him over as well, inspecting him from his close-cropped dark hair to his worn work boots. Her eyes flit over his tattooed arms shown off by the cut off sleeves of his tee. I've never thought of Jet as competition before, not because I'm an arrogant asshole, just that we tend to attract different types. But for the first time I'm jealous of him being admired. Turning to me with a smirk, Lana gives me a once over before she leans her back against the bar with her elbows resting on the surface.

"What are you drinking?" Jamila asks Lana, handing longnecks to Kaycia and Shane.

"Just a club soda with lime, please," she answers over her shoulder, smiling softly at Jamila.

"Not a drinker?" I wonder aloud, sipping my beer.

"Not often, or in new places." She squeezes the lime wedges into her glass, then licks her fingers free of the excess juice. I catch myself swallowing as I watch her pull each digit between her lips. She bites her middle finger with a grin when she catches me staring, showing off the little gap between her front teeth. "When do you go on?"

"In about fifteen, gotta let them get warmed up first." The jukebox is playing a slow song, but I spy a group of women in their early twenties pointing at some of the song options. I guarantee they're going to pick a few fun ones to follow.

From the corner of my eye, I watch Lana sway subtly to the melody of the next song, an oldie that I remember listening to on my granny's radio as a kid. She lets a little smile tug at her lips, sipping her drink and watching the crowd, and her body seems to relax as the music takes hold.

The oldie ends and the first few notes of a well-known, upbeat country tune take over. Lana's small smile stretches wider as the same group of women dash out onto the dance floor, lining up in preparation to dance.

"Hey, Kaycia!" Lana calls out. Kaycia and Shane are cuddled up, whispering into each other's ears, but Kaycia immediately turns her attention to Lana with a curious expression. "Do you dance?"

"What do you mean?" Kaycia giggles, tossing her long blonde hair over a shoulder and taking a long pull from her beer bottle.

"Come on! I'll show you." Lana grins broader than I've ever seen, a gleam of mischief sneaking in as she nods toward the dance floor and grabs Kaycia's hand. Kaycia's a good sport and doesn't fight her as Lana drags her to a parallel line forming behind the other women. As the song picks up, and the dancers begin to move in unison, stomping their boots in time with the music, the smile remains plastered on Lana's face.

"Did you know your sister could line dance?" I ask Shane incredulously, finishing my beer.

"I sure as fuck did not." He chuckles as he watches Kaycia miss a step and bump into Lana. Both of them are laughing fiercely now, as though neither of them has a care in the world. "But it's damn good to see her smile like that."

It sure is.

Chapter 8
Lana

I can't explain what possessed me to grab Kaycia and drag her out on the dance floor, but as we move to the music an old familiar joy returns to my heart. Maybe it's the acceptance she's offered me since I moved into Shane's place, or maybe it's the comfort of knowing my brother and his friends are close by watching my back, allowing me to let my guard down. From the moment that old song started playing, I felt a sense of relief. Like all I needed was a reminder of the good things I enjoyed once, and line dancing with friends was one of them.

It's been months since I've danced or allowed myself to get lost in music. To feel something *good*. To let loose in public. I hadn't opened my fiddle case since I moved home, fearing what melancholy might escape the strings when the bow touched them. It felt nice to practice the other night, but I certainly haven't let loose like this. Kaycia misses a step—again—and stumbles into me. Her laughter is contagious as she brushes her hair away from her face and finds her footing. Clinging to each other's arms we stand in the middle of the floor giggling like children.

When I glance toward the bar, I find both Max and Shane watching us. Shane's focus is completely on Kaycia, but Max catches my eye and winks. Resisting the urge to blush, I roll my eyes and throw my head back with a laugh, hugging Kaycia as the song ends.

"Gods, that was fun!" Kaycia cries over the next song. Her cheeks are flushed and her blue eyes shine in the lights. It's easy to see why Shane loves her with her gentle heart and sweet disposition. She's treated me like she's known me forever, like a sister, even though she's seen what violence simmers under my skin.

When we reach our friends, I give her a little twirl and send her into my brother's arms. Shane wraps her in a tight embrace, kissing her deeply with no concern for who's watching. Turning away quickly, I find Max close at my back. We are nearly the same height so it's impossible to avoid meeting his eyes. I should have sensed him there, but my guard was down completely and now our breaths mingle for a tense moment before Jet claps Max on the shoulder.

"We're up, buddy."

"Be there in a minute, man," Max answers, still staring at me with a sideways smile. "Have fun out there, darlin'?"

I school my face into what I hope is a relaxed expression, erasing the wild smile that had overtaken it while out on the floor. Pushing my messy, sweat-dampened hair from my forehead I offer a small smile, taking a glass of water

Jamila offers me, and reply, "Always do. You gonna put on a show for me now?"

"Only if you'll dance for me." His eyes flick over my face, then lower, making my breath stutter.

I look toward the stage where Jet is taking a seat at the drums and Ryan picks up his bass. An acoustic guitar waits for Max.

"You only have three members?" I change the subject.

Max shrugs. "All we need right now. We have a couple of guys who rotate in here and there to fill in when someone needs off, but no one's stuck full-time."

"Hmm... lead singer a pain in the ass?"

"Something like that." He winks, brushing off my joke, and flashes that damn smile.

"Well, I'll give y'all a chance to impress me. No promises I'll become your groupie though. I have pretty high standards." I sip the water, trying to pretend his flirtation doesn't effect me.

"Good to know." Max reaches up and brushes a few sweaty strands from my forehead.

He doesn't let his touch linger long before he gives another wink and heads to the stage. I hate that his eyes flicked down to my throat, knowing his keen falcon sight surely noticed my heartbeat galloping as his fingers grazed my skin.

I exhale forcefully, trying to ignore the butterflies in my stomach as I track his tight tee and jeans through the crowd, admiring the way his muscles flex as he picks up his guitar and slips the strap over his head. Everything about him screams "heartbreak", and the people in the crowd love it. I might like it a little, too.

It's been a while since I've been attracted to a man, but I have to admit I'm attracted to this one.

Taryn and I spent the last three years together, and she was feminine to the core. Despite being a wolf, she balanced my quick temper and emotional reticence with her mild-mannered personality and soothing sensitivity. Even when she shifted, she was as playful as a puppy. Until I did something she didn't like.

She never approved when I let loose, when I pulled out my fiddle or got a little messy. She always tried to make me rein in my less proper attributes. Would get pissed if I spoke up about a slight or got too drunk or too loud. She was from a pack on the coast; they must have been mellower than the wolves who raised me. More refined in their human forms.

I finally found myself as a silent chaperone, sipping water or club soda and giving tight smiles when we'd go out to prevent conflict. I never knew what I might do to embarrass her. So, I tried to avoid attracting attention, becoming a passionless sentinel except when she was out and I could play my fiddle in peace. She turned me into a different person. One she didn't like in the end. Someone I didn't like much either.

I came home one night from a late shift at the diner to find her shit packed into her car while she waited on the front porch to tell me it was over. That it had been over for her for months. She cried as she pulled away from me, but my lack of tears at that moment seemed to solidify her decision.

How could she possibly stay with someone so stoic? she had asked. I couldn't even cry when she was leaving me.

I didn't cry or fight her decision in the moment. She'd spent years telling me not to fight. Training me to control myself.

But she didn't see me after she left. She didn't see me collapse on the porch sobbing harder than I had the night I found out Ethan Cameron was dead, and Shane was exiled.

I didn't *want* her to see me like that. Weak and broken and scared.

My emotions were for me to process alone, scribbled in notebooks, or exorcised through the strings of my fiddle. Not for someone to fawn over and feel sorry for. I didn't want her to stay with me out of pity. To be someone's project.

I'm clenching the glass of water with white knuckled fingers by the time Max's soothing drawl comes over the microphone. My eyes snap to where he romances the crowd, the opening notes of his first song pulling me from the painful memories of that night. As if he senses me watching, he shifts his gaze from the dance floor to smile at me. That smile, and my brother's voice at my side, remind me where I am. Standing in a room full of half-drunk strangers, not somewhere safe for me to think about my broken heart or messy life.

"You okay, Lana?" Shane asks. Concern is written

plainly on his face as though he's tried to get me to answer before this.

"Yeah," I croak, clearing my throat of any lingering regrets and finishing my water. "They're pretty good, huh?" I nod toward the stage.

"Yeah, they are."

Shane glances between Max and me suspiciously, his brow furrowing deeply as he studies me for clues as to what I'm hiding from him. Before he can say anything else, Raquel ropes him into a debate, leaving me to puzzle through my feelings and enjoy the music in peace.

Chapter 9
Max

Tonight's show is a good one. The crowd is electric, their energy fueling me and pushing me to give my best on stage. Lana's presence doesn't hurt either. Each time I look in her direction she's watching me with a thoughtful little smile on her lips. She doesn't dance outright, but she sways or taps her toe, always moving.

When our set ends, I use the hem of my shirt to wipe my brow with my back turned to the audience, then hop off stage to head to the bar. Halfway through the crowd, a rough hand lands on my forearm, pulling me around to face its owner. The handsome man bites his cheek when I turn, a familiar expression.

"Hey, Aidan," I greet my sometimes fling.

"You looked good up there tonight," Aidan says, running his hand down my forearm and tangling his fingers with mine. I swallow, knowing where this usually leads. When one of us is lonely we often find comfort in the other's bed. "How you been?"

He steps closer, the scent of whiskey and cologne reminding me of the last time we were together. But instead of making me want him like before, it forces my steps backward.

"Doing all right, man. You?" I pull my hand free from his grip and look over my shoulder to where Lana and Raquel are talking. Lana catches my glance and arches a brow in curiosity.

"That's all I'm going to get from you?" Aidan looks over my shoulder, following my sightline and raking his dark eyes over Lana. "Oh. I see. You're chasing pussy this month, then? Who is she?"

"Fuck off," I snarl and push past him.

"What's your problem, asshole?" Aidan calls out, but I don't respond. He and I haven't been more serious than a shared joint and a good lay. He has no right to be pissed beyond the fact he'll have to find someone else to get him off tonight.

I've never spent more than a few weekends with someone, rarely more than a single night really, embarrassing as it is to admit. If I keep things casual no one will get hurt. Or so I tell myself.

I never want to be left a broken husk because someone decides they don't want me anymore. I saw what that did to my mom each time a different man left us. I felt it myself when she left me with my granny one weekend and never came back. I haven't spoken to my mother in years. I wouldn't know what I'd say to her if I did. The only permanent person in my life was my grandmother, but she passed on two years ago. Now, the only family I have is the one I picked.

Lana hands me a beer when I finally make my way through the room to her side. She's leaning back against the bar, observing the room like I've seen Shane do numerous times. The similarity makes me chuckle as I take a swig. "What did you think?"

"I think you pissed off your ex—" she jerks her chin toward Aidan, now standing with his friends near the pool table. Before I can correct her, she adds "—and you need a fiddle."

"He's *not* my ex. And do we now? Are you a music expert?"

She just cuts her eyes toward me with a sly smile. "I know a few things."

Well, that's cryptic.

"I bet you do." I whisper, catching her gaze and leaning closer.

She chuckles a bit breathlessly, taking a long drink of the club soda with lime she's holding. The ice rattles against the glass and she wipes her lips on the back of her hand, but I notice she doesn't move away from me.

"Lana!" Jamila calls over the music of the jukebox. She's drying a pint glass while her manager, Carson, stands with his arms crossed over his chest at her side.

Lana gives me one last look, then devotes her attention to Jamila and Carson. Shane and Kaycia have both started drinking water, a sure sign they're ready to head back to their apartment. I wonder if Lana will leave with them, or if she might want to stay out a little longer. Raquel will stay until Jamila's shift ends. They usually have breakfast before dawn at one of the 24-hour diners around the block. The band and I join occasionally. Maybe I can tempt Lana to come with us this time. Chicken and waffles sounds pretty good. The company sounds even better.

Shane watches closely as Lana nods and shakes Carson's hand, then Jamila grins and gives her a half hug. Lana smiles when she makes her way back to the little circle we've created.

"Well, step one is complete. Jamila got me a job," Lana announces.

"That's great!" Kaycia beams.

"Want to go have a celebratory breakfast?" I ask, receiving curious looks from Raquel and Kaycia. Shane stands with an arm wrapped around Kaycia's shoulders, rubbing a strand of her blonde waves between his fingers. He can't seem to help rolling his eyes at my obvious bid to flirt with his sister.

"You know," Lana answers, "I think I do."

"We're going to head home," Shane tells her. "Max"— he turns his attention to me—"can you make sure she gets back?"

"I'm not a child, big brother. I can find my way home. And I can certainly handle myself against these city boys."

"I know you can, but you're still learning your way around." Shane's big brother attitude is amusing; Lana's annoyance is even more so.

"I'll get her home," I reply.

When Lana glares at me in false irritation I give her a wink while my stomach does a little flip-flop.

Chapter 10
Lana

Jamila finished her shift around 1:30 in the morning, leaving Carson and another bartender to finish closing up. She and Raquel, Jet, Max, and I all headed a few blocks away to a little diner that I was assured would be just as comforting as the one I'd left behind in Woodbine Hollow. I wasn't convinced that the food could compare to what I grew up with, but I was willing to let it slide after tonight.

I hadn't expected to have as good of a time as I did when Shane knocked on my door and Kaycia practically dragged me out with them. I wasn't sure how I'd feel in a crowd, but I realize now that hiding in Shane's apartment, wallowing in the bedsheets and my miseries isn't what I need to heal from the past few months. I still haven't told Max, or anyone, that I know even more about music than I do about line dancing, which they all seemed very impressed with. I haven't figured out a way to drop it into conversation, instead remaining quiet and listening to the different discussions happening simultaneously.

Jet is quizzing Raquel about scooters—he's thinking of buying one.

Max is asking Jamila if she's had any luck on a project he gave her—whatever that means.

And I'm hanging onto Max's arm, so I can stare up at the sky while walking without getting lost or falling off the curb. Street lamps, glowing advertisements, night owls' apartment windows, and headlights all blind me as we walk. No hint of the stars here like back home. But tonight, the artificial glow is exhilarating instead of exhausting. The city, or the company at least, is growing on me.

As my focus shifts back to the sidewalk, I catch Max watching me from the corner of my eye. Before I can remark on his quiet admiration he stops, opens the door with a grin, and declares, "Here we are," holding the smudged glass door wide for the others to pass through.

———

After a breakfast filled with laughter, maple syrup, and Jet warbling a surprisingly good, albeit slurred, rendition of the latest pop princess anthem, Max stays true to his word and insists on driving me to my apartment, despite my protests that I don't need a chaperone.

"I have my truck parked in the alley near the bar, why wouldn't I just drive you?" he insists.

Sighing, I relent without a fight, saying goodnight to the group bathed in the neon glow of the diner's "open" sign and start strolling back in the direction we came from. The odor of trash, spilled beer, and piss in the alley has me crinkling my nose as I open the passenger door of Max's truck and climb in. The clean smell of freshly oiled leather and Max's familiar scent is a soothing cocoon, erasing the stench of the city. I relax into the passenger seat and close my eyes as I inhale deeply. I hadn't realized how tired I was until Max put the truck in park and whispered my name, waking me from a doze.

"Lana?" He places a palm on my forearm. "You awake?"

"Yeah, sorry." I try my damnedest to stifle a yawn. "Didn't mean to doze off. I haven't been sleeping well since I got here." Glancing out the window, I add, "Or before that really."

"You wanna talk about it?" He cocks his head to the side, his wavy hair a dark halo in the streetlight. "Is it from that night?"

"I—" My words die in a broken exhalation. I haven't spoken about any of this to anyone. Why would I admit how I'm feeling to my brother's friend whom I barely know? But I don't stop too long to think about it before the words tumble out.

"It's everything," I confess. Then it's like a dam breaks, and I blurt, "Everything's gone to shit over the last few months. My girlfriend leaving. Moving back home with my parents. The kidnapping and whatever the fuck they drugged me with. Killing one wolf with my bare hands and Colton with a single shot." I'm panting, my eyes reflect gold in the tinted glass of the windshield. "I can't stop it from all flooding in whenever I close my eyes."

Though my chest rises and falls rapidly, I feel lighter. As if sharing what's been haunting me has relieved some of the burden. Like Max is shouldering just enough to let me breathe again. I rest my face in my palms. "I have no idea why I just told you all that. I'm sorry. Way to be a buzzkill." The small laugh I choke out is anything but convincing.

"You don't have to apologize, darlin'. We all have demons. I'll listen any time you want to tell me about yours, okay?" Max is facing me across the truck's center console now and reaches one hand out to stroke my hair and then cups the side of my face. I lean against his palm, letting the warmth of his touch soothe me while my breathing evens out.

For a moment, I think he may kiss me.

And for a split second, I think I may let him.

But I ruin it moments later when I realize, "*Shit!* I don't have my fucking key." I pull away, searching the pockets of my jacket and my shorts, but I already know that all I'm going to find is my phone, ID, and a tube of lip balm. My cash is long gone, and my key is hanging on the stupid hook inside the door of the apartment. When I left with Shane and Kaycia I locked the door, but didn't consider that I wouldn't be coming back with them. Shane has the keys to both apartments on his keyring, so I didn't bother putting mine in my pocket. "I'm a gods damned *idiot.*"

"Is your slider locked?" Max asks. His eyes glitter in

the dim light, no longer the grey-green of his human form. Now, their gold mirrors mine.

"I have no idea." I try to remember the last time I went out on the balcony and whether I flipped the lock down.

"Let me find out." Max grins before he reaches overhead and pulls his shirt off with one smooth, effortless motion. After the rush of heat that floods my face at his sudden nakedness, I can't help trailing my eyes over his bare chest, following the dark hair that dusts his pecs and down his abdominal muscles. I freeze for a second when he unbuttons his jeans. Max's chuckle snaps my attention back to his glowing eyes. "I would have made you buy my breakfast if I knew you'd be getting a show."

Before I can answer, Max has swung the door open. "Bring my clothes to the door." He turns the truck off and tosses me his keys with a wink, kicking off his boots before he slides out of his seat. Glancing up and down the empty street, Max shifts into his falcon form letting his jeans and socks crumple onto the pavement. He gracefully flaps his wings up to the third-floor balcony and disappears beyond my line of sight. I hop out of the truck, gather his discarded clothes, and lock the doors with a jarring *beep*. Within a few minutes, the entry door of the apartment building opens. Max grins with a blanket wrapped around him as he holds the door for me.

We scurry up the stairs—me clutching Max's wadded up clothes and him wearing the little fleece throw around his waist. What a sight we would be if any of my new neighbors decided to investigate our pounding footsteps. I push into my temporary home and Max shuts the door behind us. Standing in the dim entryway, the tension between us is thicker than in the cab of his truck. Maybe it's because he still hasn't pulled his jeans on and I can scent the subtle change in his smell. I'm certain he can scent me, too. Swallowing, I turn my back to him and empty my pockets, then shrug out of my jacket to hang in the little entry closet. The soft thud of the blanket hitting the floor and the whisper of denim catch my attention, sending my heart into a rapid rhythm.

A moment later Max clears his throat, saying, "I'm decent," when I continue to face away from him. Glancing over my shoulder, I find him barefoot, but fully clothed. I'm almost disappointed.

Exhaling a little laugh, I turn back to face him completely. "Thanks for saving me from having to wake up my grumpy brother." I try to remain nonchalant, but goosebumps rise on my bare arms now that I'm in just a tank top, the security of my favorite jacket discarded like my guard was in the truck.

"Any time." Max cards his fingers through his loose waves, shaking his hair out with a grin.

Without letting myself think too long, I close the distance between us, placing a tender kiss on his stubbled cheek, breathing in his scent with a shudder. "Thank you, Max," I murmur. "Please don't tell Shane about what I said in the truck."

I'm still so close to him that I can feel his cheek move as he smiles, his arms circling me in a gentle embrace. I hold my breath, anticipating what's next, but he just holds me close and runs a palm over the back of my head, smoothing my hair before tracing down my spine.

"You're welcome, Lana. I meant what I said. You can call me anytime. I'll be there. And I'll keep it to myself."

When he kisses my forehead, lingering for just a little longer than might be proper between friends, I bite the inside of my cheek to keep my emotions from spilling over at the kind of tenderness I've missed for a long time.

"Good night, pretty bird."

"Good night, darlin'."

Chapter 11
Max

Keys dangling from my fingers, I look back at the closed door of Lana's apartment. The claw marks still marring the wood are an ugly reminder of what pulled her into my orbit. I wonder if she's reminded of everything she went through each time she comes and goes, or if she can ignore it.

I have a suspicion she can't. Not after that moment of candor in the truck. But I bet she'd rather have her claws removed than admit it.

Her sudden confession made my heart ache for her. I look back one more time when I reach the bottom of the landing before I can't see her door anymore. I worry about what kind of nights she's been having all alone with everything weighing on her. I told her I wouldn't tell Shane what she told me, but I wonder how I can make sure he knows she needs support.

It was hard to keep from kissing her tonight. When she kissed my cheek, I was tempted to turn so our lips would touch, but something held me back. I could scent her arousal, but as soon as I remembered how sad she looked when she told me she hasn't been sleeping, I couldn't bring myself to follow through.

For the first time, I wanted to be more than just a rebound or a good time. I meant what I said, I'll be there for her if she'll let me. However she wants. But I'll let her show me what she needs. I won't be the next person to take something from her or cause her more pain.

Feeling her relax into my arms was enough for tonight.

———

"Do you guys think we need a fiddle?" I ask Ryan and Jet the next time we meet to rehearse. We all chipped in and spent a weekend soundproofing my garage after we solidified our core trio, now it's our rehearsal and hang out space.

"Do we know someone who plays? It would add a great sound, but we're already searching for a permanent guitarist." Jet twirls his drumstick aimlessly and sips a beer.

"Speaking of that, my cousin's been talking about moving to the city. He plays guitar and might work in well. But I could ask around about a fiddle player," Ryan offers. "I agree it would be an interesting addition. What made you think of it?"

"Just something someone mentioned. I think it would work well with some of the new songs I've been working on."

Memories of Lana dancing at the bar and laughing in

the bright light of the late-night diner come to the forefront of my mind when I hum the melody of one of said songs.

"How're they coming along? Did Jamila help you out?" Ryan questions, his voice cutting through the tune I'm still trying to figure out.

"She said she has some ideas. She's been picking up some extra shifts with her catering gig though, so she hasn't been around as much lately."

Ryan and Jet are good guys, we've been bandmates longer than any of my other human relationships, but I still keep them at arm's length. They don't come to our regular hangouts and don't know about shifters. I'm not ready to tell them about me or my friends. I don't know if I ever will be.

It doesn't impact our music, and I've managed to explain about mine and Shane and Raquel's habits and quirks in other ways. We've had a few other band members come through in the years we've been playing together, but none have meshed. But now that Lana mentioned a fiddle, I can't seem to get the idea out of my head. I'll add "fiddle player" to my list of things I need to figure out.

"We're still on at Lucy's tomorrow night, right?" Ryan confirms, looking at his phone and scrolling through the calendar.

"Yeah, I'll meet y'all there," I reply.

"McKinley's sister gonna be working?" Jet asks, he glances at Ryan with a raised brow, still fidgeting with his drumsticks.

"I have no idea," I answer, hoping to sound casual, but knowing I don't. "Why?"

Jet and Ryan exchange glances again before Jet shrugs. "Just wondering. Heard she was gonna be working with J."

"Shane will skin you alive if you fuck his sister, dude," Ryan warns, but his shit-eating grin tells me that's what he expects me to do.

"I'm not fucking anyone."

"Yeah, okay," Jet scoffs. When I glare at him, he raises his hands in faux surrender. "It's your funeral. McKinley scares the shit out of me. I never know if he's going to shake my hand or rip my head off."

"Shane's a good guy. He's never done anything to you," I defend Shane. I know that Jet and Ryan think he's a moody dick because they don't know it's his wolf that makes him overprotective. They just view him as a possessive prick.

"He looked like he was going to jump me when we first met Kaycia. There's no way I was even going to glance at his sister." Ryan cracks open a beer with a laugh.

"She'd be more than happy to rip your balls off herself if you did." I laugh at the idea that Lana needs Shane to protect her honor.

"Well, with those legs I might let her if it meant she'd be near my balls. Damn, she's good-looking," Jet muses. When he finds only my irritated glare in response he amends, "I mean, respectfully. And if you're interested in her, I'd never—"

"You don't have a chance, man." I interrupt. "She's fresh off a break-up, she's not looking. Trust me."

"Mmm hmm, trust you." Ryan laughs, rolling his eyes as he and Jet share another look.

"Fuck off." I change the subject and stand to start our newest song again for one more round of practice for the day. "Let's run through it again."

When the guys have packed up and left for the evening, I recline on my sofa ignoring the game on the screen with the volume barely audible. Instead, I stare at the wrinkled and dog-eared notebook where I've scribbled song after song, a pen hanging out the side of my mouth.

The one I showed Jamila is still only partially complete:

Here I sit in the neon light, pour one out on a lonely night
Turning over things I've said and shit I've done
Wondering... wondering when regret became by favorite drug.

So, I'm...
Composing elegies for a hopeful youth
When I never doubted or needed proof
That my dreams would spark and that good would win
Now I'm left here wrestling with all my sins.

I know I want to repeat the opening verse somewhere, but I'm blocked on the rest. My songs are usually more upbeat and fun, but this one has a mournful quality that I'm stuck on. Since the night Raquel and I helped Shane deal with his rival packmaster it's been hard to shake this lingering heaviness, even if I manage to shine it on. That night was one of the first times I'd felt truly afraid since I was a little kid waiting for my mom to come back to get me from my grandma's front porch.

Once I got over the shock of being abandoned and matured enough to start shifting—a surprise for my granny and me both—I knew it would take a lot to hurt me physically. I never thought twice about the fights I got into as a teen. I always used humor as a first line of defense, but I was never afraid to finish a fight with my fists when needed. But that night at Shane's cabin all I could think about was getting Lana free, keeping Kaycia from getting hurt beyond what a human could heal from, and making sure Shane wasn't slaughtered in front of both of them.

I had confidence in Shane's skills, but one against six are never good odds.

I didn't even consider that I might be injured until the wolf I attacked caught hold of my wing with his clawed fist. The bones breaking were excruciating, but being unable to shift back before losing consciousness was terrifying. The only thing that made up for the fear was waking to see Lana smirking at me, eyes glowing in the night.

I shake off the memory, shuddering at the phantom ache in my arm where the bones have more than healed. I rub my palm against it out of habit, then chuck the notebook onto the coffee table and head to bed.

Chapter 12
Lana

I swipe on an extra coat of mascara for my first night working at Lovely Lucy's and smile through the layer of clear gloss on my lips. That's about all the extra work the customers can expect me to do. Sighing at my reflection I run my brush through my hair once more, it hangs just below my shoulders, the honey color highlighted with lighter streaks from the summer.

I consider chopping it all off.

Maybe getting bangs. Or growing it out.

Anything to distract me from the little tingle of apprehension at the anticipation of a new job in this clusterfuck of a city.

Why the hell are you nervous, Lana? Jamila will be there and so will Max. You're a big girl. Nothing is coming to get you.

Gods, I'm shitty at pep talks.

I never used to have anxiety like this. I know I'm more than capable of taking care of myself, but my hands still tremble slightly as I push the applicator back into the tube and screw on the mascara lid. Since the night Max brought me home, I've actually been getting some sleep, as though finally admitting to someone that I've been struggling helped to numb the pain. *Go figure.* Shifting to sleep as my wolf has helped, too. It's easy to feel less vulnerable with sharp teeth and claws.

I hear Shane leaving the neighboring apartment before he ever knocks on my front door. The light taps come shortly after Kaycia's door closes.

"Come in!" I call, taking a final look in the full-length mirror as I pull on my jacket. It covers a tight black tank top tucked into equally tight, ripped jeans. They're my favorite pair and one of the rips is strategically placed on the back of my upper thigh. I'm not above flaunting a little skin to get tips, okay?

"Nice shoes. Questionable jeans," Shane teases. I laugh when I turn to face him, noting we're wearing matching sneakers. They're popular, gender-neutral, and versatile. I'm fairly certain Kaycia has the same ones, too.

"Aren't we just an adorable little matchy family?" I offer a sarcastic, sideways smile at Shane, wondering why he's stopped by. He already told me that Kaycia was working on a painting, and he was staying in when I asked him if they were coming out tonight.

"I wanted to wish you luck on your first night," he tells me, running his hand over the nape of his neck. A nervous tic from youth he still hasn't discarded. "You doing okay, little sister? I feel like I barely see you."

"You've seen me more in the last month than you have

in the past ten years, Shane." I bite my tongue to try to stop the acid in my tone. Shane just winces at the dig.

"You know what I mean."

"I'm fine."

"*Lana.*" His tone forces me to look up to where he crosses his arms, his lips tight as he gives me a look entirely too similar to one our father makes. "I hear you at night. I hear you whimpering when you're a wolf, sobbing when you're not. I also hear you sawing on the fiddle you refuse to acknowledge you play."

"You need to invest in some earplugs." I try to brush him off, grabbing my thin wallet to slip in my back pocket and palm my keys. I learned my lesson from forgetting them last time, even if I was blessed with an eyeful of falcon for my trouble. "I mean, what're you gonna do if I decide to bring someone home one of these nights?"

Shane growls in irritation and when I try to skate past, he blocks my path. His eyes flash the same gold I know mine are, frustration clouding his face. He's not going to let it slide this time.

"I know you've had to deal with a lot of shit on your own because of me, Lana." I glare at the scarred forearm blocking me from escaping. "I'm trying to tell you that I'm here if you need me, damn it. I'm sorry about missing so much, and I'm sorry you got dragged into the bullshit with Colton, but I love you. I want to help you if you'll just let me."

"Have you been talking to Max?" I snap.

Shane recoils, his brows furrowing at the question. My heart is hammering, why is he bringing this shit up when I need to leave to start this stupid job? Did Max run his mouth to Shane about what I told him?

"Max?" He blinks in confusion, eyes hazel once more. "What does this have to do with Max?"

"Nothing." I clear my throat and change the subject. "Look, I appreciate the brotherly concern, but I really do have to go if you expect me to be able to afford rent—here or anywhere else in this overpriced hornet's nest of a city." I offer a forced smile, then, surprising both of us, give him a quick hug. "Let's plan on doing lunch, just the two of us soon? We can catch up and talk, okay?"

"Yeah. Okay." He runs his hand through his already mussed hair, like he was worrying before he ever came over. "Good luck tonight."

"Thanks. My shift isn't over until two, so you and Kaycia won't hear your noisy new neighbor until late." I feel a little guilty snapping at him for checking on me, so I add a playful jab to his ribs, right where I know always tickled him. He jumps with a surprised chuckle. "Don't wait up."

"Be safe. Get a ride home from Max. Or give me a call if you need one."

"I'll be fine. Goodnight, big brother."

I slip out the door, leaving Shane standing in the kitchen of the apartment I've commandeered from him before he can offer any additional words of caution or support. I didn't mean to make a jab about him being gone for so long, but they just escape sometimes. I know it wasn't entirely his fault, and that he suffered far worse than I did from the separation.

But there's still a part of me who isn't over it. The teenage girl who felt the weight of responsibility alongside the loss of the brother she adored and the death of the boy she thought she was in love with. That part can't let go so easily.

The absence of Shane and Ethan broke my heart more than anyone knew. I couldn't bring myself to add my sadness to what my family was already dealing with. A teenage crush was nothing to the loss of a son.

From that moment on, I vowed that I wouldn't hurt like that again, no matter who I lost.

And I hadn't. Until Taryn blindsided me.

Walking toward the bar in the fading dusk light, I blink back the tears that have welled, threatening to smudge the extra coats of mascara I stupidly applied.

Get over yourself, Lana. I grind my teeth together, hands shoved deep into the pockets of my jacket as I swallow my emotions. It doesn't help that the damn thing still smells like Taryn's perfume. I can't bring myself to wash it. Not yet.

At this point, I can't tell if I even hurt over her leaving or if it's just the loss of the person I trusted and found comfort in for the past few years. The betrayal at her sudden departure from our shared life. I make a disgusted sound in my throat at my wallowing.

Rounding the corner, the neon sign for Lovely Lucy's comes into view. It's early and no one is out front except for the bouncer and a familiar silhouette in slim jeans and a band tee. My heart skips a beat when I hear their laughter before they see me, warmth coursing through me as I wonder if Max was waiting for me. I shake off the idea, he's friendly with nearly everyone. I don't want to get ahead of myself with the little crush I've developed.

I pause, letting the pedestrians who seem to crowd the sidewalks no matter the hour pass me while I watch Max. He throws his head back in glee over whatever the bouncer is saying. The sound makes my heart skip a little and loosens my jaw enough to allow a smile to slip across my face by the time I reach the door. He's good at that. Making me smile and forget the bad things that tend to drag me down when I'm left to my own thoughts for too long.

"You waiting to welcome me on my first night?" I greet Max with my arms folded over my chest. He'd already turned to watch me walk up, having scented me before the bouncer saw me in the low light. His smile is wide, reaching his grey-green eyes.

"Sure am, darlin'. You know Rodrigo?" Max turns to introduce me to the bouncer. "Rod, this is Shane's little sister, Lana."

"Heard you got hired, welcome to Argent," the big man says, reaching out a meaty palm to shake my hand. He has a cigarette dangling from his lips, which he takes between his index finger and thumb before continuing, "Shane's a good guy, he's been working on my bike for years. Glad to have you here."

"Thanks, it's nice to meet you. Well, better get in there." I fake a big smile and point my thumb over my shoulder toward the door.

I take a deep breath, but end up regretting it between the smoke, the scent of piss from the alley, and the street's oily asphalt aroma. I stifle a cough before pushing through the door of the bar. Max follows close behind, his scent and presence becoming a familiar companion as we weave through the room. There's a happy hour crowd but it isn't as full as when I visited the first time. Perhaps I'll get to ease my way into my new role as a bartender.

"Hey, J! Our girl is here!" Max calls down the bar to where Jamila talks to one of the servers at the end of the well. She waves and holds up a finger for me to wait there.

"Wish me luck," I tell Max with a nervous laugh.

"You'll do great. And if anyone fucks with you send them my way." He winks and looks hurt when I scoff. With a squeeze to my shoulder Max leaves me to wait for Jamila, making the rounds to flirt and smile, chatting with people he must know as he heads toward the stage where Ryan and Jet are setting up. I try to ignore the lingering warmth on my shoulder where I can still feel his touch.

"Hey!" Jamila greets me with a wide grin and a quick hug. I'm getting used to all the physical affection from her and return the gesture. "Let's put in an order for the guys— I'll show you how the system works."

She guides me through the ordering system. It's much more sophisticated than the handwritten tickets I used at the diner back home, but easy enough. The menu is small and the labels are simple to follow. After an hour that consists of a tour of the back of house, introductions to the line cooks, bussers, and bar back, and a rundown of how to know when a keg's tapped out, I'm ready for the influx of people that Jamila warns me is inevitable for a Friday night.

Max, Ryan, and Jet have taken up spots at the end of the bar, munching on fried food and sipping drinks until their set time approaches. I'm pleased with the flow behind the bar. It's surprisingly easier than I anticipated and I've shed my jacket to get more comfortable, a bar towel shoved in my back pocket to mimic Jamila. Max's eyes snag on me every once in a while, raising a blush on my skin that could be blamed on the neon glow of the beer signs, not his attention. He smiles at me when I catch him watching and I can't help but roll my eyes and smile back. This only widens his grin while his bandmates catch one another's eyes conspiratorially.

The bar is busy until the guys take the stage, but then attention focuses on the music, giving J and me a little break. Jamila downs a glass of water and sneaks some chicken tenders and fries while I sip a mineral water from the bottle and watch from the edge of the bar. My toe taps almost involuntarily as Max woos the crowd with his deep voice, gentle drawl, and quick fingers that run over the guitar strings. He's magnetic and mesmerizing as he paints a picture with his words and urges the audience to sway and dance.

Several songs in and the patrons are thirsty again, crowding the bar while Jamila and I open bottles and pour liquor. Jamila is making change in the register while I mix a trio of cocktails when a drunk slurs, "What the fuck is taking so long?"

I put limes on the edge of the glasses and glance over my shoulder to find a clean-cut blond with a bleary expression propped up at the bar.

"I'll be with you in just a minute," Jamila answers, smiling as she accepts a tip from another patron. She moves on to the next person waiting, ignoring the drunk.

"Not you. I want the pretty blonde one," he answers, head swinging my way. I swallow a snarky remark and hand over the mixed drinks to the server waiting in the well. Ignoring him, I move to the next order that comes through the machine.

"New girl! Yeah, you!" he calls when I turn my head slightly. "Let me see those pretty eyes!" I bristle at the way he leers.

"I think you've had enough," Jamila tells the man. Her sweet demeanor has morphed into stern confidence as she prepares for him to give her a hard time.

"Fuck you," he dismisses her, then murmurs, "Stuck up bitch." The man sloppily knocks an empty glass toward Jamila, spilling melting ice across the bar and sending the glass shattering on the floor.

Between Jamila's gasp and his amusement, he has my full attention now. My blood is hot, my temper rising at the disrespect. His friends laugh uncomfortably as they pull at his arm, but he brightens when he sees me turn toward him.

"Yeah, you. The hot one," he crows, bragging to his friends as though I've come running at his request. "Bring me a beer."

His expression changes quickly as I approach, his eyes widening with fear when I give him a feral grin instead of a longneck. I reach across the bar, quicker than he expects, and grip his hair between my fingers before slamming his face into the bar top with a bloody thud.

"You wanted *me*, you dumb son of a bitch?" I smash his face into the wood once more for good measure, despite the blood running freely from his nose and the busted lip that's already swelling, before I let him go. "You got me."

Jamila is gripping my arm, pulling me away as I breathe raggedly, while Carson appears, as if from thin air, to do damage control. My blood tingles through my veins, my wolf begging to slip free at the scent of the blood and the pull of violence. Rodrigo pushes through the crowd. People look around stunned at the pause in the music. That's when I realize Max has stopped singing. He hands his guitar to Ryan without taking his eyes off me, before hopping off the stage and following in Rodrigo's wake.

Well, I've fucked up this job already.

I'm so used to being around shifters, or people who know about them, that I forget my temper is a liability in this city. I just behaved exactly how Taryn hated. *This is why she left you*, I scold myself. I steady my breathing and soothe my wolf while Max takes Jamila's place.

Rodrigo yanks the drunk from the floor, catching a beer-soaked bar rag from J for the guy's nose, and drags him stumbling through the room. Carson speaks softly with Jamila while Max stands at my side. His hand hovers near me, like he wants to place it on my back or take my hand, but instead he clenches his jaw watching Carson with narrowed eyes. He looks more serious than I've ever seen.

"Are you okay?" Max finally asks me, studying me as closely as his falcon form would.

"I'm fine. Probably just lost my job." I sigh, scraping my palms over my face before I remember I wore mascara and lip gloss tonight and cringe. "May have overreacted a tad, but no one gets to treat her like that."

"You good, Lana?" Carson questions. I'm waiting for the axe to drop. He holds my jacket out to me and I take it with another exhale. "Take the rest of the night off. Rodrigo will handle that guy and I'll help Jamila behind the bar. We'll see you at your next shift."

"What?" I ask, looking between Carson and Jamila.

"You thought I'd fire you? He's lucky you caught him and not Rod. He would have done worse." Carson hands me a wad of cash from the tip jar and pats my shoulder with a sideways smile. "We'll see you in a couple nights. Can't wait for word to get around that our newest bartender will put you on your ass if you talk shit."

Jamila wraps me in a soft hug, whispering, "Way to kick some ass," before tightening the squeeze for a moment then releasing me with a smile. Then she returns to the bar and pulls the tickets that have started to print again now that the excitement has died down, Carson reaches for a broom I hadn't noticed before, and everyone else is distracted by the jukebox, which is back to playing loud music that fills the dance floor.

"You need a ride?" Max asks as I shrug my jacket on and shove my cash in my pocket.

"What?" I glance at his bandmates who stand off to the

side waiting to see whether their next set is on or not. "Don't you have a set to finish?"

"I didn't ask about my set. I asked if you needed a ride."

My heart has calmed since Rodrigo dragged the drunk guy out the front door and I found out I wasn't fired. But it speeds up again, responding to the way Max's eyes linger on mine. How they flit to my lips and linger on the pulse point on my throat. I know his falcon sight has clocked my heart rate. If the look hadn't confirmed it, the little smirk lifting his pouty mouth does.

"I need a drink. Somewhere that's not here," I blurt. Surprising us both.

"I thought you didn't drink?" Max cocks his head with a little crease between his brows.

"I don't drink in new places when I don't feel safe. But after that bullshit I'm making an exception. Let's see where you pick."

I push past him before he can answer. The crowd parts as though I'm a snake in the grass, giving me a wide berth while whispering things they don't think I can hear. When I reach the front door, I look over my shoulder to find Max catching up. He gives a little salute toward the band before holding the door open for me to step into the cool night air.

MAR
GA
NA
2025

Chapter 13
Max

Lana climbs into the open door of my truck and I'm proud of myself for averting my eyes from the strip of skin showing through the rip in her jeans just below the curve of her ass. Rounding the front of the truck I hop in and pause to grin at her once before starting the ignition.

She glares at me, but her lips are curled into a sarcastic smirk. "What?"

"Oh, nothing. Just wondering where's the best place to take you to drink away that aggression." I shake my head with an appreciative chuckle. "Damn, darlin'. You busted his face up good. Made me proud as hell." I pull out into the light traffic and head toward the part of this neighborhood that's full of bars, clubs, and other nightlife. Exactly what she needs.

She barks a laugh, and I catch her shaking her head at me from the corner of my eye. "Asshole got what he deserved. I'm sick of men thinking they can fuck with women just because we don't jump as soon as they snap their fingers. I was surprised Carson was so chill about it though." She's staring out the window now, watching the neon lights passing by as I make a few turns.

"Carson's a good dude. Jamila's been working there for a long time. He'll always take her side over a customer's."

"Good to know. Wait! There!" Lana points, her fingertip smudging the window.

"Seriously?" I question, pulling up to the curb in front of the strip club she's pointing at. "You looking for a little more than a drink to take the edge off?"

"I'm looking for a good time for once and I bet you're just the guy to show me one, aren't you?" She grins broadly. A wink of her hazel eyes is all the convincing I need to put it in park and feed the parking meter. By the time I'm done, Lana stands at my side. We're nearly the same height so she just cuts her eyes to me as she threads her arm through mine and lets me lead her through the door.

"Twenty bucks for you, hon. But ladies are free," the door girl announces, smiling at Lana while holding out her hand for our IDs. Two men in suits stand silently behind her, waiting for anyone to give her shit. I pass the brunette a few bills while Lana's eyes drift over the entryway, taking in the velvet and neon.

Music throbs from behind the opaque divider separating the club from the entry, barring any curious, non-paying visitors from getting too much of an eyeful before they've handed over cash and proof of age.

"Go on through," the young woman jerks her chin toward the divider, raking her eyes over Lana.

The flush on Lana's cheeks at the interest makes me jealous and frustratingly aroused all at the same time. I wave her ahead of me, fighting the urge to place my hand on her lower back.

"Ladies first."

She rolls her eyes but strolls on ahead of me.

The club looks the same as always. No matter the time of day, the interior is kept dim with just the right amount of black light and neon to accentuate the beauty of the dancers while masking any flaws. It's one of the more upscale strip clubs in this part of town, so I'm resigned to the fact that I'm about to shell out a hell of a lot more on drinks than I would have back at Lucy's. But to be invited by Lana—for her to trust me enough to want to come here and drink after she explained her hesitation to let loose— makes it worth it.

"Where should we sit?" Lana asks over the bass thumping through the club. Her eyes scan the room, flitting between the dancers on stage, the ones who mill around talking to patrons, and the cocktail servers. It's hard to tell, but the flush seems to still be tinting her skin, and her pupils are wide in the darkness.

"Anywhere you want. I'm along for the ride tonight," I reply.

She guides us to a small round table with two velvety chairs facing one of the smaller stages and plops down, her gaze fixed on the voluptuous dancer performing on the stage. Her hair, so blonde it's nearly white, is streaked with purple and shimmers as she moves. Tattoos snake over her bare skin, curving under her breasts and twisting down her sides. I glance at Lana with approval. I can see the appeal.

"What can I get you, love?" a cocktail waitress asks as my ass hits the seat.

"I'll have a be—"

"Two tequila shots, dressed," Lana cuts me off. "And two beers."

"And a couple of waters," I add to the waitress' back as she saunters off to ring up our overpriced alcohol. "I hope that's to share." I raise my brows at Lana.

She chuckles and pulls out part of the cash Carson gave her from the tips at Lucy's, peeling away the singles and a few smaller bills. "Of course it is." She cuts her eyes to the woman still dancing in front of us, her nostrils flaring a little like she's scenting the room. "She's gorgeous."

"Yeah. You should go get a dance." I look around to see if any of the women I know are working. Most I'm on good terms with. A few might give me some well-deserved shit.

"Oh—" Lana looks shy suddenly. "I dunno, I've never..."

"You've never been to a strip club before?" I don't hide my surprise. *She's* the one who wanted to come here. I wouldn't have thought in a million years this is where we'd be hanging out.

"I have. I just haven't ever gotten up the nerve to get a dance before. I used to go with my ex and some friends. I didn't know how she'd react to another woman grinding on me."

She's saved from having to say anything else when the waitress drops off two bottles of water, two beers, and two tequila shots complete with salted rims and lime wedges.

"Well," I say, leaning closer and taking one of the shot glasses between my fingers. Our knees bump under the table playfully as I grin at her. "She's not here, and I'm not your keeper, so I say you do what you want and have a good time, darlin'.'"

With a chuckle Lana looks up at me with the shot glass held aloft, her honey-colored hair hangs over one eye as she smiles. "To good times!"

We lick the salt—I have to drag my eyes from the sight of her tongue flicking against the side of the shot glass—shoot the tequila, and suck on the limes with grimaces before laughing together. The waitress clears the glasses, and I'm surprised when Lana orders another shot, sipping her beer as she continues to glance around the room. After the second shot, she seems to relax, sinking into the chair, her shoulders dropping and her posture reclining so her knees fall apart slightly while she watches the next dancer. A few songs later she sheds her jacket, and I discretely observe her lightly muscled shoulders and biceps displayed by her tight black tank top.

Fuck, she's pretty.

There are women walking around in next to nothing and all I can focus on is the fully clothed one whose knee keeps grazing mine under the tiny round table.

She motions for the waitress to bring her another round and raises her brows at me in question. "Do you need another beer?" Her expression is playful, like she's removed armor I hadn't realized she donned.

"No, thanks." My beer is still over half full, I'll drink water the rest of the night to make sure she's safe. "At the risk of sounding like your father, or Shane, are you sure you shouldn't slow down? You trying to drown out more than just the asshole at the bar?"

"I'm good. Promise." She winks and changes the subject. "So, what do I do if I want someone to dance for me?"

"Well, you go stand up at the stage like those guys are doing," I reply, using the neck of my beer bottle to point toward the men near the stage. "Or, if you want a lap dance, you can get their attention and they'll come to you. See someone you like?"

Lana's breath hitches and her eyes drop to my lips for a heartbeat, stilling the beat of my own for that moment. But she blinks a few times, clearing whatever she was thinking, before answering. I lean closer as though I can't hear her over the music—we both know I can—when really, I just want to be near her. Lana's wild wolf scent punches me through the haze of vanilla and coconut, and the various other artificial perfumes that remind me of tropical vacations and pastries, making me want nothing more than to pull her into my lap and kiss her. Instead, I clear my throat and explain the etiquette while our server brings Lana her drinks.

"Her," Lana nods toward a woman who just stepped off the other small stage. A curvy redhead wearing a black G-string and garter. She's gathering the money that was left on the stage and tucking it into the little bag she wears on her wrist. I flag our waitress as she passes, offering her a tip and whispering that we'd like the other woman to come over for a dance.

Lana pulls out her wad of tips, but I lean over and push her hand back into her pocket. "I got you."

Chapter 14
Lana

I'm so nervous. I rub my sweaty, trembling palms down the denim on my thighs, then curl my fingers in to hide it as much as I can.

I'd never admit it to Max, but I can't decide if the idea of him seeing me with a woman straddling me is one of the most erotic or the most embarrassing things I can imagine. I've been to a strip club before, but it was nothing like this. It was a small-town affair where Taryn and I knew some of the dancers. I never dared to ask for a dance for fear that Taryn would feel jealous or disrespected. That was nothing like this club with its beautiful dancers, high-priced drinks, and upscale ambiance. If I wasn't so drunk I'd almost feel bad about how casual my outfit is, but currently, I don't really give a fuck. I bet none of the men are worrying about whether they're dressed nice enough to be here.

It's been months since anyone's touched me with any hint of sexual intimacy. Paid for or not. Watching the woman sway her hips on her tall heels as she approaches sends heat coursing through me. Max shifts in his chair almost imperceptibly, but I know he can scent the change with his sharp senses. He knows I'm turned on. I think it turns him on, too. Dragging my eyes from the woman approaching us, I catch him lick his lips and look away, rubbing a palm over his facial hair. But I know he was watching me. I inhale deeply, trying to confirm it, curious if he's as attuned to me as I am to him. He smells like tequila and beer, falcon and a light cologne, but before the dancer steps between us I can tell he's turned on. I just can't tell which of us he wants.

"You wanted to see me?" the redhead croons, running a hand over Max's chest.

"Hey there," he says, shifting away from her touch slightly. "She wanted to have her first dance." He nods toward me, redirecting the dancer's attention.

The woman turns, her perfectly sculpted brows lifting in curiosity. I catch myself biting my lip, mirroring her as she pulls her lush lower lip between her teeth, inspecting me. Her hips sway as she takes the few steps that separate me from Max, then rests her palms on the back of my chair, one on either side of my head, so she's bent forward, breasts on display for me and ass toward Max.

Leaning closer, her breath is warm when she whispers in my ear, "Hey, love. I'm Holiday." Her curled red hair tickles my shoulder and upper arm, raising goosebumps and sending a jolt of arousal through me. "You want a dance?"

"Yes," I whisper, wondering if she can hear me over the

music. She smells like a cupcake undercut with sweat, her breath minty as she runs her nose against my hair and side of my neck. I can barely breathe, gripping the velvet seat of the chair.

Gods, she's sexy. Through the haze of lust, I catch Max's eye. He's pretty damn sexy, too.

"It's fifty dollars," she says, looking over her shoulder. Max nods in response as he pulls out another couple of bills and places them on the table.

Why the fuck are you so nervous? I think again, then over and over when Holiday sits across my thighs. I can't figure it out until I look over at Max who is trying his damnedest to avert his eyes. *Oh.* He's *definitely* as attuned as I am. No matter how quickly he looks away, I still catch his gaze. And I like it.

"You're so pretty," Holiday whispers as she straddles my lap, trailing her fingers over my bare arms as she grinds her hips to the beat of the music.

"Thank you. You are too," I manage to murmur while I melt into the softness of her skin, the curve of her bared breasts against my chest, the tingle of her breath against the column of my throat. A little sigh escapes my lips as I close my eyes. I'm not trembling from nerves anymore.

"If you want to go back to the private room we can. Your boyfriend can watch," she says, taking my hands from where they're still gripping the chair and running them over the smooth skin of her thighs, then up her belly and between her breasts. I shudder with desire, my eyes closed as I savor the sensations, but through the haze of tequila and hormones I realize what she said.

"Oh, he's not my boyfriend." I still and blink, meeting her brown eyes while she still holds my hands.

"My mistake." She smiles at me seductively. "He just seems like he's way more interested in you than any of us tonight."

I scoff a half-hearted laugh. "He's a friend trying to help me get over an ex and a shitty night at work." Even if I like his attention, am beginning to crave it as the alcohol soaks in, I don't want him to think I have any expectations.

"Lucky you," she giggles.

I look over her shimmering shoulder to catch Max's hooded gaze flick toward us and then back across the room. Seeing his sly smile, and catching his eyes when they drift back over to mine, has my confidence soaring as much as the liquor coursing through me while Holiday continues her dance. When the song ends, she takes Max's money from the table, then pulls out a little pen from her bag. She scribbles on one of the extra drink napkins and slips it into my palm before sauntering back through the tables to her next patron.

My skin is hot from both her attention and Max's eyes resting on me. I glance down at the napkin to find Holiday's number scribbled in blue ink.

She's written: *My real name is Caroline. Give me a call sometime. 555-232-3890 xo.*

"Lucky night for you, huh?" Max teases, but something is different in his smile this time. His eyes are heated, and his scent has changed. It's just as aroused as mine, and I'm no longer questioning who's responsible. I expected him to be turned on the moment he walked through the door, but his scent hadn't been this strong until I met his gaze.

"You tell me," I say, standing on legs that are far wobblier than I expected. Screwing up all the liquid courage I've drank, I stagger the few steps that separate our seats. I brush back his wavy dark hair, bringing my lips close enough to his ear to brush the shell of it when I whisper, "You asked me to dance for you that first night at Lucy's. Let me dance for you now."

Chapter 15
Max

I tried to not watch while Lana got her lap dance.

I tried to be respectful and look anywhere else while the curvy redhead slid her hands across Lana's scarred knuckles and over her bare arms.

I tried to not imagine what the woman felt when she stroked over Lana's breasts and down her sides, or what it felt like to be that close to her, what it sounded like when Lana gasped against her ear.

I tried.

I really did.

I failed.

Now I'm trying to hide how hard I am when Lana whispers in my ear that she's going to dance for me. The scent of wolf is drowned by the smell of her arousal and alcohol. I should tell her to stop. That she's had too much to drink and I need to get her home. That Shane would kill me if he saw this.

I'm going to tell her that very thing. I even open my

mouth to do it. But then she turns her back to me and sits in my lap.

She presses that perfect ass right against my cock and any hope that she won't feel how turned on I am dies. But if she's surprised, she doesn't show it. Instead, she leans her back against my chest so I can watch her tits in that tight fucking tank top rise and fall as she grinds against me.

My umpteenth failure of the night happens when I catch myself nuzzling my cheek against hers, drunk off her scent and the sound of her heart pattering as wildly as mine.

"Max?" Lana breathes, turning her head slightly toward me. So close our mouths will brush if I lean any closer.

"Yeah?" I barely manage to say without groaning.

"I don't work here. You don't have to keep your hands to yourself."

I'm a dead man. My tombstone will read: Max Acheson. Murdered by Shane McKinley because he was a horny dumbass.

I fight my desire to run my hand up her thigh, to press against her abdomen to make her grind harder against me, to tease her taut nipple through the thin fabric of her tank top. When I don't take her up on the offer, she shifts slightly, turning her body so she can wrap one long arm around my neck.

Lana mimics my earlier motion, nuzzling her face into my hair and against the side of my neck. I hold my breath, longing stealing it when she opens her lips against my throat. She stills, then leans away from me, studying my face with mild confusion as though she doesn't understand why I haven't touched her.

"Don't you want me?" she asks.

"I think you know the answer to that, Lana. I just—"

"Max?" she interrupts, pulling away abruptly, her voice wavering.

"Yeah?" I ask. Lust has my brain so muddled that I nearly confess that I've wanted her since the first night I saw her. But better sense kicks in, reading her tone and leaving me apprehensive at what she's going to say next.

"I'm going to be sick."

The next few moments are a blur as I register what she said and what's about to happen, my desire pivoting to concern. Lana tries to hoist herself from my lap but stumbles and knocks over one of the empty beer bottles. When she rights herself it's only a moment before she's covering her mouth and trying to push her way to the door. A few of the dancers and patrons swivel to watch us, some with sympathetic expressions as if to say, *"Been there, buddy."*

I toss a few bills on the table, grab her red jacket from where it's splayed over her chair, and try to catch up. Just outside the entrance, Lana is heaving onto the sidewalk. I have no idea how she made it out the door, but I just place one palm on her back, helping to gather loose strands of hair out of the way until she stands to face me.

"You all right?" I ask, averting my eyes from her wiping her mouth with a downcast look.

"Does it look like I'm all right?" she slurs. She places a palm against the side of the building and empties her stomach once more. "Please take me home. I'm so sorry."

"Hell, darlin', we've all had a night like this. I've got you." I wrap my arm around her waist, brushing a stray tear from her cheek, and help her to the passenger side of my truck. She staggers, leaning against me with a pathetic moan as I open the door and help her inside.

Before we can turn the corner, she fumbles with the window. I match her groan when she doesn't get it rolled down in time. "Okay, now *that* you may need to apologize for."

"Shut up," she mumbles, but there's no venom to it as she lays her cheek against the door with the wind blowing in her hair. At least there wasn't much left in her stomach.

"It's all right. I'll take care of you." I'm not sure if she hears me, as I'm met with silence. When we stop at a red light and I look over at her, her eyes are closed and her hair whips around in the soft city breeze.

I sigh at the mess on her shirt and pants, and my door. It's going to be a very late night.

———

Two hours after pulling up at my condo, I finally collapse into bed.

I felt guilty taking Lana's shirt and jeans off, but I didn't think she'd want to wake up with tequila-scented vomit covering her in the morning. Her clothes are in the dryer and she's sleeping it off in one of my band tees and gym shorts in my guest room. It's a good thing I kept the air mattress when my last roommate moved out, otherwise, her long legs would be hanging off the end of the couch to add insult to injury.

My truck has been wiped down. Hopefully, it won't smell like rancid tequila when I get in it next. I left the windows cracked, just for good measure.

I debated taking her to her apartment, but I didn't think it was worth the risk to wake Shane by carrying his passed-out sister up the stairs. It would explain how her scent was all over me, but I'd rather not have that conversation right now.

I toss and turn until dawn starts to peek around my blinds.

The memory of Lana asking if I wanted her replays over and over until I finally drift off in a fitful doze.

Chapter 16
Lana

Fuck, I feel like shit.

The mattress squeaks as I roll over, sending a wave of nausea coursing through me as the inflated plastic shifts. My mouth tastes bitter and rancid and the faint smell of tequila makes my stomach flip distressingly.

What the hell was I thinking?

Max's heady falcon scent rises to my nostrils as I move. When I crack my eyelids, I look around the unfamiliar room, half expecting to find him next to me. I'm disappointed to see that I'm in an almost empty bedroom. All that accompanies the air mattress are a few instruments stored in the corner and a couple of cardboard boxes with the tops taped shut. Disappointment turns to embarrassment when I discover that the scent is due to my attire—an oversized band shirt and gym shorts weighted with Max's detergent.

My confusion lifts in fits and starts and I think I might be sick again at the memory.

I puked in front of him. I puked *in his truck.*

Wracking my brain for more, I groan inwardly when glimpses of the evening return.

The pretty red-haired dancer stroking her fingers over my skin. Me sitting in Max's lap. The feel of his desire against my ass. *My* desire to feel him all over me.

When I remember asking him if he wanted me like a desperate teenager, I cover my face with my hands, as if there's anyone to hide from.

Lana, what were you thinking?

I know *exactly* what I was thinking. I've been attracted to Max since I saw him naked in the rain at Shane's cabin. His easy smile and deep drawl send little chills over me whenever they're aimed in my direction. The tequila last night just killed any inhibitions I might have been clinging to and did the talking for me. That mouthy bitch.

I manage to stand from the wobbly edge of the blow-up mattress and make it to the door of the bedroom, determined to find a bathroom. My hair is stiff, and I shudder, wondering if I can sneak a shower before I go home. I have no idea what time it is, my phone is dead on top of a box and there's no charger to be found in this room. But the glass of water and bottle of aspirin make up for it.

I pop two of the pills in my mouth and drink half the glass of water, my stomach churning, when the sound of someone pounding on the front door tells me it's later than I expected. My brother's voice bellowing through said door confirms my suspicions.

———

"Calm down, man. She's okay," Max mumbles sleepily down the hall as the door opens and closes.

"What the fuck, Max? Jamila texted this morning asking if Lana was okay because she hadn't heard back from her. I can't reach her because her phone is off. What happened?" Shane's tone is slightly calmer than when he was yelling through the door, but it's tinged with panic and frustration. I stay out of sight down the hallway, eavesdropping.

"She's a grown woman, Shane. You need to loosen the leash a little."

"Seriously? She doesn't know the city, doesn't come home, and J tells me she got into a fucking fight on her first night at work? What am I supposed to do, kick back and watch the game without giving a shit?"

I swallow my lingering hangover and wince at the worry in my brother's voice. I can't tell if I should be pissed that Shane is acting like I'm still a fifteen-year-old or touched that he's concerned about me.

"No," Max sighs. "Fuck, I'm tired. Look, she left with me. I made sure she was okay. She's just sleeping it off."

"What? Sleeping what off? What did you do?"

"She wanted to go get a drink. I took her where she wanted and showed her a good time. No harm done. Except for the gods awful hangover she's probably nursing."

Silence. I can scent the shift in the air as Shane's temper builds. I need to go out there.

"Showed her a good time, huh?" Shane snarls. "*Great.*

She's on the rebound and is nursing a hangover. I can guess what kind of *good time* you showed her."

"Hey!" I interject, stalking out into the living area. The light streaming through the open blinds makes me squint, but I stand my ground. Shane tosses his hands up and sighs when he spots my outfit, which seems to back up his assumptions. "Don't you dare talk to him like that. If I want to fuck him, or anyone else for that matter, it's my business. I'm not a little kid you need to protect anymore, *big brother*." I can't help but sneer at what should be an endearment.

Max is sitting on the arm of his sofa with a wary look, eyes flitting between Shane and me. "Shane, we didn't—"

"You expect me to believe that she's wearing your clothes, reeking of liquor and your scent without you having been in bed together?"

"Yes," Max answers solemnly, his expression serious. "Whatever you may think of my personal life, you know *me*. I like to have a good time, but you know I wouldn't sleep with your drunk sister, asshole. She puked all over herself *and* my truck and I washed her fucking clothes for her instead of dropping her off unconscious on your doorstep."

"I slept on an air mattress, Shane. Get off your fucking high horse. You haven't been around to protect me for ten years. Now isn't the time for you to start."

That may have taken it too far. Shane looks like I punched him in the gut, wincing and clenching his jaw so tight I fear his teeth might splinter.

I try to soften the blow a little, even if the anger and

resentment that fueled it is real. "I know you're my alpha, and my older brother. I understand that you're looking out for me. Yes, my phone is dead. And yes, I didn't make it home. But remember, I'm your second. You have to trust me. I think I've proven I can take care of myself."

"I'm sorry," Shane says, first to me, then to Max. "I shouldn't have barged in like this."

"No, you shouldn't have," I answer. "Now, I'm going to take a shower if that's okay."

"Of course, down the hall on the right. I'll get your clothes out of the dryer," Max says, cutting a glare at Shane.

"Can coffee and better attitudes be waiting when I get done?"

"Yeah. You want one, too?" Max asks Shane.

"I'll take you home after if you want," Shane directs to me. Not really a question, but not an order either.

"Okay."

I linger in the hallway for a moment once I'm out of sight, listening to see if the bromance is repaired before I slip into the bathroom.

"Listen, man—" Shane begins.

"It's fine," Max sighs, the scent of coffee beans floating through the air. "I know why you were worried and thought what you did, but I wouldn't do that."

"I know. And I mean it, I'm sorry. I overreacted. I feel so fucking guilty about being gone so long and what happened with Colton. I just want her to be okay. But she throws those jabs like that, and it guts me." My brother's voice is rough with emotion and it makes me feel shitty, even if I was in the right for defending Max. "It's like she thinks I wanted to leave them all behind. I think she blames me for Colton taking her and I know she thinks I'm a coward for not coming back to challenge him sooner."

"Have you thought about talking to her about it?"

"I mean, I've tried. She just changes the subject or makes some sarcastic comment and brushes it off."

Max's voice drifts farther down the hallway, followed by a dryer door opening and closing. If I don't get in the bathroom soon, he's going to catch me listening.

"I think you should take her to breakfast and have a chat. It would do you both good," Max explains, voice inching closer.

"Maybe I will," Shane replies.

I slip into the bathroom and turn the water on before Max can catch me. He knocks softly at the door, startling me. Instead of letting him leave my things in the hallway I crack the door and meet his gaze.

"Hey," he whispers with a soft smile.

"Hey," I reply shyly. The memory of his warm breath against my neck brings goosebumps to my skin and my stomach flip flops in a much more pleasant manner than it had earlier this morning.

"You okay? Can I bring you anything?"

"Something to make me forget what an idiot I was last night? I'm so sorry about your truck."

"It's fine. No harm done. And it was worth it, just wish you didn't feel like shit."

"I'm not feeling *all* bad." My cheeks heat as I avert my eyes.

"That's good then." He winks, then offers me the bundle of clothes. When our fingers brush as I take them from him, I let out a shaky breath and bite my lip. "Coffee will be waiting for you, darlin'."

"Thank you. For taking care of me," I whisper as he turns away. He pauses and looks over his shoulder with that damn grin.

"It's about time someone did."

Chapter 17
Max

After twenty minutes spent silently sipping coffee across from Shane with sports highlights quietly playing in the background, Lana reappears refreshed and smelling like my soap instead of day-old tequila and strip club. She's tied her damp hair back, scrubbed the smudged mascara remnants from her eyes, and washed away the traces of Holiday's glitter. I suspect she's still a little queasy.

Something seems softer about her when she takes the steaming mug I offer, refusing cream and sugar with a little smile.

"Feeling better?" Shane asks cutting his eyes between the two of us. Even if he knows that I wouldn't take advantage of his sister, he definitely suspects there's more going on here than we're admitting. He's not stupid, or deaf, and both our hearts skip and stutter when we stand close.

"A little." Lana grimaces when I offer her an everything bagel, wrinkling her nose at the pungent spices and shaking her head.

"Well, drink up and get your shoes on. I'll take you to my favorite place for a hangover cure. The wind in your face will fix you, even if biscuits and greasy hash browns don't."

"Oooh, are you taking her to Ruby's?" I fight to keep my drool in my mouth at the thought of the big breakfast platter at one of our frequent breakfast spots.

"Yep." Shane finishes his coffee and rounds the counter to wash out his mug. He might be an overprotective dick sometimes, but no one can say he isn't neat or remorseful. He'd probably even invite me along for breakfast if he didn't want to be alone with Lana.

I'm not complaining, my coffee is doing nothing to wake me up and I plan on going right back to bed once they leave.

Lana sighs, finishes her coffee, and slips off the stool where she's been perched at my bar. I can't help but watch her graceful movements, so unlike her vulnerable clumsiness last night, as she hands Shane the mug to wash and then retreats to the entryway where she pulls her sneakers on and grabs her jacket from the wall hook. She remains quiet as she digs through the pockets of the bomber, checking and rechecking them, pulling out cash and keys. Shane notices with a cock of the head as she starts to panic, heart rate speeding along with the search. She pats her jeans, as though something might have been left in the pockets during the wash.

"Something missing?" I ask her. "Your phone was in the pocket, but I put it by the mattress."

"Uh, yeah. I found my phone." Her eyes are slightly watery, but she gives a tight smile. "It's fine. I thought I had a little notebook in my pocket, but I bet I left it at home. Shane, you ready?"

Shane and I share a curious look.

"I'll look again in the truck for you," I offer, standing and reaching for my keys.

"It's no big deal. You can just check whenever. Thanks again for a fun night and a place to crash." She adds the last part so casually that I almost convince myself this is still platonic, even though the memory of her body pressing against mine screams a different story.

"Anytime. I'll see you both around."

Shane and I share a handshake and he pats me on the shoulder—all angst buried once again, all harsh words forgiven—as he holds the door for her. Lana wraps her arms around me, holding on a moment longer than expected before dashing through the threshold, leaving me sipping my mug of cooled coffee with a set of feelings more tangled than my bedhead.

———

Hours later, I've woken from my nap, stripped the bed Lana slept on, and sit on my couch with my guitar and notebook of half-finished lyrics. Instead of writing, I keep glancing at my phone, wondering if I should text her to make sure breakfast went well. Or to see if she found the little notebook she said she'd lost. I wonder why she carries it with her and what secrets it holds for her to have seemed so concerned, yet so secretive about its contents.

Maybe I could find out more if I asked her out for dinner sometime. Tonight, even.

I'm debating with myself and what I'm even thinking, trying to start something with Lana when I don't even know if she's going to be staying in town, when I'm startled back to reality by a text from Jamila.

JAMILA

Heard things got wild after you and Lana left last night.

Ha Ha. Just giving the lady what she wanted.

JAMILA

I hope that just sounds dirty. She doing okay?

Yep. Shane picked her up this morning.

JAMILA

How's the songwriting going?

It's not. How's it going on your end? Any inspo on those lyrics?

JAMILA

I've got a little something planned, I'm not going to show you until it's done though.

Tease.

JAMILA

Takes one to know one. Can you take a
call in a bit?

Sure thing, I'm around.

We have off from playing at Lucy's this week, so I should take the opportunity to finish one of the new songs I've been working on. It's been one of our regular standing gigs and while I look forward to our nights there, I'm starting to wish for something bigger. Something different.

I make good money with my design jobs, it pays the bills, but music has always been what I love most. If we could cut an album or go on tour, I think it might open possibilities beyond a weekly bar set for the same crowd. The guys would be game, but they haven't offered to help with logistics or bookings. A manager would be helpful, but so far, I'm wearing all the hats and they're getting mighty heavy. We still haven't found an extra member to round out the band, and I'm not sure if we should broaden our set list to allow for more prospects, or what that would even look like. Maybe Lana was right. A fiddle player *would* spice things up.

My eyes drift back to my phone, thinking about texting her again. The last thing I need to add to my plate is a new relationship, especially when I've never had any real relationship to speak of. But gods know I've never been one to shy away from a little challenge. In the end, I compromise, sending a casual message checking to see how she's feeling and asking how breakfast went. Just being friendly.

What I need is for Lana to let her guard down a little,

without the help of black lights and tequila. A way to figure out if she's interested in me romantically while she's sober, or if this is just fun between friends. I'm happy to support her either way, but I need to prepare myself in case she really is just looking for a rebound like Shane suggested. I'm not sure I'll be able to take it if things get more serious and she up and runs on me.

Chapter 18
Lana

Shane may have been out of line this morning, but he made up for it with the ride on the back of his bike and the promise of an enormous homestyle breakfast. The wind yanked my hair free from its tie and dried it into a pitiful bird's nest on the way to the restaurant, leaving me to scrape the tangled mess back into a bun as we walked through the door.

Shane ordered for us both at the counter, smirking when he asked if I wanted a mimosa for a little "hair of the dog".

I almost puked on his shoes. It would have served him right.

He carried our waters and led me to a booth in the back by a window overlooking the side street, far from anyone else. The waitress came and filled the empty coffee mugs on the table, leaving creamer in a miniature cow-shaped pitcher for Shane.

Now, we're left alone staring into the depths of our slightly burnt, very strong, coffee.

"Look," Shane begins. I bristle, wondering what lecture he's about to serve as a side with my meal. He glances out the window, wiping his palms on his thighs under the table, as though we're about to have the birds and the bees talk. "I want to apologize to you."

"What?" I'm confused.

"It was my job as your older brother to protect you and because of my bad decisions I put you in Colton's crosshairs. I'm sorry I wasn't there for you. If I could have stayed in Woodbine Hollow and prevented all this shit, I would have. Guilt has eaten me up over the last decade." He runs his fingers through his too long hair before wrapping both hands around his mug. "You know I haven't been living it up all these years, right?"

"Oh. I—" I do. It had to have been excruciating for him to be sent packing all those years ago. But it doesn't mean I haven't suffered, too. "Yeah. I do."

"Do you though? It feels like any time I try to reach out to you, you bite back with some comment like I gave up on you." Despite being an alpha, he doesn't look me in the eye.

"I haven't been fair to you, but this isn't just about you being gone. The hits keep coming and I'm not dealing with any of this shit very well."

Shane gives me a look that says "no shit". But when he opens his mouth, he says, "Then talk to me about it."

I swallow down the lump in my throat, then take a sip of my coffee to keep from answering or meeting his eye.

"Lana, I've missed out on a lot. But I'm here now. Max told me to talk to you. That you're hurting. Let me help."

My cheeks heat, wondering what exactly the falcon has spilled.

Looking up from the depths of my diner mug, Shane gives me a soft smile. With that expression he resembles the older brother I've missed far more than the somber man I've come to know the past few weeks.

I'm relieved when the waitress delivers the massive plates of greasy food, my stomach growling despite its recent misery. Distracted by bacon, hash browns, and eggs served alongside a fluffy biscuit, I can avoid the conversation that may expose the raw emotions of the last few years. Shane swipes butter on his biscuit and eats in silence while I shovel food in my mouth, groaning like I've never tasted anything better.

"Lana..." he finally says.

"Fine." I sigh, wiping homemade jam from my mouth. "It wasn't just that I missed you. Mom and Dad were both a mess after the exile. Mama focused on Aubrey; he didn't really understand that you weren't coming back and kept asking about you and wanting to see you. Daddy focused more on his duties as second in command. I was kind of left on my own. To pick up the slack and take the place you vacated. No one seemed to notice that I lost both you and Ethan." My voice breaks on his name, and I wish I hadn't smeared jam all over the napkin now that I could really use it to wipe the stupid tears that have appeared.

Shane's jaw flutters, but he silently holds his napkin across to me. "What do you mean you lost Ethan?"

"I loved him." I whisper at my plate. "It was stupid teenage love. Unrequited, secret, cliched. Of course, the first boy I thought I loved was my big brother's best friend." I roll my eyes. "But that doesn't mean his death hurt any less."

"Did he know?"

"No. Of course not! I would never have confessed that to him. He would never have wanted me."

Shane gives me a look that says I shouldn't sell myself short. "I never knew you had feelings for Ethan. I didn't know his death affected you like that."

"No one did. And it doesn't matter now."

Shane swallows thickly and I can't help but reach across the table to squeeze his hand.

"It's not your fault. I know that. I need to grow up, but you also need to understand I have a lot of hurt bottled up from those years. I do realize you were forced to leave. It's just taken me a while to accept it. And what Colton did isn't your fault either."

"Then why is there so much blame to lay at my feet? If I had reacted differently against Logan, you wouldn't have suffered from my mistakes. I have so much guilt, Lana."

"I can relate," I mutter, giving a pathetic attempt at a smile.

"You don't sleep, do you?" Shane asks, and the question has me pulling my hand back to hold my coffee cup again, giving me something to focus on so he can't read my expression. Shane doesn't stop his train of thought though. "I can hear you screaming and crying through the apartment wall. The first couple of nights I got up and sat in the hallway to make sure you were okay, but I didn't think you'd welcome me barging in. Kaycia told me you'd come around when you were ready."

"Kaycia's a smart one."

"I'm a lucky guy." His expression brightens, clearly thinking about the woman he loves. "She's shown me things can get better. That someone can love me in spite of all my bullshit."

I don't reply, a sting of heartache searing through my chest.

"You'll find that, too."

My cheeks flush, remembering last night with Max, our almost kiss before I ruined it. Remembering how comfortable I feel around him and how he seems to enjoy the parts of me that aren't always pretty.

"Is that what's happening with Max?" Shane gives me a pointed look and I realize I was daydreaming a little.

"No!" I answer too quickly. "No. There is nothing *happening* with Max. He's just someone I feel comfortable with."

I'm irritated at Shane for bringing it up, but my frustration dissipates when I realize that last night was the first time in months that I slept through the night in my human form. Even though I embarrassed myself thoroughly, safely snuggled in Max's house and wrapped in his scent, I slept soundly, alcohol or no.

"Let's do a better job at this, okay?" he blessedly changes the subject.

I raise an eyebrow in question.

"Communicating. If I do go back to take over the pack,

you're my second. We need to trust one another and know when the other needs something. You've gotta let me get to know you again, little sister. To trust me."

"I do trust you, Shane," I argue, but he frowns at me like I'm the annoying little sister I used to be. "Okay, fine. I can get on board with that, but you have to remember that I'm grown. I don't need you busting down doors and protecting my honor."

Abashed, Shane holds his hands up in surrender and we smile at one another in mutual agreement.

The waitress refills our coffees and takes our empty plates once I'm too stuffed to even consider eating any more. The silence lingers, but I can't stop myself from asking a question I've been holding back. Hesitantly, I ask, "Does it get easier? Do you ever stop seeing them?"

"Who?"

"Ethan. Logan...."

"Oh." He sighs and leans his head back for a long pause, as though the ugly diner ceiling holds the answers to a mystery. "It becomes manageable. I used to have night-mares about that night. Not as often anymore, but some-times things will hit me wrong and it comes flooding back. The fear, the anger, the blood. Is that what's been keeping you up?"

"Yeah," I answer, looking away and out the window, watching traffic to hide my emotions. "I've been in fights before, but never like that. Sometimes I dream I have that fucking hood on again, or I see the wolf I killed in the woods, grinning over me without being able to fight back."

"Did they..." Shane's lips are drawn tight, as though he might be sick if he says what he's thinking.

"No. They knew better than to do more than take me and hold me hostage."

"Next time you have a nightmare, come next door. Kaycia won't mind."

"Thanks."

I appreciate the offer, but I know myself better than to think I'd ever come crawling over to my brother and his girlfriend because I've had a bad dream. The offer stands though, and knowing it's there lifts a bit of the weight I've been carrying.

Chapter 19
Lana

I say goodbye to Shane at the doors of our apartments with a tight hug before he goes home to Kaycia and I slink into mine. My phone starts chiming with text notifications once I plug it into the charger.

Max messaged to ask how things went with Shane, bringing a smile to my lips, but it's Jamila's message that I'm most excited to see.

JAMILA

Hey! Hope everything went ok last night! Raquel says she owes you a drink for standing up for me.

I grin, but the idea of a drink makes me want to gag.

JAMILA

By the way, you missing something?

The next message is an image of Jamila's ring bedecked hand holding my notebook.

Oh, thank the gods.

YES! Where the hell was it?

JAMILA

On the floor behind the bar. It must have fallen out when you left in such a hurry. We need to talk about this, my friend.

Uh oh. Maybe I said thanks too quickly, I think, fingers flying as I message her back.

That's debatable.

JAMILA

It is NOT. Can I come over in a couple hours?

Exhaling in a loud puff I reply:

OK.

———

An hour and a half later, Jamila is sitting cross legged on my couch with a megawatt smile.

"You didn't tell me you're a poet," she chides.

"Because I'm *not*. I write lyrics here and there. I'm not a *poet*," I insist, handing her a glass of water and sitting across from her in a leather accent chair. I feel immensely better with a full stomach, and after another shower and fresh change of clothes.

"Girl—" she gives me a look that says I'm full of shit "—

whatever you want to call it, *this* is poetry," she insists, gesturing to the battered little notepad that blew my cover. "Do you have music for it?"

"Maybe." I hedge, but I can't help my eyes drifting to where my fiddle case is stashed. I'm not sure if Shane has told her my secret now that I know he's heard me playing.

"*Maybe*," she mocks. "Stop holding out on me!" Jamila chuckles, clapping her hands to accentuate each word. She's kind enough that I know she won't press me if I refuse, but I'm surprised to find that I don't *want* to refuse. I want her to hear my music. I want to share it with her.

"Okay." I give an exaggerated sigh as I unfold myself from the chair and retrieve my fiddle. It belonged to my grandfather on my mom's side, and was passed down to me since I was the only one in his family tree who was interested in playing. Mama tried to force Shane to learn piano when he was small, but he didn't have the inclination, spending most of his time in the shop with Dad. Aubrey was always a sports nut and couldn't sit still long enough to learn. But I learned, and I listened to Grandaddy play and sing the old ballads and coax the music from his fiddle. I knew I wanted to do it, too. I would sit for hours listening to him, whether it was a quick tempo number made for dancing and clapping your hands, or a lonesome mountain tune that felt like each pass of the bow was tugging directly on your heart.

It wasn't until Shane was exiled that I really focused on playing. I'd toyed with it in my youth, but I discovered it helped me to be lost in the music when I needed a respite from the world. I finally felt like I'd mastered the instrument when Grandaddy couldn't do it himself anymore. By then we'd changed roles. He would sit and smile listening to me on the porch. I even played at his funeral, four years after Shane left. Since then, I've continued to improve, sitting in with a few bands in bars and small venues that dot the mountains near Woodbine Hollow, to Taryn's dismay. She tolerated my style of music, but it didn't speak to her soul like it always has to mine.

The nights I've pulled my fiddle from its case since coming to Argent have felt like clandestine meetings with a lover—hidden away and kept secret for fear of judgment. But as I run my fingers across the polished wood and settle it between my shoulder and cheek, a surge of pride takes over. I'm excited to show Jamila what I can do, to share this peek of my soul with her.

"Fast or slow?" I ask, running the bow across the strings, tightening them as needed to make sure they're in tune.

"Both! Play it all."

I start with a slow mountain ballad, switching to a quick tempo favorite before I play a small sample of one of my own creations. Jamila sits forward to listen, her eyes never straying from my bow sawing across the strings. When I'm finished, I don't hide my smile as she applauds.

"Do you sing too?" she questions, glancing again at the shabby notebook she's returned to me.

"I can. I'm not spectacular or anything, but I can carry a tune." A wide smile breaks across her lips, making me narrow my eyes as I place my fiddle back in its case. "Why are you looking at me like that?"

"Oh, no reason." Jamila flips through my notebook coyly.

"Jamila…" I drag her name out, disbelieving.

"I have an idea," she confesses. She pulls her phone from her bag and opens it, swiping through until she finds something that makes her smile, impossibly, grow wider. Then, she turns the screen toward me so I can see scrawling handwriting.

"Is this yours?" I ask, reading the lines of the poem.

"No. It's Max's."

"Max's?"

"Yes. He's been writing more and asked me to help him with this one. He's stuck, but said he had a tune. I think it would be perfect for you to help on."

"He doesn't even know I play, let alone write." Despite telling him about my nightmares, and being more than happy to rub all over him last night, I haven't felt ready to share this part of me yet. I intend to decline, but instead, I ask, "What's the tune?"

"Hold on. Stay quiet for a minute," Jamila instructs, she's been texting off and on, but now she clicks the call button on the screen. She places a ring adorned finger against her lips to remind me to remain silent while the phone rings on speaker.

"Hey, J. How you doing?" Max answers. I roll my lips together to keep from making a little gasp at the sound of his voice.

"I'm well, thanks! What are you up to?"

"Oh, just toying with this song." He strums the guitar he's apparently holding to punctuate his words.

"What a coincidence, I was just looking over these lyrics and was wondering if you could sing them for me a time or two? I'm trying out a few things and want to see how it might sound." Jamila grins at me as though we share a private joke. I bite my lip and listen closely.

"Of course. Good timing." I can hear the smile in his voice.

Max strums a few chords, clears his throat, and begins singing in his warm baritone. The song has a melancholy sound, the lyrics about loneliness and regrets. It's more emotional than the dancing songs and flirtations he sang to the crowd when he last performed. He sings through it twice, my heart squeezing in response, then he speaks to Jamila. This time she takes him off speaker so I can't hear him anymore. The echo of the song he just sang repeats in my mind. I tune Jamila out, focusing on that mournful melody.

"Well, what do you think?" Jamila asks once she hangs up, jolting me back to the present.

"Text me those lyrics. I have a few ideas."

"Thought you might," Jamila beams.

Chapter 20
Max

"Thank the gods," I mutter, reading through a final client email for a design we've been hashing out for the last two weeks. I upload the files and hit send with a relieved sigh, reminding myself that these headaches fund my music.

I've been swamped for the last few weeks, designing and redesigning for a few different brands when I really want to be working on merch for the band. As though we're big enough to warrant merch.

My phone lights up and my heart speeds, hoping it's Lana texting me. *Shit, when did I become so desperate for a woman's attention?* Instead, it's Jamila.

JAMILA

Hope you're ready to try out this song tomorrow night. Did you look over the lyrics I sent earlier this week?

Yeah, sorry. I've been swamped. I'm ready if you are. Let's add it to the end of the set, right before the closer. You singing with me or is it just me and my guitar?

Jamila doesn't often take to the stage, but she's no stranger to readings or open mic nights, and she has a nice voice when she does sing, so I hope she'll duet with me like we've brainstormed.

JAMILA

You won't be alone. Just keep the tune the same.

You sure you don't want to swing by and run through it a time or two?

JAMILA

Positive. If it's just you and the guitar we should be good.

Whatever you say. I'll give the boys a break on this one until we see how the crowd responds. Looking forward to it.

JAMILA

Me too! See ya then.

Lana working tomorrow?

JAMILA

Yep!

The urge to text Lana is strong, but I pocket my phone with a smile knowing I'll get to see her soon.

I haven't talked to Lana outside of a few text messages over the last week. I had to miss happy hour at Kaycia's last night because of a deadline, and she was working the night before. I hope Shane didn't pull some overprotective big brother shit and warn her off me. Her texts haven't been all that different than before our tequila-soaked evening, but I have this worry in the back of my mind that she regrets that night.

Shane took a flight out this morning to Woodbine Hollow for "pack business". At least he won't be there to give disapproving stares tomorrow night at Lucy's. I was afraid Lana would go with him, but she told me she needed to work, otherwise Carson wouldn't be as forgiving the next time she breaks a customer's nose. I'm a little surprised she didn't leap at the chance to go back to the mountains though. She's mentioned how hard it is to be without them and the fresh air while living in the city. She texted that, in consolation for her missing the trip, Shane agreed we should all go up to his cabin for a long weekend on the next full moon.

I cleared my schedule.

I'm excited to see what Jamila is up to. The newly added lyrics have been dancing around in my mind and I'm anxious to see how it sounds as a duet. Pacing around my living room, I end up with my guitar in my lap, strumming the tune that's been playing over and over without its second half. It's similar to how I've been feeling since I met Lana, lonesome and lacking. Missing something. Guess I'll see how it feels after tomorrow evening.

———

Saturday nights at Lucy's are some of my favorites. The crowd is excited to be out on the town and the jukebox blares everything from nostalgic oldies to dance and pop. Lana and Jamila are both already behind the bar, talking to Kaycia and Raquel who take the end barstools closest to the stage. The glances Quel and Kaycia share are suspicious when I walk up, grins too broad and eyes too bright. Maybe they've had a few more than I realize. Lana is all smirks and sideways glances, handing me a beer without me asking and then turning to make drinks from one of the tickets from the waitstaff.

"How are you ladies doing tonight?" I ask, giving them all a close inspection to try to get a read on what they're plotting.

"Doing just fine," Jamila answers quickly. "You excited for the new song?"

Kaycia giggles but hides it by tossing her long hair and sipping her beer when Raquel shoots her a stern look.

"I am," I reply, raising a brow. I don't say anything else, but I continue to sneak glances at Lana who remains oddly quiet.

Ryan and Jet arrive within the next hour. Our set is soon, so they grab drinks, and we make sure everything is ready for us to play. The regular crowd starts to settle in their places.

"How y'all doing tonight?" I greet the audience through the mic. There's a round of clapping and shouts.

"I'm Max Acheson and this is Fairweather Creek." Another round of applause. "Let's go!"

And with a countdown in time with the clack of Jet's drumsticks, we start to play. We cover a few old-time favorites to get the crowd warmed up and singing along. Then we follow up with a couple of up-tempo numbers to pull them out on the dance floor. When we begin the second one, my eyes drift to Lana watching from behind the bar. It's the perfect beat to line dance to. Once I saw she knew the steps that first night I'd hoped she would dance to it, but she didn't take the bait then. Tonight, when I catch her watching, her lips tip up and she stuffs the bar towel from over her shoulder into her back pocket. She leans across the bar to shout something to Kaycia who grins and hops from her barstool.

Kaycia meets Lana at the opening of the bar before they wind their way through the edges of the crowd to the dance floor. Lana meets my eyes while I sing, and I almost forget my own damn lyrics. She grins at my stumble and then pulls Kaycia onto the floor to dance with the rest of the crowd. The two of them laugh when Kaycia misses a step here and there, but she seems to remember most of them from last time. Their happiness is contagious. Seeing Lana smile so broadly makes something in my chest ache. I almost wish the song didn't have to end. When it does, they wave to me and return to the bar, Lana giving one last little glance over her shoulder.

Two more songs pass, and we've reached the point where I told the guys they'd get to take a break. It's time to introduce the new song with Jamila and I'm nervous as fuck. It's always a challenge to keep the crowd's interest when you introduce something new, especially when it's gotten rowdy and you want to slow things down. It's going to be extra tough tonight since we haven't practiced together.

"Thanks so much everybody," I say to the crowd. "I've been working on a few new songs these days, and tonight I want to play one for you. A very special lady has been helping me out, and this will be our first time playing it together. I hope you'll be kind to her, and that you like it."

People take seats and go grab drinks, but most of the regulars still stand watching from the dance floor. I strum the first few bars, looking toward Jamila in anticipation. She's still serving drinks, wearing a wide grin, but Lana is nowhere to be found. I wait patiently for her to finish and hand Carson her bar rag. As she winds through the crowd I search again for Lana.

The crowd is getting distracted, starting to walk to the bar or talk amongst themselves. I know I can't wait too long to start playing or I'll lose them.

Raquel has her phone up like she's filming, and Kaycia has taken up a spot closer to the stage doing the same. *What are they doing?*

Jamila takes my hand so I can steady her as she hops onto the stage, her smile suspiciously big. With one last look around for Lana, I strum the first chords again. I hope I hide my disappointment, at least from the crowd. I don't have time to wait any longer, so I begin to sing:

Here I sit in the neon light,
Pour one out on a lonely night
Turning over things I've said and shit I've done
Wondering... wondering when regret became my favorite
drug.

And I'm
Composing elegies for a hopeful youth,
I never doubted or needed proof
That my dream would spark and that good would win
Now I'm left here wrestling with all my sins.

This is the part where I expect Jamila to start her verse. I keep playing and bore holes into her with my stare. She's still smiling but hasn't stepped up to the mic. If anything, she's moved *away* from me.

My heart starts to pound, and I'm about to mouth "what are you doing?" when the cry of a fiddle jerks my attention away.

Lana stands to the side of the stage. I somehow missed her while I sang, expecting her to be back behind the bar, not near the stage. She sways as she moves the bow across the strings, like she's part of the instrument and it's singing with her emotions. How did I not know this about her? That *she* is the fiddle player I need.

I keep picking my guitar while Lana steps up on the stage, taking Jamila's spot and moving closer until she shares breath with me at the mic.

Her voice is smoky and sad as she sings:

You came to me on a cold dark night
Kindled a flame that I couldn't light
Turned fears to passion and loss to action
Made me claim my place, but I still can't be sure

How long til you see the cold hard truth?
When does this end? I'm not bulletproof
Will the moonlight fade on a starless night?
Will the bulbs burn out like my wasted life?

Am I holding my breath? My fingers have kept playing, muscle memory taking control as I watch Lana sing. She plays another bit on the fiddle before singing:

So, I sit in the neon light,
Pour one out on a lonely night
Turning over things I've said and shit I've done
Wondering... wondering when regret became my favorite drug.

As she starts playing again, she meets my gaze and gives a little nod. I understand what she's telling me, and I join her to sing side by side. Jamila had sent over the lyric additions and the sneaky woman had even sung it to me a time or two so I at least know what do. We'll sing another verse together before we repeat the opening lyrics as a duet this time.

As our voices harmonize, our eyes stay focused on one another, ignoring the people watching, our friends recording. Right now, it's just Lana and me.

Now I'm
Composing symphonies for a fiery love,
Burning much stronger than the stars above
Where our dreams are shared and our hearts can win
Cleansing me of all my sins.

Here I sit in the neon light,
Pour one out on a lonely night,
Turning over things I've said and shit I've done
Wondering... wondering when regret became my favorite
drug.

The guitar and fiddle harmonize for a few more bars before they're as silent as we are, standing side by side and looking at one another with the mic between us. Lana's eyes are misty, her chest rising and falling quickly, and it takes every ounce of willpower I have to keep from grabbing her and kissing her in front of the audience. The applause finally reaches me through the tension that holds us in place, and I blink, turning to face everyone with a smile.

"Let's give a round of applause for Lana McKinley, everyone! She and Jamila over there really held this little surprise close to their chests."

Lana dips her head as the applause grows louder, then laughs when Jet shouts from behind his drum set: "Holy shit, y'all! We really *do* need a fiddle!"

"What do you say, darlin'? You wanna play with us?" I ask. Though I ask only her, I'm too close to the mic and it picks up my question, causing the crowd to cheer louder.

Lana laughs, waving at them and then nods back toward me with a smile.

All she says is, "I told you." With a confident smile and a deep exhale, she lifts her fiddle back to her shoulder for another song.

Chapter 21
Lana

I've never experienced the kind of high I felt on stage playing and singing with Max. Even when I used to run with my siblings or Taryn in our wolf forms, I hadn't felt such joy. At least not in a long time. Max's look of shock and delight when I started to play could keep me floating for days. I accompany the band on the last song of their set and stay with them for two extras as an encore before returning to work. I thought Max was going to kiss me right there in front of everyone with the way he stared at me at the end of our duet.

I had secretly hoped he would.

Something about singing together, creating together, seems more intimate than being physical with him. The way I could almost feel him through the lyrics. The way our emotions were laid bare in front of everyone.

"Jamila, I have to put this in the office real quick!" I call out as I walk past the bar toward Carson's office where my fiddle case waits.

"No problem! Great job!" Jamila calls, waving me off.

The door closes behind me and I gently place the instrument in the velvet lining, latching the sides of the case. As I turn to leave, the door swings open again and Max is there, standing in the doorway. The neon light from the hallway's signs limns his broad shoulders and high-lights the way his shirt hugs his biceps. I want to run my fingertips along them.

"Why didn't you tell me?" he asks, his voice raspy in the quiet of the office, secluded from the rowdy bar.

"It was a surprise. Jamila thought you'd like it. Did you?"

Why am I breathing weird? Why do I sound so out of breath? Why is my heart about to explode?

"It was a surprise all right. And of course, I liked it."

The door clicks shut behind him when he steps into the room. Max closes the space between us quietly, moving swiftly as only a shifter can when they don't have to hide their true nature.

"I like everything about you, darlin'."

His hand cradles the back of my neck, tickling the sweat-dampened hair, tilting my head back slightly. My breath hitches and our bodies instinctively close the space between us. Max's eyes glow gold and I'm certain mine match.

"I sure wish I could kiss you," he breathes against my ear, running his nose across the delicate skin below it, inhaling deeply and making my tummy flip.

"I sure wish you would," I reply on a shaky exhale, burying my fingers in his dark waves.

He grins that damn smile that draws me in every time before leaning in and pressing his lips against mine. His touch is gentle, even if I can feel the tremble in his muscles telling me he's holding back as he wraps an arm around my waist. His facial hair tickles my skin, so different from any recent kisses I've had, but I relish it. When Max starts to pull back, I grip his hair tightly between my fingers holding him closer and deepening the kiss.

My insistence unlocks whatever hold he had on himself and his fingers at my lower back grip tightly, pressing my hips against his and pushing me against Carson's desk. I groan as his tongue flicks against my lips, opening them immediately for him to explore. The hand that was at my nape has drifted down to my side and Max grazes the bare skin above my jeans before he slides his guitar string calloused fingers under the fabric of my shirt.

Footsteps outside the door halt our embrace, freezing us both in place. The creak of the doorknob has us launching away from each other, and by the time Carson sticks his head in, Max is leaned against the wall with his arms crossed over his chest and I'm pretending to be closing my fiddle case. Surely Carson won't notice how frazzled we are.

"You two all right in here?" Carson asks, a gleeful glint in his eyes. It doesn't take shifter senses to know what we were up to, and Carson's very human expression tells me we haven't fooled him in the least.

"Yep," I rasp, clearing my throat and smoothing my hair.

"Well, it's getting busy again, so J needs your help if

you're all packed up." He looks between us again, chuckling as he closes the door behind him.

"I guess I have to get back to work," I whisper to Max, fighting to keep from tracing my fingertips over my tingling lips.

"This isn't done," he promises, crossing the room as though the tug of our connection has pulled him from the wall.

A steady ache started between my thighs when he first touched me, and it's going to distract me for the rest of my shift. Biting my lip, I meet his hooded gaze. "No. I don't believe it is. But it'll have to wait, pretty bird."

I brush past him, heading toward the door when he snags my wrist and pulls me back to him, our chests pressing against one another, hearts thudding in complementary rhythms.

"I'll wait however long I have to for you, Lana."

He presses a kiss to my forehead before releasing me and walking through the door first, leaving me to fight the butterflies that have erupted in my stomach.

———

Rounding the bar, I snag a new towel to toss over my shoulder while searching the room for Max. I find him exactly where I expect, packing up on stage with Jet and Ryan. When I step behind the bar his eyes immediately find mine and he gives me another wide grin that sends my heart stumbling once again.

Raquel is grumbling while Jamila chuckles with

Kaycia. When I sidle up to them, I spy Raquel handing over a wad of bills to Kaycia. Kaycia tries to hide her smile when she catches me watching and shoves the money in her little purse resting on the bar.

"Hey!" she says brightly, unable to mask her giggles. "That was great!"

"Mmm hmm..." I reply with a sideways glance, narrowing my eyes at Raquel. "What's up?"

"Nothing!" Kaycia insists, but she bursts out laughing. "Raquel is just grumpy that she lost a bet."

"I thought you'd string him along at least a little bit." Raquel purses her lips with a look of mock disappointment complete with a slow head shake.

"What is happening right now?" I ask, beginning to catch on.

"Don't be mad," Kaycia prefaces, then explains, "We all had a little inkling that something was going on between you and Max. After that set, it was pretty obvious. Raquel thought you'd play hard to get, but I know how things are when the chemistry is that intense. I knew *something* would go down."

"And what makes you think something happened?" I ask, trying not to look at Max or smile. And failing at both.

"Ahem, shifter remember?" Raquel clears her throat and raises her eyebrows. "I can smell you all over one another. You're not fooling anyone."

"And you have whisker burn on your upper lip, which I don't need to be a shifter to see," Kaycia points out, scrunching her nose and tapping her face where mine is apparently reddened.

My face heats and I catch myself before I touch my fingertips to my sensitive skin.

"Okay. New subject," I announce before escaping to the printer to grab a drink ticket to avoid their cheers.

I catch Max staring at me again when I pull a bottle of vodka from the well. I don't even try to hide the matching smile on my face as I pour the liquor.

Chapter 22
Max

When Shane got back from his trip to Woodbine Hollow, he sent a group text out to confirm the invite for everyone to come to his cabin for the weekend. I'm packing gear into the bed of my truck when Lana texts.

I'd hoped we might meet up after our kiss, but she was closing that night and we had to put off any further affections due to shitty schedules. We were able to squeeze in one band practice with Ryan and Jet this week, but it was rushed because Ryan had to pick up a shift during the day and Lana had to work that night. She meshed well with the guys, both musically and personality-wise. While the practice solidified my certainty that we needed her fiddle, it also made it even more impossible for me to get her out of my head. The couple of quick kisses I stole before she went home didn't make it any easier.

To say I'm looking forward to this weekend, and some alone time with her, is the understatement of the year.

I keep reminding myself that this is just for fun, not to

get too attached, but my head and my heart can't seem to agree. And when my heart jumps into my throat and my body flushes at the sound of a text message ping, I give up on them reconciling.

LANA

Want company for the road?

My pulse ratchets up at the prospect. *Play it cool, buddy.*

I'm always up for anything you have in mind. Figured you'd ride up with Jamila, though. Something happen?

LANA

Nah, she's riding with Quel. Shane and Kaycia are taking the bike.

Y'all are all using me for my truck bed, huh? Did they put you up to it?

LANA

Not necessarily, but could you meet over here and squeeze in a few bags? ;)

Anything for you, darlin', but it might cost you later.

LANA

I'm willing to accept that. We can discuss the terms on the way there.

I usually rough it at the cabin, sleeping in a tent in the woods or crashing on Shane's couch. Now that Kaycia is in the picture, none of us are going to want to sleep in the cabin. Especially after they've been apart for a little while.

I've planned ahead and packed an air mattress, extra pillows and blankets, and a little strand of twinkle lights. Just in case the mood strikes for a sleepover. Wishful thinking and all that.

Glancing back at my phone before I toss it into the console, I add a few extra blankets to the back seat. Pouring a couple bags of ice into the cooler is my final chore before locking up the condo and heading toward Shane's building.

Lana is waiting for me, her duffle, fiddle case, and two backpacks on the steps next to her. Shane and Kaycia appear in the doorway as I climb out of the driver's side grinning at Lana. Shane's carrying a new tent package and Kaycia has sleeping bags rolled under her arms.

"Hear Jamila's braving it on Quel's bike this time," I say, greeting Shane with a handshake and offering a sideways hug to Kaycia. "How was the trip?"

"Yeah, she said she's willing to use my extra tent this weekend since they won't have the car. They headed out earlier to stop for lunch on the way." He adds as an afterthought, "The Hollow was fine."

Shane carries the tent to the truck and finds spots for everything, taking the sleeping bags from Kaycia. She runs to grab the other bags while Lana brings her fiddle, duffle, and purse to the passenger door. "Is this an air mattress?"

Lana peeks into the bed, meeting my eyes across the way and raises her eyebrows. I try to ignore my cheeks heating, locking eyes with Shane as he furrows his brows. I shrug.

"Gotta be comfortable, man. I didn't think you wanted me crashing on the couch with your girl there."

"That's where I'm supposed to be sleeping anyway," Lana adds with a grin.

"Good luck. If I know those two you won't be getting much sleep," I tease. My plan works, Shane chuckles before tugging Kaycia along with him toward his motorcycle. Her cheeks are flaming, but she gives him a look that could set the whole block on fire.

No one will be sleeping in that cabin tonight. I'm really just doing Lana a favor. Zero ulterior motives here.

Shane leaves Kaycia buckling her helmet by the motorcycle and strides back to the building to grab a cooler from the front stoop, stowing it in the bed of the truck and slamming the tailgate.

"That better have those steaks you promised."

"It does," Shane replies. "We'll grill tonight before we run. Drive safe."

"Will do."

Lana is already waiting in the passenger seat when I slide behind the wheel. She has one leg curled under her and her body is angled toward me as she flashes a lazy grin. My eyes can't be stopped as they run over her cropped tee under her bomber jacket, then lower to note every rip in her worn jeans.

"Hey there."

"Hey, darlin'." I swallow and glance out the windshield, watching Shane pull away from the curb and around the corner as I start the engine. When he and Kaycia are out of sight, I don't fight the urge to lean across the console and pull Lana closer, cradling the back of her head in my palm. She meets me halfway, pulling me by the front of my shirt until our lips meet for a soft kiss.

"I'm not sleeping on the damn couch," she whispers against my lips, sending heat coursing through my blood, straight to my cock.

"I hoped you'd say that."

"Now, let's get going. I'm itching to be out of this freakin' city." She sits back, pulling a bag of sour gummy bears from her purse and tearing into the package.

"Yes, ma'am."

The drive to the cabin is full of shared candy and singing along to the radio. At some point Lana snaked her hand across the console and placed it in mine, holding tight as we rolled past fields and into the forested area near Snow Fern Tarn.

"It's pretty out here," she observes, gazing wistfully through the open window. She's pulled her hair back into a bouncy ponytail and I catch myself imaging it wrapped around my fist. My own hair catches the breeze and blows around my face. I revel in the feeling of the wind, not as fast as when I'm in my falcon form, but close enough for now.

"You excited to run tonight?" I ask. The moon is full this weekend so Shane, Lana, Raquel, and I will all take advantage of the freedom of the woods. Kaycia and Jamila have assured us that they're content to drink by the fire while we "frolic", as Kaycia calls it, and get the wildness out of our system.

"Gods, yes. I needed to get away from The Hollow, but

I am so sick of concrete. I don't know how the hell y'all do it."

"You get used to it. But, then again, Raquel and I can shift whenever we want. I know y'all can't." No one blinks an eye at a peregrine falcon or raccoon in the city beyond pointing at us and occasionally snapping a photo on their phone.

"Do you think it's going to be weird to be back at the cabin? After what happened?" Lana pulls her hand away and studies her fingernails, as though she doesn't want to look at me while talking about the night we first met.

"Honestly?" I stop at the flashing red light, remembering the stormy night I pulled off the road nearby to circle Shane's land. The first night I saw Lana lying on the lawn bound by her captors. "I'm not sure. I haven't let myself think about it. But listen, if you need to get away... If you need anything at all. You just let me know, okay?"

Lana looks over at me, biting one of her nails. Her hazel eyes are glassy, but she offers a little smile. "Yeah. Same."

"Almost there," I announce, turning on the gravel drive to make the climb to Shane's cabin.

Chapter 23
Lana

"We're going to play some music tonight, right?" I change the subject from the night I shot Colton as the gravel crunches under the tires. The little frisson of excitement I get when I think of us playing together almost kills any bad vibes that linger around the cabin.

"Hell yeah we are. I'm glad you brought your fiddle." He coaxes a smile from me by patting my leg before throwing it in reverse to back into a spot on the edge of the lawn.

I'm glad my brother found this place as a substitute for Woodbine Hollow while he was in exile. I'm happy he has a place to escape to, and I'm thrilled to get to relax here this weekend for my own escape from the high-rises and asphalt. It reminds me enough of home to ease the tension in my shoulders and steady my nervous heartbeat. It's a relief to focus on the comforting parts of this place, not on being tossed in the back of a strange car with a hood over my head.

Even knowing this is supposed to be a relaxing week-end, I've been worried about the news Shane brought back with him from back home. He'd mentioned that Aubrey had been even more distant with him since I wasn't there, even distant with our parents. Texting our little brother directly did little to quell my concerns. He insisted he was "fine" and didn't answer when I tried to call to force him to talk to me.

Max grins at me when he cuts the engine, his eyes sparkling in the dappled light peeking through the trees. Their color is like fresh sage until he gets too excited and lets his falcon's gold shine through. He's always so happy, so carefree. I can pretend with the best of them, but with Max it's easy to feel lighthearted without acting. I don't have to be guarded or worry about protecting myself all the time.

It's nice. But as I return his smile a little tug of doubt throbs in my chest.

I only planned on staying in the city for a few months to get my head right, but sitting in the cab of the truck with Max, thinking of our time on stage and the friends I've made in Argent, I'm torn. If I go back home, what will I be giving up just to be back in the familiarity of The Hollow? I won't have the musical opportunities that might open up for me in Argent, now that I've finally gotten up the courage to play for a bigger audience. To play my own songs. And I won't have Max's flirty smiles and soft touch to cheer me up. But until I know Shane's plans and what they mean for me as his second, I can't make any decisions. So, I shine on a smile again as we step out of the truck behind Shane and Raquel's motorcycles. This weekend is for letting loose, not for contemplating the future.

Jamila and Raquel give me tight hugs when I make it to the deck. They're lounging on chairs with beers already in hand. Shane and Max unload the truck, carrying the tent and sleeping bags for Quel over to a little clearing. Kaycia pops out of the cabin with bags of snacks and a glass of wine, plopping down on a little outdoor sofa.

"How was the drive up?" Kaycia asks me. She waggles her pale eyebrows while Raquel sneaks some of the chips from one of the bags.

"Good," I reply noncommittally. "Excited to be here."

"Mmm hmm..." Raquel hums between crunching. "And what's the latest with you and bird boy?"

"As soon as there's something to report, I'll be sure to share. Max and I are friends," I tell Raquel as I settle on the little couch next to Kaycia. Crossing my legs under me, I ask Jamila, "Is she always this nosy?"

"Yes," Jamila and Kaycia answer as Raquel says, "No."

By the time the guys make it back to the front of the cabin all four of us are laughing and the bag of chips is demolished.

Max smiles at me as he climbs the stairs of the deck and I can barely hear Raquel whisper, "Friends my ass."

Three hours later we've all pitched in to put together Jamila and Raquel's tent, complete with cozy sleeping bags, and Max has parked his truck down on the edge of the pond with an air mattress and pillows filling the bed. He shoos me away, making me carry my fiddle case and his guitar back to the house while he "finishes up". Shane has the grill heating and a fire burning in the fire pit when I reach the deck.

"Anything new to report from home?" I ask, setting the instruments down and taking a seat next to him in one of the chairs. Shane had filled me in on Aubrey, but we haven't had a moment to really talk about the trip yet. Since he's technically acting alpha for the Galax Ridge pack, he's required to make decisions, depending on Alpha Cameron and our father to make sure they're carried out when he's away. Through the window Jamila, Kaycia, and Raquel are seasoning steaks and chopping vegetables, music thumping beyond the glass, so we have a few minutes to talk pack business without anyone interrupting.

"I decided that the three remaining pack members who assisted Colton would be forbidden from participating in any pack activities for the next two years. They'll need to stay out of Woodbine Hollow and Galax Ridge. I still don't trust them, even if they swear they were just following orders. It went about as well as you'd expect when I announced it." Shane takes a swig from his beer. "They're pissed, but they'll have to get over it. It's a temporary exile, but better than a permanent one."

"It makes sense, even if they see it as a slight." I'm beginning to question Aubrey's behavior more now that I know Shane's decision. "How are the rest of the Ross pack taking the change in leadership?"

"So far no one has made a fuss, but I'm bracing myself

for it. Especially once Cameron announces his intention to name me as heir. They'll see it as too much power for one alpha." Shane looks out across the lawn, drawing my eyes with him to the place where he and Colton Ross fought. Where Colton died. "They aren't wrong. But I don't have a solution yet as to how I can get out of it. No one challenged me at the meeting between both packs, so I'm letting it lie for now."

"How do you think you're going to keep this up? You're going to be needed back in Woodbine Hollow and across the mountain in Galax Ridge more than just a weekend at a time here and there. Are you going to move back?"

"I don't know. Dad's pushing me to come stay for a while, but I need to talk about it with Kaycia. I really don't know what to do," he answers, sighing deeply and leaning his head against the back of the chair. "What do you think I should do?"

"I can't tell you that. You've been gone a long time, though. A lot of the wolves don't know you like they did, especially the wolf you've become. It would do you some good to stay and get to know both packs again."

"Are *you* going back?" Shane cuts his eyes toward me.

"I don't know."

"I ran into Taryn Rogers when I was home."

Taryn's name catches me off guard and makes my lip curl into a snarl. I try to hide the reaction, but only manage to say, "Oh?"

"Yeah. She asked about you."

"What did you tell her?"

"I told her you'd moved to Argent for a change of scenery and that you were doing well. Playing music and getting some space from the pack." Shane cocks his head, studying my reaction. "Was I wrong to tell her?"

"No. I'm shocked she'd even ask to be honest. When she left, she didn't seem to give a shit about me anymore."

The memory of taillights and dust following her away from our place makes me grimace. I don't want to think about Taryn anymore. Especially not here. I can't remember the last time I let loose like I have in the past few weeks. It was easier to keep that part of me locked away, to keep her happy, stop any fights before they started. In the end, it didn't make a difference. She wasn't happy with me either way.

But I don't think I was happy with her either, now that I've had time to think about it.

"I'm sorry. I didn't mean to bring up a shitty topic."

"It's fine. I'm over Taryn." I hide my expression by digging around in the small cooler for a bottle of mineral water.

"I heard about you and Max's song. Kaycia sent me a video of it."

Interesting subject change, big brother, I think, hiding my smirk.

"What did you think?"

"I think you've been holding out on me with your music. You killed it. Granddaddy would be proud of you," Shane replies, smiling softly. "I'm proud of you too, little sister. You sounded good together."

"Gods, Shane. This is supposed to be a fun weekend,

why are you making me cry with all this praise?" I chuckle, poking his shoulder in jest. "But thank you."

"Is music what you want to focus on?" he asks, more seriously.

"I really don't know what I want to do with it." I shrug. "Think Max will let me join the band?" I try to keep my question light, hopefully hiding how I feel about Max and our music.

"I think Max would let you do just about anything you asked." Shane's brows raise and he glances pointedly over his shoulder to where Max is a small figure approaching from the pond. "You don't need my permission if you want to date him, I just don't want either of you to end up hurt and pissed off."

"Good to know, now let's change the subject, please?"

"Perfect timing. The grill's ready." Shane stands, stretching his long arms overhead before tossing his empty beer in the trash can. He checks the grill and retreats inside the cabin to grab the steaks before Max has even reached the deck.

I smile at Shane's soft acceptance of what might be brewing between Max and me, watching him through the window of the cabin as he wraps his arms around Kaycia while she's mashing potatoes. Seeing them together and hearing him worry about their future when it comes to pack dynamics, makes my smile falter. If I want to play in Max's band, or to see where things might go with us, how can I possibly be my brother's second?

Chapter 24
Max

I'm pleased with the results of my makeshift bedroom for the night. The air mattress Lana slept on at the condo fits perfectly in the bed of the truck and it's actually pretty damn comfortable with the blankets and pillows I brought along. Time will tell if she meant what she said about not sleeping on the couch. Hell, she might plan on sleeping in the woods alone for all I know. Better to be prepared for a best-case scenario, though. It's a clear evening and should be comfortably cool, so I didn't bother with planning any kind of canopy over the bed. The full moon and stars can keep us company.

Strolling toward the cabin, I spy Lana on her own, craning her head back to stare at the sky. Her eyes flutter closed as the breeze tickles her cheeks, blowing wisps of her honey-colored hair from her forehead. Gods damn, she's beautiful. I step into the draft, sending my scent toward her and she smiles broadly without moving or opening her eyes.

The aroma of the grill warming tells me Shane will be back out shortly with the steaks. He already had a heart-to-heart with me when we were unloading everything earlier. After Lana chewed him out at the condo, I assumed he was open to me seeing his sister, but it still surprised me when he admitted it, saying, "You did me a solid by pushing me toward something with Kaycia. I won't stop you from being with Lana." What didn't surprise me is that he followed it up with: "But if you break her heart, I'll break you."

I'd rolled my eyes and laughed, but I knew he was serious. "And if she breaks mine?" I'd asked. "You giving her this speech, too?" It was a joke, but only partially. I've already let my heart open wider to Lana than anyone else who's come through my adult life. If we get more serious, her leaving would hurt worse than I'd like to admit.

"Nah," Shane had replied, looking toward the house with a smile. "I'll let Raquel handle that." We both laughed, knowing Raquel is as protective of us as we are of her. "Seriously, though. If you make each other happy, you should see where it leads. You could be good for each other."

And that was the end of it.

We made it close enough to the cabin that the girls would hear us if we kept talking, and Shane is never one to chat for longer than needed. He gave me a firm pat on the shoulder and started putting the groceries away. After a couple beers, I decided to head down to the pond in the truck to set things up while everyone else prepped dinner. Washing dishes is on me tonight.

I climb the stairs of the deck, leaning against the railing

to face Lana with my arms crossed over my chest. She's got her long legs tucked under her, but I can see her feet are only covered in wool socks. Already getting comfortable in the woods. It's rare to see her so relaxed, especially when we're in the confines of the city.

"Hey, pretty bird. You make a nice little nest down there?" Lana asks, exaggerating her movements as though she's trying to see down to the pond. She bites her bottom lip when her gaze locks on mine, smiling softly.

"You'll have to wait and see, won't you?" I drop into the chair at her side. "Figure we'll eat, have some dessert, and play a little music if you're up for it. Then we can all run, or fly, once the moon's up."

"I can't wait." Lana's breath hitches, but before she can say anything else, Shane returns with steaks on a plate and Lana excuses herself to help set the table inside.

I prop my feet on the stone edge of the fire pit while Shane watches the meat, sipping my beer and letting my sharp eyes stray to Lana through the glass. She smiles more now, relaxed amongst the others. She's still fierce, alert, but nothing like the feral woman I woke to find the last time we were out here. I'd take any version of her, but seeing her like this does something to me.

Kaycia brings out ears of corn to add to the grill, tucking herself under Shane's arm once they're cooking. The looks they share aren't secret or guarded like that first night she met us, and there's nothing to tease either of them about this time. What they've found is rare, especially between a shifter and a human.

Seeing everyone coupled up makes me yearn for what

I've been missing all these years, filling my nights with superficial hook ups. The comfort and safety found in knowing someone. I've always had a good time, and most of all I've kept myself from being hurt. But I think I might finally be willing to risk being broken again for a taste of permanence. If Lana wants the same thing.

She catches me staring at her through the glass, raising her brows with a purse of her lips. She sips mineral water, leaning against the counter while Raquel snacks and Jamila dries her hands and turns off the stovetop. The next time she looks over she mouths, "Do you want another drink?" as though I'm watching her to get something instead of just admiring her sharp beauty. I just shake my head and turn my attention back to the setting sun.

———

Dinner is a joyful affair. It's been months since we've all stayed at the cabin, shifting and running at will and enjoying the freedom and peace from the city. Not since spring when the leaves were first coming back out and the nights were still cold. Now, the forest is dense, autumn just beginning to turn the leaves the color of flames. The pond may still be warm enough for a swim.

"Jamila, that was probably the best mac and cheese I've ever eaten," Lana groans, rubbing her stomach after a second helping. "Someone please take it away before I'm too full to shift."

"Just wait for dessert!" Raquel is giddy, lighting up at

the timer going off and announcing that the berry crumble Jamila made is ready.

Lana responds with a melodramatic groan, but we all laugh. No one's passing up dessert.

I collect the dirty plates and pile them in the sink for later, then refill any glasses before digging into the steaming crumble topped with melting vanilla ice cream.

"And now *this* is the best thing I've ever eaten. Period," Lana compliments Jamila. She cuts her eyes to Shane, adding, "Don't you dare tell Mama I said that."

Shane chuckles around a mouthful of crumble.

When everyone's bellies are full, I collect the bowls and add them to the sink, running hot water and soaping them up.

"We'll meet you on the porch when you're done," Raquel calls from the front door.

"Be out in a few," I answer, scrubbing and rinsing a plate.

"Want some help?" Lana asks, bumping my shoulder with hers. "I can dry if you wash."

"Sure."

We work in tandem, silent except for the clink of ceramic and silverware. My breath catches each time our fingers brush when I hand her a clean plate, forcing me to focus so I don't let one slip free. I feel like a hormonal teenager, navigating a first crush and desperately hoping she likes me too. When the last dish is dried and put in the cupboard, I glance over my shoulder to where everyone sits on the porch. Almost all of the kitchen is visible to them, except one small corner. I look back at Lana to find her exactly in that corner, eyes gold as she reaches a hand toward me.

Heart galloping, I take her offering and let her pull me close, pressing her against the counter as I circle her bare waist with exploring fingers.

"They're expecting us to play something for them," I whisper, running my nose against her jaw. The shiver that runs through her muscles would have me ruffling my feathers in pleasure if I could.

"I need you to do me a favor first," she answers, hands on my shoulders.

"Oh?"

"Kiss me."

"Yes, ma'am." She cups my face in her warm palms and draws me closer as I pull her hips against mine. Our mouths slant against one another, sweet with the remnants of berries and melted sugar. Lana moans softly as she opens her mouth, tracing my lips with her tongue as I slide my hands lower. One of the rips in the denim is just below the curve of her ass and I graze bare skin, sending a current of need through me. She becomes pliant in my arms, melting against me so that our bodies mold to one another as our kiss deepens.

"Are you two coming out or what?" Kaycia calls from the front door. Lana's gasp turns into a muffled giggle when she meets my gaze.

Breathing deeply, I step back, letting her slip past to poke her head around the cabinets so I can adjust my now too tight jeans before I face Kaycia.

"Ah, yeah," Lana answers, clearing her throat. Kaycia

grins and sneaks past as quiet as a human can, heading toward the bathroom.

"Come on, let's go make some music," Lana says before biting her lip. With one last quick peck on the lips, she leaves me panting in the kitchen as I watch those ripped jeans skirt the counter and slip through the door.

Chapter 25
Lana

Shane and Raquel both turn to watch me walk through the door, raising their brows with a knowing look. Can't do anything around freaking shifters without them scenting it. I ignore their pointed looks and flip the latches to open my fiddle case. I stroke my fingers over the wood and strings, lovingly tracing them like I always do. Tucking it under my chin, I run the bow over the strings a few times, then play a short melody to get warmed up.

By the time I finish, Kaycia is back, sitting in Shane's lap, and Max has joined us with his guitar. I smirk at him wondering if it's helping to hide what I perked up in the kitchen. He grins at me, his eyes glittering as though we're the only two people on the porch.

"Stop flirting and play already!" Raquel jeers, popping open another beer bottle. "Otherwise, I'm heading to the woods, so my lady isn't alone in the cold more than she has to be."

"Don't even act like you could run after stuffing your-self on a second helping of dessert. Kaycia and I will be just fine here by the fire, don't use me as an excuse to rush," Jamila chides and smiles when Raquel curls her lip at her.

We start with a classic, upbeat mountain song that lends itself well to my fiddle. Max keeps up, strumming and singing while I play. It was fun to find out he knows a lot of the same old songs I do. After another fast one, I play the opening notes of the one we duetted at the bar.

Max breathes deeply and I can sense the shift in him, his mood settling from flirtatious to serious as his eyes find mine and he strums the opening chords. No one moves, but for me it's just the two of us now. He sings his verse and first chorus, then I sing mine. When our voices weave together on the next verse, we're only singing to each other, like everyone else has faded away.

Something changes between us, some kind of recogni-tion that what's happening here isn't just flirtation. When the final notes are sung and the melody stops the only sound is the crackle of the flames in the fire pit. Even Raquel holds her tongue.

"Let's run," I breathe, so low I don't know if I even said it aloud.

"Yeah," Max agrees, eyes golden as they remain fixed on mine.

"Are we still invited?" Raquel whispers to Shane. Her voice breaks my concentration, and I look down, blinking as I pack my fiddle back into its case. My cheeks are so hot you'd think I'd pressed them up against the metal of the firepit.

"We'll be back," Shane murmurs to Kaycia, kissing her before she stands and takes a seat next to Jamila with her legs tucked under a blanket.

"Take your time and have fun!" Jamila holds her wine glass up in a pretend toast as Shane and Raquel bound down the steps. Max ushers me ahead of him with a smile, following behind all of us.

At the edge of the tree line, we both pause, momentarily awkward. Shane and Raquel are farther ahead, and judging by the piles of clothes separated by several trees, have already shifted. Shifters don't usually flinch at nudity. A body is a body, and stripping down is a necessity if you don't want to ruin all your clothes. Plus, I've already seen Max naked. The last time we were here covering up was the least of our concerns. But now, I *want* to see him naked and the thought causes blood to rush to my cheeks.

"You okay?" Max asks. "I didn't know if this place would bring back bad memories."

His line of thought would make sense, and now that he's mentioned it the excitement *is* a bit deadened. We aren't in the exact same spot as the night I killed two men, but we're close enough for me to need a few moments.

"I...ah..." I exhale deeply, then shake off the regret. I was the one who was defending myself and my family. I did nothing wrong. "I'm fine."

To divert his attention from my temporary remorse, I strip my crop top off and toss it aside, my fingers popping open the top button of my jeans.

"You gonna watch me?" I ask, smiling at the hunger in his eyes.

"Only if you want me to."

"Flirt."

"Tease."

"Strip already, pretty bird." I kick off my shoes and push my jeans past my hips.

"Yes, ma'am." He pulls his shirt overhead, tossing it aside quickly before kicking out of his boots and jeans.

I turn my back before unclasping my bra and stepping from my underwear. In a blink I've shifted. A low howl greets me in my wolf form, Shane calling to us to hurry up. I stretch, luxuriating in my wolf. It's been too long since I've shifted for the sheer joy of it, to scent the earth and water and wilderness and forget the troubles that plague me as a human. I missed the freedom that always comes with this form.

Within seconds Max screeches and circles overhead. I let my tongue loll as I trot in the direction Shane howled from, Max dipping from the canopy to snap his talons at my fur in jest as we make our way deeper through the forest. Any sadness I might have felt before shifting was shed with my human form and the joy of running with my friends takes its place.

I catch up to Shane quickly, wagging my tail and snuggling against him like when we were pups. All that's missing is Aubrey tagging along and it would feel like nothing had changed. Except for the blood on our hands and the emotional turmoil of Shane's exile and now reentry to the packs.

Raquel is perched on a low tree branch nibbling on something with a satisfied purr.

Are you still *eating?* I think to her.

Mind your business. These are good this time of year, she scolds back, shoving fruit from the tree in her mouth with a sharp little raccoon grin.

Max swoops down to harass her like he did to me the entire run to find Shane. Raquel hisses at him and makes a swipe with a paw, but he avoids her easily and lands on a branch above.

We bound through the woods, enjoying the night scents enhanced by the cool weather—the wild animals and pines. Savoring the soft flex of decaying leaves and pine needles under my paws. The strength in my muscles is a reminder of how much I love this, but a little pang in my heart reminds me that I also love making music. And that the joy of doing so over the last few weeks has made staying in human form more bearable than I'd imagined it could be. Perhaps I can find a balance between the two.

I yip with glee as we start trotting back toward the pond an hour or so later. Moonlight illuminates the forest and the amusing scene before me. Max can fly at incredible speeds in his falcon form, and Shane and I can cover ground easily, but Raquel isn't nearly as quick. To make up for her short raccoon legs she stands with her little hands grasping the air in Shane's direction.

What are you doing? I mentally chuckle toward them as I watch Shane stop next to her so she can climb on his back.

You didn't see this, he thinks back, then takes off at a quicker pace with Raquel clinging on like a child hanging on to their first pony. If I were human I'd shake my head, but I just laugh inwardly and follow along snapping my jaws at Max when he comes too close.

Don't get any ideas, pretty bird. You're not riding me when those wings get tired.

Max circles, flying low and close to me as the trees begin to clear and the pond ripples ahead.

Don't give me any ideas, darlin'.

My heart flips at the innuendo and my tail wags before I can stop myself.

Shane runs into the pond without stopping, Raquel still hanging on as he paddles toward the middle. I follow his lead, the water sluicing off my fur as we splash in the chilly depths. Max circles twice, crying out once before suddenly plummeting toward the surface of the pond, his wings tucked tight to his body.

My heart stutters as he nears the water, falling faster than seems safe. He dips below the surface in a quiet dive, then resurfaces, tossing his shifted hair out of golden eyes and sending droplets flying. His chest and shoulders are pebbled with the chill, but he doesn't show any other signs of being uncomfortable, grinning at us as we splash around.

I dip under the surface and shift, surfacing with a gasp as the chill of the water seeps into my human skin.

"Shit, it's cold!"

"Need someone to warm you up?" Max splashes me before diving under to avoid my returning volley of water.

Shane growls at the flirtation but starts swimming to the bank.

"Where are you going?" I call to him. Raquel lets go and swims to the shore, shaking her little body when she reaches the edge. Shane looks toward the cabin, tilting his head as if asking me if I'm coming back yet.

"I think I'll stay a little while. It's been too long since I've been out in nature." It's not a total lie. "Don't wait up for me, I might sleep in the woods tonight."

Shane cocks his head and even though he's in his wolf form I can tell he thinks I'm full of shit. I'm certain he and Raquel can scent the change in the air between Max and myself, even with the water to mask it, and I fight to hide my flushed cheeks. He doesn't say anything though, just swims to shore and heads up the hill toward the cabin with Raquel scurrying nearby.

"You know, a gentleman would go get a lady's clothes so she could get dressed if she wants to sit on the shore."

"I don't see either of those around here. But I'll go get your clothes." He laughs, then makes his way to the bank, squeezing the water from his dark hair. I watch as it runs down his bare back and over his round ass. He glances over his shoulder, catching me staring with a little laugh. Shifting, he ruffles his feathers, then takes flight toward the tree line where we left our clothes. He's weighted down by the time he returns, dipping under the weight of denim and our tee shirts.

Shifting with his back to me, Max slips his jeans on before he turns to face me. In my wolf form again, I shake the water from my fur, then grab my clothes in my jaw and move a little farther away before I shift. "Missed my underwear, huh?" I call out as I pull on my jeans and crop top sans undergarments.

"I'm only one bird. If you need them that badly you're

welcome to run on over and get them." He tosses his tee over his shoulder, striding toward me with that damn grin that makes my knees weak. "I'd rather show you something though."

"Lead the way."

Chapter 26
Max

I start walking toward the other side of the pond where I parked my truck, feeling a little silly acting like it's a surprise since I know Lana can see it from here. But she saunters up next to me, and any doubt I feel disappears when she slides her palm against mine. My breath catches, heart thrumming like I'm a hummingbird instead of a falcon when our fingers clasp, and she gives a lazy smile when I look over at her. In the light of the moon, I can see her pulse throbbing just as quickly as mine, the flutter of it making me want to run my tongue along her slender neck.

"Is this what you've been working on?" she asks when we reach the truck. The quilts are piled on the mattress, and I click on the battery-operated twinkle lights I've wrapped around the edge of the truck bed, sending a soft glow over everything. She giggles when I lead her around to view the bed from the tailgate. "Looks awfully cozy for just one person."

"You told me you weren't sleeping on the couch, don't change your mind now, darlin'. Shane can't make that fold out this comfortable no matter how hard he tries." She gives a shy smile, and I worry I'm being too assertive. "I mean, unless you want to sleep inside. I didn't mean—"

"Max, this is perfect."

My name on her lips does something to me, sending my heart swooping. A wave of desire runs straight to my cock and tightens my stomach. She doesn't let me respond before she's kissing me. Her fingers tangle into the damp strands of my hair, tugging slightly as she presses herself against me. This time when I run my hands against her waist, I let them travel upwards, brushing against the curve of her bare breasts under her loose cropped tee. A whimper escapes her at the caress, and she deepens the kiss, nipping at my lower lip. She breaks our embrace just long enough to boost herself onto the tailgate, the motion giving me a glimpse of the parts of her I just touched. She slides back so she's on the air mattress, keeping her eyes locked on mine as she gives me a sexy smile.

"Get up here," she orders , pulling the top quilt back and scooting under it to make room for me.

I toss my shirt aside, then climb onto the tailgate, smiling alongside Lana's chuckle at the air mattress squashing and rocking under my weight as I crawl to her side.

"Hi," she whispers when I grin at her.

"Hey," I breathlessly reply.

This is where I'd hoped the night would lead, but now I tremble with nerves. What the hell is wrong with me?

I've been with... well, we don't need to list exactly how many partners I've slept with, but it's been quite a few. Why does this feel so different?

Because I don't want this to be just one night with Lana. But I don't want to scare her off by telling her that. She doesn't need to know about my abandonment issues, especially not right now. Especially since I know she's Shane's second and she might return to her life back in Woodbine Hollow at any point to support his leadership.

"Max?" Lana slides her palm up my arm. "You okay?"

"Yeah, darlin'."

"You sure? Are you cold? You're shivering." She sits up and strokes her hand over my cheek, fingers running over my beard as though she's soothing a pet.

"You've got me nervous."

"Ha!" Her laugh seems to surprise us both, but it makes me chuckle, too.

"Wanna know a secret?" Lana asks, tracing her fingers down my throat and over my chest before resting it over my pounding heart.

"Sure."

"I've been imagining this moment since... well, I'm not sure if it started when I saw you half naked in the rain, or strumming your guitar and flirting with the whole damn dance floor, or grinding on you at the strip club. Regardless, you've been on my mind." Her fingers trail lower, her hazel eyes flashing gold as they watch while she explores the plane of my stomach and down the thigh closest to her. "But..."

"But what?" I urge her to continue, arching into her

touch as my body responds to her. Our breathing has become ragged, matching the other's as we lean closer.

"It's been a while since I've been with a guy," Lana murmurs and my breath hitches as she slides that same exploring touch against the zipper of my jeans, pressing firmly against my cock.

"It's not like you forget how it works," I tease, gasping when she grips me through the denim.

"No, but I want it to be good for both of us. Can you take it slow? And tell me what you like? I'm pretty sure it's not the same as what my ex enjoyed."

"I'll take it as slow or fast as you want, Lana. And I'll tell you what I like if you promise to do the same." Cupping her cheek in my palm I lean toward her, easing her down against the mattress and wedging a thigh between her legs. "And what on earth did your ex like that I wouldn't?" I ask against the side of her throat as I nibble and kiss down to her shoulder.

She clears her throat and answers with a broad grin coloring her tone. "Being choked while I fucked her with a strap on."

I nearly choke.

But instead, I huff a laugh against her skin. "Well, that's a hell of an image to put into a man's head. But you know, I'm willing to try anything once."

"Max?"

"Yeah?"

"Can you please put your mouth on me?"

I'm no longer trembling when I press her into the air

mattress and claim her lips. Even if she might leave me lonely one day soon, it'll be worth it.

Everything is wobblier than I'd prefer, the mattress shifting precariously under our movements, but I manage to slip my hands under her shirt to cup her breasts. She sighs and arches into my touch, her nipples pert and practically begging for my attention. I slide down her body, kissing over the fabric until I can push her cropped tee higher and bare her breasts fully. With a smile, she grips the torn hem and pulls it off.

I'll never get tired of the sound of Lana's soft moans of pleasure when my tongue traces against her skin, or when I pull one of her rosy nipples into my mouth. She grips my hair between her fingers and guides my mouth lower, down her taut belly and to the top of her jeans.

Grinning up at her I find her eyes blown almost black and assume mine look similar.

"Tell me what you want, remember?" Groaning she arches her hips toward me, but I just pull back with a smirk. "Use your words, darlin'."

"Damn it," she laughs, unbuttoning the top of her jeans. "I screwed myself on that little promise, didn't I?" In the moonlight I can just make out the flush on her cheeks and chest. She drags the zipper down, keeping her eyes locked on mine.

"Now's not the time to be shy. A promise is a promise."

Exhaling a shaky breath she replies, "I want you to take my jeans off and fuck me with your tongue and fingers. Let's see what all those years of playing guitar have taught you."

Holy gods, I might come in my pants before I even finish getting her off. I grip the open waistband at her hips and pull them down. "With pleasure."

Chapter 27
Lana

Max's hot mouth between my legs has me panting as he slips his fingers over me, then slides them inside, matching the speed of his tongue on my clit. My body responds immediately, bucking and grinding, seeking the exact friction I need. What I've been craving since that night at the strip club.

When I whimper with pleasure Max's eyes dart up to meet mine, the corners crinkling in one of his constant smiles. I'd smile back but I can barely control myself. His other hand grips my thigh, almost bruising while holding me close so he can wring everything from me. It feels better than I would have imagined. His facial hair scratches against my inner thighs, a pleasant way for him to claim me that I've never experienced before.

"Right there. Please—" I stumble over my words, throwing my arms over my face and chasing my release as he speeds his fingers. "Please don't stop. Oh, gods." Any hope that we'd be stealthy in our hook up is dead when my climax takes over, leaving me a moaning mess. As I catch my breath, I stare up at the night sky, my breaths are little panting gasps as I smile at the chirping of the crickets and frogs nearby. I can't stop the breathy giggle that escapes my lips when I glance down at Max's messy hair.

"Did I pass the test?" Max teases, kissing my inner thigh, then dragging open mouthed kisses back up my torso until he's covering me and nibbling on my neck.

"With flying colors," I answer, pulling his mouth to mine. He tastes and smells like my desire, a little claiming of my own that fuels me to lift my hips to press his hard cock where I want him. His jeans are rough against my sensitive skin, and I want to know what it feels like without denim between us. "Now, it's your turn. Tell me what you want."

"I want that pretty mouth wrapped around my cock," he answers without hesitation, gripping my chin between his thumb and forefinger and staring into my eyes. The heat behind his gaze sends my stomach flipping and I want to push him down and ride him. But I'll take my time, we have all night. I push him onto his side, then his back with a grin. The air mattress creaks, making us both huff a laugh, but the laughter dies and Max's breath hitches when I run my hands over him, my nails scraping through the dark hair on his chest and stomach. The cute twinkle lights he strung around the truck bed glitter in his golden gaze as he watches me unfasten his jeans and slide the zipper down.

Without his underwear, he's bared to me quickly, his size surprising me as he springs free of the denim. He raises his hips enough for us to pull his jeans off before I wrap my fingers around him and offer a tentative stroke, watching his expression the whole time. My chest is hot, heart pounding, flushed with my release and with the excitement of finally being with him. When he tilts his head back, breathing a moan, I run my palm down his length again, biting my lower lip before I kiss along his hip bone.

"Gods damn, Lana," Max whispers, gently cupping the back of my head. I meet his gaze, our eyes the same molten gold, then run my tongue across his tip. His breath is a hiss between his teeth, and he tangles his fingers in my hair when I take him fully into my mouth, sliding along his length and testing how deep I can pull him into my throat. His moans fill the night, joining the sounds of the night birds and chirping insects as I explore his body with my tongue, stroking him until he groans and pulls me away.

"Fuck, darlin'," Max murmurs. "You look prettier than I imagined sucking my cock, but if you keep going I'm not going to last." He pulls me up his body so our bare chests press together. "And I want this to last," he whispers against my mouth before he claims it, pulling my hair with a gentle grip as his tongue parts my lips and he devours me.

Breathing heavily, I push up, straddling him and pulling him up to kiss me again. He groans when I tug the dark waves at his nape, deepening our kiss as he runs his hands over my back before resting them on my hips.

"Do you have a condom?" I whisper, pulling back slightly.

He nods, then wraps an arm around me, holding me

steady while he leans across and digs through the pockets of his jeans. The foil packet crinkles in his fingers when he pulls a strip of three free.

"Someone was prepared." I laugh at him as his eyes sparkle, and he grins and rips into it with his teeth. "Am I that easy to read?"

"A guy can dream. And I've been dreaming about this for a while now, darlin'." Max presses a kiss to my breastbone, looking up at me. "You sure about this?"

"Very," I reply with a grin, leaning down to nip at his throat.

He groans, slides the condom on quickly, then kisses me more gently than before, caressing my skin and planting tender kisses down my throat and across my collarbone.

"You're leading the way here," Max whispers against my skin, the tickle of his breath and whiskers raising gooseflesh with their sensation. With a sigh, I push him back so he reclines on the collection of pillows he's piled at the head of the mattress and raise up over him. I slide against him a few times before lining him up with my entrance, then slowly lower myself onto him. I'm still slippery and eager, but I go slowly, adjusting to his size with a gasp as he fills me.

"*Fuck*, Max," I whimper when I'm fully seated. The sensation is so consuming that I sit still for a moment, enjoying the fullness of him inside me. When I throw my head back, I can't tell if the stars I see are the ones that have always been in the sky or the ones in my mind.

"You okay?" He slides his hands over me, not pushing

me for more, but I can feel a tremble that runs through his muscles, his need to take me trying to break through his desire to be gentle.

"Gods, yes." I murmur, rocking my hips. Max's grip tightens, his fingers digging into my hips with his moan of pleasure, encouraging me to move again and again.

We find a rhythm, our bodies working in tandem to seek pleasure from one another. I can't hold back my moans as my muscles coil and my release looms again. Somehow Max is already attuned to my needs, letting me set the pace. A low growl rises in my throat as my desire for him increases, and I let instinct take over.

Even though we're joined, I want him closer. I want more.

"Come here," I whisper and slip my hand behind his head to pull him so he's sitting with me straddling him, riding him. Our chests are flush, the warmth of our skin nearly the same as I kiss him. I hadn't expected to feel such a need for his touch.

He breaks the kiss and I almost whine with longing, but then he's kissing my throat, murmuring, "Use me, Lana." He trails his mouth down my neck, biting where it meets my shoulder. I'm so focused on the warmth coiling in my belly that I almost miss him whisper, "Take whatever you need from me." He buries his face in my hair, holding me tight as I chase my climax.

"Max," I gasp his name, my breath ragged. Reading what I need, he snakes a hand between us to stoke my clit. "Oh, *fuck*. I'm coming."

I cry out, my nails digging into his freckled shoulders

and back. I muffle my shout against his skin, unable to stop myself from biting when I come, pulsing, and rocking my hips against him. As I catch my breath, Max grips me around my waist and flips me onto my back, thrusting into me as I ride the waves of my pleasure. After a few thrusts, his hips jerk and he pants, "Fuck, Lana," when he reaches his own climax.

Our breaths are rapid and heavy as Max rests his forehead against mine. Our hearts beat in time as we catch our breath. Max surprises me when he tenderly strokes his palm through my hair, tracing a finger over my collarbone and following it with gentle kisses before he pulls out of me and rolls to lay beside me.

"That was..." I mutter, staring up at the stars, not even sure how to end my sentence.

"Yeah," Max answers.

He turns toward me, palming my cheek and kissing me gently before rolling away to discard the condom. When he lays beside me, I slide my gaze to find him studying me. He winks and then gives one of his panty-melting smiles when I take his hand in mine.

By the time he pulls the layers of quilts over me, I'm halfway dozing. In the space between waking and sleep I mean to tell him that, despite his order earlier, I would never use him. I think I tell him, but with the warmth of his body against my back, I find myself drifting to sleep, unsure of whether I've opened my heart to him or not.

Chapter 28
Max

Lana's breathing is even, her eyes fluttered shut shortly after I wrapped my arms around her and tucked the quilts tight. Even so, I don't dare confess what I'm thinking.

I may have extended an offer to use me, but I can't bear the idea that she might do just that. That Shane was right about her being on the rebound, and that I'll scratch that itch and she'll retreat back to Woodbine Hollow and her life there without so much as a second thought.

I don't think she would. I think what we're building is more than that. The music if not the sex. But I want it all. And the fear of being left behind again prickles at the back of my mind.

I want to lay next to her at night and wake with her in the morning. I want to share the stage and make music with her. I want a bond and a life with this wild wolf woman that's taken my heart in her jaws. But will I ever be able to admit that?

What will I do if she leaves? My heart stutters, my chest squeezing with misery at the thought. I pull Lana closer, her smooth skin is soft as she snuggles against me. We both run a little warmer than a human, but the air is crisp as a breeze flutters through the trees. Tonight, I can savor the scent of her in my bed, the feel of her against me. If I dwell on what might go wrong, I'll lose my mind.

Curling around her, I close my eyes and try to focus on the pleasure that bubbles within me at the sight of her so comfortable and safe. Ignoring the pangs of doubt, I focus on Lana's breathing and let it coax me to sleep.

—

Groaning, I crack my eyelids open against the bright orange glow of the sunrise. Something soft landing on me has my eyes opening fully, wondering how my boxer briefs ended up on my face.

"What the—" I'm cut off by Lana's bra flying through the air, landing between us. A chuckle follows, then Lana's panties. I left all of our underwear where we dropped them to shift last night. Another low giggle tells me Raquel is the pest returning them to us now.

"Wake up, love birds," Quel chides. She has one hand covering her eyes, like she might see something she hasn't already, when she peeks over the edge of the truck bed.

"Good morning to you too, you little shit," Lana mutters, pulling the quilt over her head. She sounds pissed, but I caught the barest glimpse of a grin before she disappeared under the patchwork. Raquel scoffs and drops her hand, leaning her forearms on the edge of the bed.

"Sorry to interrupt whatever round was on the schedule this morning," Raquel teases. She doesn't look sorry in the least. "Shane told me to come find you. Unless you're okay with cold breakfast." Raquel grins as she drums her fingers against the side of the truck and turns to hike back to the house. "Looks like I won the bet." She chuckles as she goes.

"You've got to be kidding me." Lana's voice is muffled by the quilts, but I burrow under them to join her, like two kids in a blanket fort. Like we're the only two people around.

"You okay?"

"Well, I had hoped to have a peaceful morning with you," she says, glancing over at me with a small smile tugging on her lips. "*Before* everyone was awake."

"Might not have been too peaceful then," I tease, pulling her close.

"Mmm, maybe not," she replies, wiggling against me and sending need pulsing through me when she grinds against my morning wood. Before I can say anything, she kisses me, holding me tight like I might disappear. "I had fun last night," she murmurs against my lips, more tender than I think I've ever heard her speak.

"Best night of my life," I reply, running my nose against hers.

"Fucking breakfast? *That's* what she came down here for?"

Lana sighs, sitting up so her bare back is to me as she

puts on her bra and starts searching for her tee shirt that we discarded last night. She throws the blankets off and shimmies into her panties, then her jeans before laying back down on the partially deflated air mattress next to me. "I don't give a shit if it's cold or not." She grins and kisses me.

Breakfast can be cold; I don't give a shit either. Fuck, I don't even need breakfast.

"Let's go," Lana finally says with a sigh, pulling me up with her.

I pull my jeans on and grab a new shirt from the back of the truck. We both left our shoes back at the edge of the woods, so we have to pick our way up the low hill to the cabin barefoot on the cold, dewy grass.

"Well, well, what a cute little 'walk of shame'," Raquel announces over her coffee mug from where she sits with Jamila on the porch. Jamila playfully chucks her on the shoulder, winking at me. Shane is staring into the fire pit, pointedly avoiding my eyes as we climb the stairs.

"They're biscuits!" Kaycia explains when I cock my head at the cast iron Dutch oven in the fire.

"Fancy. Please tell me this isn't what Raquel woke me up for," Lana grumbles, crossing her arms as she meets her brother's matching hazel gaze. I catch myself staring at her messy hair and the light flush on her lips and cheeks from our earlier kisses, the places my beard rubbed her skin and left proof of my affection. She doesn't give a fuck who knows what we've been doing, and I love her for it. Shit, do I *love* her? I run my fingers through my hair to hide their tremble.

"Didn't want you to feel left out. Or for Raquel to eat everything before you got some," Shane replies, ignoring Raquel flipping him off.

"Oh, they got some all right," Raquel murmurs. "Looks like you two worked up an appetite, wouldn't want you to perish." She's gleeful when Lana glares at her and sticks out her tongue, egging her on.

"All right, enough. Everyone is an adult here," Shane interrupts, looking mildly uncomfortable. "Breakfast is ready."

Lana reaches out her hand to take mine, offering a wink before dragging me inside to get a cup of coffee.

I barely taste the bacon and eggs, or the fresh biscuits smothered in honey butter that Shane literally stood over a fire cooking. Nothing can compare to the taste of Lana still lingering on my lips, or the thrill of her touch on my leg under the table. If I wasn't already in trouble, the night we shared sealed it for me. This is the first time I've let someone affect me like this, risked that they might tear my heart out. But even if I told myself this could be casual, even if this is the moment I usually call things off, I knew the first time I saw her it would never be just one night. If I was able to convince her to give me a chance, I wasn't going to be able to let go.

After breakfast, Lana washes dishes with Kaycia while Jamila and Raquel pack up their tent and I help Shane clean up the rest of the cabin and pack away the air mattress and quilts. By the time Lana wanders down to the pond, I've cleaned up all the evidence of the night we shared. The twinkle lights and quilts are tucked safely in the backseat, and the only thing that remains after our night together is the little current that threads between us.

Raquel and Jamila have tossed their tent and supplies in the bed of the truck and headed back to the city by the time Lana and I are ready to hit the road. She smiles at me when she climbs in the cab, the late-morning sun glinting off her messy bun. Shane waves goodbye when I turn the key and honk the horn.

"See ya!" I call out the open window.

Kaycia already has her sketchbook out, tucked into one of the chairs on the deck to take advantage of the scenery before they return home. She smiles and waves in our rearview as our tires crunch down the driveway toward the main road.

Lana leans her head against the window, watching the trees fade into neighborhoods, which fade into skyscrapers and bridges as we approach Argent. I wove our fingers together when the gravel was still noisy under the tires and haven't let go since.

"Do you miss it?" I ask, waiting at one of the red lights behind a line of cars. Horns honk and construction noise pierces the glass over the music playing low on the radio. I hope she doesn't read between the lines of my question. Doesn't sense the pathetic need to ask her to stay here. With me. In this noisy place so different from the peace she's used to.

"Hmm?" she questions, brow furrowed as she studies me.

"Woodbine Hollow. Do you miss it?" I keep my eyes on the road, turning when the light finally turns green.

"My family? Yes. The mountains and being away from crowds? Yes. The drama that inevitably comes along with being part of a pack or the pitying looks I got post-breakup? Not really. No."

I want to ask her more about her ex, but I don't want her to think I'm prying, or comparing what we have with their relationship.

Before I can ask anything, she continues, "It's hard because I feel the pull so strongly. To check in with Shane because he's my alpha, to be near my family because they're my pack and my loyalty should be there." She glances over at me, at our joined hands, but I pretend I don't see it, focusing on the drive. "Sometimes I wish I could tell them to figure it out themselves. Even if that's against everything I grew up knowing. Does that make me a bad wolf?"

I don't have an answer for her. Falcons aren't bound to packs like wolves, so I can never understand the draw of the pack, or the urge to obey an alpha. I've been on my own so long, no one to answer to really, that I just squeeze her hand before bringing her fingers up to my lips. She's the only one I want to answer to.

"I don't think so. I think you just need to work some things out, I think that's the human part of you."

"Maybe." She smiles as I squeeze her hand, returning the pressure and keeping our fingers laced on the console as she turns to look out the window again.

When I pull up in front of her building, I leave the engine running, turning to her instead of getting out to unload anything. "What's your schedule look like this week?"

She seems surprised I'm asking but doesn't hesitate with her response. "I'm scheduled for doubles Wednesday and Thursday, then lunch Friday. I thought about picking a shift up Saturday since we aren't playing. Why?"

"Well, I thought we could set up a full rehearsal so you can get more comfortable with the guys. See how we all really fit together. What about Tuesday?"

"Oh, sure. I'll put it in my phone." She reaches into her pocket to pull out her phone, the little glimmer of excitement fading from her eyes. I stop her, taking her hand again and hoping the disappointment in her voice means she won't break my heart with my next question.

We just spent the night wrapped up with one another, I don't know why my hand shakes like a teenager.

"And how about you don't pick up anything Saturday." She narrows her eyes, but I keep talking before I lose my nerve. "Since you're off, I thought maybe I could take you on a real date."

Lana's eyes flash gold as a smile spreads across her face, that look sending my heart sputtering and my stomach flipping.

"I'd like that."

Chapter 29
Lana

"So, what kind of date are we talking about here?" Kaycia asks, hands on her hips as she stares into her closet. Shane's clothes are shoved in one side, his boots and sneakers piled in the corner by the bed, jeans draped across various pieces of furniture. I need to find my own place soon, me being in his apartment is really ruining the vibe here.

"I dunno?" I look over at Jamila as though she has an answer. She's kicked her sneakers off somewhere and sits with her legs crossed at the ankles on the bed reading through the lyrics of a new song I've been working on since I got home from the cabin. "What kind of dates are there? Back home you either eat at the diner, grab a beer at the local dive, or party around a bonfire and end up making out in the woods."

"Well, you've pretty much done all those things already. You sure it's a first date?" Kaycia teases, throwing a wry glance over her shoulder.

"Ha. Ha." I toss one of her velvet throw pillows across the room, bouncing it off her legs.

"Just come take a look and borrow whatever you want," she finally says, pulling her phone from the back pocket of her cut off denim shorts and checking a text. It's starting to get chilly in the city, and she's wearing one of Shane's sweatshirts to battle against the crisp breeze blowing through the open slider, making it look like she's only wearing a shirt and socks. I can hear the street sounds blaring over her soft music, and it makes me long for the silence of Shane's cabin again.

Unfolding my legs from beneath me, I stand and stretch. The new velvet accent chair Kaycia bought after Colton's guys trashed her place is cozy. Just like almost everything else about her apartment. It's easy to see how she's taken the hard edge off my brother, I'm practically turning into a kitten after only twenty minutes here.

A full-length mirror is mounted to one of the walls between the closet and bed. I won't think too much about that, but I do take a look at myself standing in front of it. I'm wearing my usual ripped jeans and a tee. I don't have many dressy things. I really never needed them back home. But I want to at least try to dress up for my date with Max. It's been almost a week since our little camp out and I can still imagine his hands on my skin, his scent all over me. I'm nearly squirming just thinking about what we might get up to tomorrow night. Luckily, Raquel and Shane are both at the shop. Kaycia and Jamila can't scent what I'm thinking about like another shifter could. I blow out a breath, refocusing on the task at hand.

"This is pretty." I pull out a red floral sundress, its straps so delicate I'm afraid I might break them if I borrow it.

"Oh, uh—" Kaycia chokes a little, clearing her throat before blurting, "—*not* that one!"

Jamila holds in a laugh, but starts cackling as Kaycia blushes nearly as red as the dress.

"I don't even want to know what you and my brother did while you were wearing this." I hang it back up immediately.

"Another first date." Jamila chuckles. Kaycia pours a glass of wine with a smile.

I flip through the hangers, studying the different options. Kaycia is several inches shorter than I am, and built slimmer, but she wears a lot of her clothes loose, so I'm sure *something* will fit. Out of the corner of my eye I see that Kaycia is engrossed in her texts, but it's really none of my business who she's so preoccupied with.

"Wait, what were those?" Jamila asks, stopping my hands from their aimless hanger scraping.

"These?" I pull out a pair of leather shorts. "These look very adventurous for you Kaycia."

"They were for a costume party a few years back." She laughs. "I had it in my head that maybe I'd have the nerve to wear them out once I moved, but I kind of forgot about them."

"What were you dressed up as?"

"A sexy black cat. *Obviously*," she replies.

"Obviously."

"Try them on!" Jamila insists.

"I'm not sure my thighs will squeeze into these," I inspect the size, but they actually might fit.

They both avert their eyes, Kaycia laughing as she mutters, "still not used to naked shifters," when I strip out of my jeans and wiggle the leather shorts up and over my hips and zip them up.

"Not bad." I look over my shoulder in the mirror. They're not as a short as they looked, but they're not long either. And I have to admit, my legs look great. "But what would I wear them with?"

"Tights and boots!" Jamila announces. "And damn, those are perfect on you." She nods approvingly. "He's going to lose what little mind he has left in that bird brain."

"But like, what shirt? I'm terrible at this."

"One of your cool vintage band ones. Here, look." Jamila clicks around on her phone for a moment, then turns it around to show me a few photos of women wearing similar shorts with tights, various styles of boots, and tees or sweaters.

"And we can curl your hair and really play up the eye makeup!" Kaycia does a little wiggle of excitement and claps her hands.

I can't help but grin, her excitement is contagious. Is this what female friendship feels like? "Okay, I think I know which shirt and I'm sure I can pick up tights somewhere tomorrow."

"I know exactly which boots," Jamila says. She and Kaycia share conspiratorial grins. I wonder if they know they don't have to work this hard to get Max and me together, but I keep my mouth shut. "But I'll swing back by tomorrow with some options, just in case."

"Not too tall though!" I insist. "I can't walk on stilts like you do, J."

"I know, I know." She waves me off and glances down at her phone. "I have a couple of jackets you can try with it too. I have to get going. I'm meeting my mom for dinner after her class is finished, but I'll be back tomorrow. Here, I made a couple of notes on the song. It will be good for you two to sing together."

She tosses my notebook toward the foot of the bed for me. I snag it before Kaycia can peek at the lyrics written inside.

"Thanks, just text me when to expect you tomorrow."

Jamila hugs Kaycia, then me, before grabbing her bag and letting herself out of the small apartment. I realize this is the first time I've hung out with Kaycia all on our own.

"I'll just change back into my jeans." Kaycia turns away from me again as I shimmy out of the shorts and yank on my familiar denim.

"You want something to drink?" she asks over her shoulder. "I have sparkling water or iced tea if you don't want anything with alcohol." She holds her glass of white wine up with her head tilted a bit.

"I'll have a glass of wine with you, if that's okay."

"Of course!" Kaycia walks across the room to the kitchen and grabs a clean wine glass, pouring in the cool liquid. By the time she's returned the bottle to the fridge, I'm back in the comfy chair with my legs curled under me again.

"I only avoid drinking in crowds or new places. I've had a few times where it caused me to be a little too... out of control. It used to embarrass my ex, so I pretty much stopped drinking altogether." I shrug, taking a small sip of the wine. It's crisp and refreshing, a little tart, and so good. "That and then the shit Colton and them did to me, makes me extra leery of letting go in strange settings. I'm still not totally okay with feeling out of control."

"Ah, I see." She nods, taking a seat on the small sofa. "Shane mentioned you'd broken up with a long-term partner recently. I'm sorry. About all of it. What Colton did. What happened... it was fucked up. How are you doing?"

"It's fine. I'm fine. Most of the time."

She gives me a look that practically screams, *I know damn well you have nightmares and are totally not fine.* But she doesn't press me about it.

"But you were okay drinking with Max." Kaycia's eyes crinkle, the bright blue filled with curiosity over the rim of her glass as she takes a delicate sip and steers the conversation to a lighter topic. She tilts her head and arches her brows as she adds, "At a strip club."

"I see Shane has told you all kinds of things."

"I think his words were: 'I accused Max of sleeping with Lana when she was drunk and she handed my ass to me'."

I can't help the laugh that bursts from my lips. "An honest man."

"Yes. And a good one. So is Max."

"Yeah, he is. They both are. And yeah, I did. I got

wasted. Embarrassingly so. But I feel safe with Max. Comfortable. Like—" I pause, taking a sip to keep myself from spilling all my thoughts to my brother's poor girlfriend who probably wants me to leave her alone. "I'm sorry, you don't care about all that."

"Yes, I do! You don't have to tell me anything you don't want to, obviously. But I'm your friend, Lana. You're Shane's sister, we're practically family. So, if you want to share, please do. About anything you need to talk about. We were both there that night. You can talk to me."

"I just...I don't know. I feel like Max won't make me feel shitty for having a good time and being myself. If I lose my temper or get too drunk or hell, want to sing an old song around a campfire, he's not going to make me feel like an idiot. He'd probably cheer me on. Or join me."

"Absolutely," she says with a smile. "He would definitely join you. And, no, he would never make fun of you. *We* won't either. I felt so alone in this city at first. Shane and his friends really took me in. Took me for who I am. We're all embarrassing sometimes, it's just part of...well, I would say it's part of being human, but only Jamila and I are really just human. It's part of being alive. All those things that light you up, you shouldn't dim them. And no one who loves you should either."

"Yeah," I take another deep drink of the wine, finding it difficult to swallow around the lump of emotion in my throat. "Thanks, Kaycia. I'm really glad Shane met you."

"I'm glad too. And I'm glad you're here. It's been really good for him to have you around in Argent. So, please don't think you have to rush back home or move or anything too quickly, okay? Find your footing and figure out what's best for you."

"Thank you." I sniffle, unable to keep the tears away now. "It's nice to know someone cares."

"Awww! Don't cry! Come here," Kaycia exclaims, crossing the tiny room to wrap her arms around me. "And Shane and I aren't the only ones who care. Max *really* cares, too. He's been texting me all afternoon trying to plan your date."

"*What?*" I laugh, wiping at my nose with the back of my hand, feeling like a gross little kid as I blink the tears away.

"He's so nervous, you'd think he's never been on a date before."

"We already slept together! What can he be so anxious about? It's kind of a sure thing." I make light of it, huffing a sarcastic laugh. But my heart is pounding so hard I suspect even Kaycia's human hearing can pick it up.

"Oh, I don't think this has anything to do with getting laid." Kaycia's eyes practically sparkle. "But I do think this is the first time he's ever cared about all the rest."

I smile, matching the exuberance that radiates from my brother's girlfriend. My heart continues to pound in my ears and my stomach does a little flip flop, encouraging me to down the rest of the wine as I think about how dramatically my life has changed in the last few weeks.

By the time Shane's bike rumbles up to the curb, the sun has sunk low and the sky is a glorious pink beyond the towering city. Kaycia and I are finishing the bottle of wine on her balcony, waving and calling down to him as he approaches the front of the building.

"Hey hey, handsome!" Kaycia crows with a grin, flushed and a little tipsy.

"Hey, baby girl! Hey to you too, Lana," Shane replies with a matching smile.

He smells like oil and citrus scrub when he walks through the door minutes later, wrapping Kaycia in a tight hug in the open doorway of the loft while I stay perched on one of her little patio chairs.

"What are you two up to?" Shane asks, arm wrapped around Kaycia's waist. Their casual affection reminds me of what I used to have with Taryn, except I don't think I was ever so carefree.

"Girl time! Getting Lana outfitted for her date tomorrow!" Kaycia explains, dragging Shane out to sit amongst the plants on the patio.

"Where are you going?" Shane asks me.

"I'll tell you later, it's a surprise!" Kaycia answers while I shrug.

Now, I'm getting nervous at whatever Max has planned. I've never really been away from Woodbine Hollow, what kind of fancy date is this going to be?

"You okay, little sister?" Shane nudges my knee with the toe of his boot from where he sits across from me.

"Oh, yeah. I'm good. I think I'm going to call it a night though. Thanks for the shorts, Kaycia. I'll see y'all tomorrow."

"Wait just a minute, I need to talk to you." Shane stands and follows me through the apartment, leaving

Kaycia out on the balcony. My heart rate ratchets higher at the tone of his voice. Is he really going to lecture me about Max? Or is this something else?

"What's up?" I ask in the entryway of the apartment. "Mom already told me where babies come from... you're too late."

Shane doesn't smile. *Shit.*

"Have you talked to Aubrey?" he asks.

"No, why?" I pull my phone out of my pocket, when *was* the last time we checked in with each other? It's been over a week.

"Caleb Davidson has gone missing." Shane runs a hand through his hair with a frown.

"What does that have to do with Aubrey?" I hedge, looking up from my phone as I send a text to Aubrey, hoping my feigned nonchalance is believable. I know my little brother's secret, but I don't know what Shane is privy to and I don't want to cause problems if no problem exists.

"I heard rumors when I was back in town that the two of them sometimes hung out. Before everything went south." He shrugs. "Mama's the one who told me Caleb was missing. I guess his mom called her panicking, asking if *I'd* had anything to do with her son disappearing."

"I mean, you exiled the ones who were part of the attack by Colton. Why would him leaving be a surprise?" I slip my phone back in my pocket, waiting for Aubrey's reply.

"He didn't say anything to her. She swears he would have said goodbye before he left."

"Did you ask Aubrey?"

"Yeah, he told me he didn't know and left the house before I could get anything else out of him. Something is off, but I don't know what yet." The lines around Shane's mouth deepen, showing me he's worried without having to say it.

"I'll keep you posted if I find anything out." I open the apartment door.

"Thanks, Lana. I feel bad that I barely know my own brother."

"It's not your fault," I insist, squeezing his forearm. "It will all work out." *I hope.*

After calling out a goodbye to Kaycia, with a promise to let her know when Jamila comes over tomorrow, I slip into my apartment and flick on the television to drown out the conversation between Shane and Kaycia through the wall.

I look at my phone again, as though I might have missed Aubrey's reply. When he doesn't text back, I dial his number and let it ring through to voicemail twice before I leave a quick message. Curling up on the couch with a container of leftover takeout noodles I try to focus on the trashy reality show instead of worrying about what the hell is happening back home or wondering what exactly my nervousness about my date tomorrow really means.

Chapter 30
Max

I check my shirt pocket for the third time as I pull into a spot across from Lana's building. The theater tickets are safe and sound, just like they were the first and second times I checked.

The newest stage sensation is nearly impossible to get decent seats for without booking months in advance, but luckily, I did some work for one of the promoters a year ago and was able to call in a favor to get a pair on short notice. I hope Lana's as excited as I am about it. It will be fun to be the one in the audience for once. I'm fairly certain she's never been to a big production before either, so I'm looking forward to showing her more than just dive bars, diners, and strip joints in the city.

Kaycia seemed to think it was a great idea. She even helped me plan where to go for dinner—reservations in thirty minutes at a steakhouse near the theater—and what to do after—craft cocktails and dessert at a popular rooftop lounge downtown. I felt like a dick asking her how to plan a nice date, but when it comes down to it, I really only have hook ups and friends. Even if those sometimes overlap, I've never had someone I'm trying to impress or keep around for more than a weekend or two. But I definitely want Lana for as long as I can have her.

Sighing at my nerves and the fact that I very well may be setting myself up for heartbreak, I get buzzed into the building and climb the three flights of stairs. I run a hand through my hair before knocking on the scarred wood of Lana's door, trying to hide their anticipatory quivering.

The door swings open and I have to catch myself from gaping at Lana. She's always good looking, but tonight she's a knockout. Her hair has these messy waves, and her eye makeup is smoky and dark, so different than her usual minimal style. A vintage band tee hangs from one shoulder, revealing the lacy strap of whatever she's wearing underneath. I can't stop my eyes from traveling down, taking in black leather shorts and tall boots that stop just above her knees. The skin between the hem of her shorts and the top of the boots is covered with black mesh, the pattern not quite fishnet, not quite lace.

"Gods damn, darlin'," I manage to say on an appreciative exhale. She looks like she stepped out of the pages of a rock n' roll fashion shoot.

Lana's face has been still since she opened the door, like a beautiful statue, but now a grin breaks out across it, showing me the little gap in her teeth I adore so much. She lets out a deep breath like she was holding it as much as I was.

"Is this too much? Kaycia wouldn't tell me what we're

doing tonight." She glances down at herself, then back to me. I catch her scanning my dark long-sleeved tee and slacks, not too causal but not buttoned up either.

"You're fucking perfect. You look—" I grin at her, relaxing into our usual comfortable tones now that we're together again. "—you look good enough for me to consider calling it a night early and just stay in." I wink when she rolls her eyes.

"Flirt."

"Damn right. Hopefully I can flirt those little shorts right off."

"Good to know you're up for a challenge." She winks and smiles. "Let me grab my jacket. Come in." She leaves the door open for me to cross into the foyer. The space, once so familiar when Shane was in residence, now makes my heart race knowing it's her place, at least for now.

"I haven't changed much," she says from the bedroom portion, taking an oversized black blazer from the wardrobe.

"What's holding you back?" I swallow, looking away as I ask.

"Money. And planning," she answers. "I don't feel settled enough yet to start buying things. I still need to figure out where I'm going to be permanently."

As I turn back, she's sliding her arms into the blazer and her eyes meet mine as she cuffs the long sleeves. I wonder if mine look as sad as hers when she says it. I still don't know everything that went down with her ex, or what being Shane's second really entails. And she doesn't know any of my issues yet. So, rather than going to her and pulling her close to tell her I want her to be *here*, with me, permanently, I flash her my falsest smile, hoping she won't see through the façade of happiness. No one else ever does.

"Well, let me take you out to try to win the vote for you to stay in Argent."

She shakes her head with a laugh, golden waves hiding her expression as she grabs her keys and a little bag to stuff them in, and let's me lead her out the door and into the cool night.

We slip into the backseat of a ride share, the scent of leather and old takeout mingling with the soft hum of the city. We sit quietly as the driver has a heated conversation over speakerphone, our fingers brushing in the dark of the backseat, Lana's knee bumping mine every time the driver takes a corner too quickly. By the time we reach the restaurant my fingers have skated up her thigh and toy with the edge of her shorts. She's trembling when the driver throws it in park and lets us scramble out onto the busy sidewalk around the corner from the steakhouse.

"Good thing neither of us get banged up too easily. That was some shitty driving," Lana jokes, even though I can tell it's real relief she feels at being free from the confines of the car. My breath catches when she reaches out and takes my hand with a strained smile.

"Come on, everything else is in walking distance." I squeeze her palm in mine and lead her into the dim interior for our reservation.

"Holy shit, Max." Lana stops in the entry of Maddie's Steakhouse with her lips parted in surprise. "This is the nicest place I've ever been in."

"Come on, just wait until you taste their food." I tug her toward the hostess stand and keep hanging onto her hand as one of the black clad women behind the counter leads us to a candlelit booth in the back corner.

Eyes follow us through the tables, eliciting whispers over who she might be. Who *we* might be. In this city she could be a model or actress. She's a brilliant musician, and one day we might actually be people with names that are whispered as we walk by. But tonight, I just want her to be mine. To show her how she should be cared for, no matter what her status is in her pack is or what she's done in her past.

Our server brings us water, then iced tea, then glasses of red wine. While we wait on our salads, Lana studies the menu quietly. I sip my wine, giving her time to decide. It gives me time to admire her sharply sculpted face in the candlelight. To memorize her expressions. Just in case.

She flicks her eyes from the page, catching my gaze and raising her eyebrow with a smirk. "What?" she asks, her eyes flashing gold.

"You look beautiful tonight," I answer truthfully. Her eyes burn golden again, this time not changing back to their usual hazel while she holds my stare.

"Thank you," she whispers as she closes the menu. Blinking rapidly, she clears her throat and glances up to the waiter who stands at my shoulder.

"Have we decided?" the waiter asks.

We both order ribeye steaks—rare—with baked potatoes and asparagus. The waiter gathers our menus while asking, "Are you attending a show tonight, Mr. Acheson?"

"Yes," I reply, patting my shirt pocket.

"Wonderful, I'll be sure to have you out the door with time to spare."

"I appreciate it."

He smiles at us and departs to key in the order.

"A show?" Lana asks. "There's more?"

"Of course," I answer. I reach my hand across the table to brush my fingers against hers. "I want to show you what the city has to offer. Just in case I can tempt you to stay longer."

"What show is it?" Her eyes sparkle, but this time it has nothing to do with desire for me. I don't mind though, seeing her excited is even better.

"You'll see."

She scoffs and rolls her eyes but smiles broadly as she flips her hand over so our palms rest together on top of the tablecloth. My stomach somersaults at the casual intimacy, her grin growing wider as the pounding of my heart echoes in my ears.

Chapter 31
Lana

This is the nicest restaurant I've ever been in. And it's definitely the most expensive steak I've ever tasted. It's all I can do to keep from groaning as I swallow the first bite. Max is practically preening as he watches me eat and look around, like I'm some silly country girl who's never been to the big city.

Which I am.

And I hadn't been.

Until now.

I still hate the asphalt and steel jungle of Argent, but I must admit some parts are growing on me. I'm beginning to see how Shane can manage living here. Having friends and family around certainly makes it more appealing. The band. Max. All reasons I'm beginning to think I want to stay.

A few bites into our meals, I decide to take the conversation somewhere outside of music and flirtation. If I'm considering more, I need to know what's underneath the feathered façade. And he needs to know the mess he's getting into as well.

"So, how long have you lived in Argent? Your accent tells me you're not originally from here."

Max winks as he takes a drink of water, ruminating on his answer. "What accent?" He looks affronted, but his eyes crinkle at the corners.

"The one that drops your 'g' every time you call me 'darlin'', darlin','" I retort, letting my own accent come to the forefront more. "Or did you just figure out that twang would get panties to drop quicker?" I can't help but tease.

"I have no issues in that department, with or without pet names and pronouncing 'g's'." He laughs. "But you're right, I'm originally from Pine Valley. It's only about a half a day's drive south from Woodbine Hollow, I think."

"Is that so?" My chest warms, what if I can have both? What if I can go back to The Hollow and bring him with me. He'd be close to his people, too. "Your family still there?"

"No." He averts his eyes from mine, as though he can hide the sadness from me so easily. "My granny died nearly two—no, *shit*—nearly three years ago now. She was all I had there."

"Oh. I'm so sorry, Max."

"It's all right. She went peacefully, and it was expected. She'd been sick, so it was good that she wasn't suffering anymore. It's because of her I was able to move here in the first place. She left me her land and everything else she had. I sold it and used the money to move and get my place." He smiles at me, but it's soft, sad. He quickly looks back at his food.

I set my silverware down softly before reaching for him. When I wrap my fingers around his wrist his eyes meet mine again and the ache of missing someone is written all over his face. "And your parents?"

He offers a sarcastic imitation of a laugh, but his expression hardens. "Never knew who my father was. Don't know if Mama knew either. She left me on my grandmother's porch when I was five. Told me she'd be back soon. I waited on that porch for three days before Granny could convince me to come inside. She never did come back." His fingers grip his fork so tight I worry he might bend the steel.

"Oh, Max," I whisper, trying to soothe him. I can imagine a little boy with a mop of curly hair and sad grey-green eyes on a wooden porch like we have at home, watching a gravel driveway through all hours. I know first-hand what it's like to watch someone drive off, left behind on the top step with their tire dust sticking to your tear-stained cheeks.

"It's all right," he replies, taking a deep breath and shaking his head as though that's all that's needed to clear the years of loss. "What?" he asks, tilting his head when I huff a sad little laugh at the irony, the quick motion so like his falcon form.

"Nothing," I insist.

"No, tell me."

"I know a thing or two about being left on a porch by

someone you love. Just happened when I was older and partially to blame for the situation."

"Your ex?" he asks with a knitted brow. I don't want to be reminded of Taryn, but here we are. I guess I can't avoid telling him something about her.

"Yeah. I'm sure you can gather things didn't end great between us." I try to shrug it off by sipping some of my wine.

"Were you together long?" he asks, and I can tell he's trying to keep it casual by toying with the stem of his wineglass and not looking directly at me, but his shoulders have more tension than they did before and his jaw flexes minutely. *Is he jealous?*

"Three years. It wasn't a clean break up, but it's done now." I'm determined to change the subject to anything else. "So, was your grandmother a shifter, too?"

He studies me for a moment before relaxing and answering. "No, but at least Granny had heard some strange whispers about shifters and knew some people to talk to. Whoever my dad was must have been the one with the falcon genetics because Mama and Granny sure as shit couldn't shift. I never did know if he even knew about me. Guess it doesn't matter now."

His mood has turned somber since the start of this conversation, like talking about his past has drained away all his excitement. I don't know what to say. I can't imagine learning I was a shifter without the support of my family, my pack. No platitudes seem appropriate for the hand he was dealt. And my own moping about being lonely or not knowing what to do about going home seems ridiculous now that I know Max has no family to go back to even if he wanted to.

"Aw, shit. Did I spoil it?" Max asks, looking worried.

"What?"

"I ruined the date, didn't I? With my sob story." He has a wary look in his eye, like I might shift and run out of the restaurant or something. As though his sadness is contagious. As though he's going to be left again.

"No! No, you didn't. Thank you for telling me. I just...I feel silly now. My own mess seems a lot less important."

"Don't do that, Lana." Max places his other hand over mine where it still rests on his forearm. "Don't diminish your hurt just because I was dealt a rough hand early on. I'm doing just fine now. I have friends who are just as good as family, I know they'd go to war for me just like I would for them. I love my job and my band and my life..." He trails off for a moment, but the way his eyes flash gold and burn into mine makes me tremble at the energy sparking between us. "It's not a competition on who has the most trauma."

"Okay, sure. You're right. But just know, you can count me as part of those who care about you. Because I do. I care a hell of a lot, you know?"

I'm officially babbling. Who am I, blurting out that I care for him in the middle of dinner like a lovesick fool? It's clear we have chemistry—both musically and physically—but beyond that we haven't discussed *feelings*. I'm not sure I'm ready to admit that I think I'm falling for him. That I hope this is more than just a friends with benefits deal.

I'm certainly not going to ask him to define the relationship on our first date.

Before I spiral too far, he replies, "I kind of hoped you did." He meets my eyes with a soft smile tugging at the corners of his lips, quieting my racing thoughts with a single look. "Let's finish up dinner and head on over to the theater, okay? No more sad talk tonight."

"You mean I don't get to ask you about your exes?" I tease, trying to lighten the mood.

"Nothing to tell. I don't really have any to speak of." He shrugs with a broader smile, his eyes sparkling. "No one's been worth the risk before."

My cheeks heat and I smile as I squeeze his forearm one last time, finding it hard to pull my hand away from his warmth. We finish eating, changing the subject to favorite musicians and folk songs and movies and desserts. The innocuous everyday things that couples should know about one another. And the nice thing is I can tell him exactly what I like and dislike without wondering if he's judging me, or how it compares to what he likes or doesn't. It never feels like I have to hide parts of me like in the past.

When he's paid the check, we head out the door into the cool of the evening. Max's palm slips under my jacket to rest comfortably on the small of my back, the heat soothing me amongst the throngs of pedestrians and street noise. He guides me down the sidewalk toward the front of one of the theaters where a line is forming to get in the doors. I must admit, I feel a little star struck standing on the crowded street with the bright lights of the marquee shining brighter than anything I've ever seen before. My blood rushes to my cheeks when Max wraps his arms around me and pulls me close while we wait, chest to chest, hearts thumping in a nearly matching rhythm. With these heeled boots on I'm maybe a little taller than he is, but I still nuzzle my nose against his throat, tucking my head into the crook between his shoulder and jaw to inhale his scent.

He swallows as he runs his hand down my back, then whispers, his voice rough and needy, "You gotta be careful doing that, darlin'. I might have to take you home instead of being able to wait for the show."

"It's dark in there isn't it?" I tease.

"It's not like the back row of a small-town theater. Not with the seats we got." He chuckles, stealing a quick kiss before the line begins to move and we are ushered into the theater.

Chapter 32
Max

The smile that spreads across my face watching Lana is wider than I thought possible. She turns in a circle in the theater's lobby while we wait in line for the bar, studying the architecture of the historical building with her lips parted. Men and women in their various evening wear mill around, older couples in suits and dresses and younger groups in trendy high fashion styles, the din of humanity a constant hum. With our sensitive hearing both Lana and I can make out the conversations around us and we share secret smirks at couples flirting or fighting as they rush to their seats. I catch people glancing at Lana and me and feel a swell of protectiveness and pride bloom knowing we look good together.

"This place is *beautiful*," Lana says softly after we collect our drinks—overpriced bottles of water and a plastic, lidded souvenir cup of champagne for each of us.

"It's one of my favorite venues," I reply, pulling out the tickets to show the older man working as an usher. He smiles and shines his little pocket flashlight on the seat numbers, then leads us slowly down the aisle to a private table near the stage.

"*These* are our seats?" Lana's eyes widen, looking over her shoulder as the man retreats and leaves us to get settled. "How did you—"

"I wanted you to have a good time. I have a friend who was able to help me get them. I've heard this show is best when you're close to the action."

"Thank you," she replies, eyes flashing gold in the red stage lights. Her breathing is rapid, but the flush on her cheeks tells me it's a good thing. Thank the gods for good clients.

The production begins shortly after we toast with our champagne, dancers mingling through the audience as they make their way to the stage for the first number. It's a burlesque vibe with mash ups of modern music, and I hope Lana enjoys it as much as everyone else seems to.

Halfway through the first act I realize I don't have to worry, her eyes have been glued to the performers, flicking between the dancers and the musicians in the orchestra pit. During one song, she reached out to take my hand and hasn't let it go since, our fingers twined together under the table. Now, the last song before intermission starts. It's a slow number and the principal actress belts out the heartfelt solo under a bright spotlight. Her costume glitters in the light, drawing every eye to the stage. Every eye except mine, which drift to watch Lana's silhouette. In the glow of the lighting, I see tears welling in her eyes, lips still parted in wonder as she leans forward, enraptured. When the song is over, the last, long sustained note lingers in the silence of the auditorium and Lana's tears flow freely over her cheeks, her emotions freed by the music.

By the end of the show Lana's makeup is smudged from dabbing at her tears, but she shines with happiness. The same way she did the night we sang together at Lucy's. There's a standing ovation and she cheers as loud as the rest of the crowd for the performers. She grips my hand tightly as we walk out of the theater, jostled along with the rest of the spectators.

"Thank you, Max. That was incredible," she announces when we make it to the street out front. She laughs, wrapping her arms around my shoulders, and pulls me close.

"You're welcome. I wanted you to have a good time." I brush her hair back from her face, tucking one side behind her ear before letting my palm rest on her cheek.

"I did." She nuzzles her cheek against my hand before brushing her lips against mine, sending a spark fizzing through my blood and straight to my cock as she whispers, "Take me home."

"What about dessert?" I answer on a sigh as she presses her body against me and kisses me softly, knowing I don't give a shit about the best cheesecake in the city right now.

"That's exactly what I'm asking for," she replies, pulling back with a grin and flashing eyes.

I flag down the next cab that passes, Lana's laughter behind me as musical to my ears as the show we just watched.

"Take me to your condo," Lana whispers as we hurry

to the car. "The walls are thicker, and I don't care if your neighbors hear us."

"Let's hope this one's as fast as the last one," I tease, capturing a kiss before we pile into the backseat.

This cabbie did *not* drive as fast as the reckless one earlier, much to my desperation. Lana spent the twenty dark minutes nibbling on my ear lobe and kissing down the side of my neck while she ran her hand up my inner thigh to palm me through my pants. I spent the time thinking about anything but what she was doing and trying not to moan too loudly. I must have done a poor job because the driver turned the music up twice before we parked out front. I tossed cash in the front and practically dragged Lana out of the backseat.

She stands with her chest to my back and slips her hands under the front of my shirt as I get the key in the lock, dragging her fingernails over my abs and dipping her curious fingers beneath the waist of my pants and boxer briefs. Before she can explore any farther, I get the door open, spinning quickly and grabbing her. She squeals as I hoist her up, long legs wrapped around my waist so I can carry her through the door and into my bedroom. She peels off her blazer, leaving it discarded on the floor before I lay her across the top of the comforter, taking her in as she arches her back and smiles at me.

"Think Jamila will care if you leave these on?" I ask, sinking to my knees and kissing the mesh tights on her inner thigh as I tap on the nearly thigh high boots.

"If I leave them on, how will you get the tights off?"

"Oh, I have an idea," I reply. "Take off your shirt and shorts."

Lana moves swiftly, tossing both across the room and laying back on the bed in a black lace bralette, tights, and those fucking boots. Bless, Jamila. I pull my shirt over my head, adding it to the pile of discarded clothes, kick out of my shoes, and unbutton my pants while I watch her in the lamplight from the nightstand. Her eyes rake over my body before meeting my hungry gaze.

"What are you going to do now?" she asks, driving me wild by running her hands over her thighs as she opens them to me.

"What do you want me to do, Lana?"

"*Max*," she whines, dragging her hands up the inside of her thighs now, then over her breasts. "Come here already."

Her eyes are nearly glowing, and I know mine match, our animal sides close to the surface. I can scent how turned on she is, it drove me crazy in the confines of the cab, and it takes me only a moment to cross the room and cover her body with mine.

Our kisses are rough this time, claiming one another with actions if not words. She nips at my lower lip, and I groan when I taste the hint of blood from it. Being with another shifter is different than being with a human, I don't feel the need to hold back. Lana could toss me across the room if she was so inclined, but the way she's arching into me and dragging her nails down the flesh of my back tells me she wants this—needs this—as badly as I do.

Tonight, I'm free of the nerves I felt at the cabin. Then, I wasn't sure if what we had was just teasing and flirtation, two friends who could flirt paint off a wall having a good time, or whether it was more. But tonight, I can feel the difference between us. This is something rare. Tonight, I told her about my past, something I've never done with any of my other partners, and she comforted me without the pity I always fear.

Even if we're both craving the physical, I know this is more than just sex. More than I've ever had with anyone else.

Lana moans as she grinds her hips upward, her center pressing into my hard cock as she seeks friction where she needs it. Every worry in my mind vanishes, leaving just the feeling of her to focus on. I grind my hips in time with hers, moaning at how good it feels without even being inside her. Sliding my palm from ankle to thigh, I run my fingers against her, finding she's soaked through both her panties and tights.

"I hope you don't like these very much," I murmur against her neck. Then, I raise up on my knees, hook my fingers in the mesh of the tights, and rip them from her hips.

Chapter 33
Lana

When Max rips through my tights I think I might come undone then and there. He's a major flirt, always, but he's also usually kind and gentle and smiling.

This is none of those things. It's hot as fuck and I'm aching for him even more than I already was. I stare down at him in the dim room, his scent surrounding me on his sheets and setting my nerves on fire.

The mesh of my tights is in tatters, covering my thighs, but leaving my panties exposed. Max kneels between my legs in his straining boxer briefs. "So. Fucking. Beautiful," he rumbles, running his palms up my thighs, like he's taking inventory of what's his.

His eyes are golden, the color revealing his excitement even if I hadn't already felt how hard he was when he was grinding against me. Now, he kisses me again, one broad palm slipping under my bralette to pull it up and off, so my tits are bared to him. I arch my back, seeking release as I whimper, but he ignores me and proceeds to pull one nipple between his lips, teeth teasing it while I pant.

He continues this slow torture, dragging open mouthed kisses, peppered with little nips and licks, down my ribs, over my belly, stopping just above my clit. His breath is hot through the damp fabric of my panties, and I try to will him to slide his tongue over me. Instead, he runs his hands up my thighs, hooking my still-booted feet over his shoulders.

"Is this what you want, darlin'?" he asks just as I'm about to cave and beg him to touch me. He slides my panties to the side and teases me with his fingers, sliding two inside before his mouth joins, licking exactly where I crave. My hips buck as I pull him closer with my legs grinding against him and tangling my fingers in his hair.

"Gods, yes," I moan. Before long I'm gasping and muttering unintelligible words as I reach my peak and tumble over. My legs relax and I run my fingers through his waves, gently releasing the death grip I was wielding when I came. I'm panting and trembling from my release when he slides up my body, keeping my calves on his shoulders.

"You all right?" he whispers, but his grin tells me he knows damn well I'm just fine. His boxer briefs are gone, and he slides his cock over me, teasing me through the fabric of my panties, now back in place to cover me. The angle feels delicious, and I want to move my hips enough for him to be inside me.

"I'm more than all right. Max, I want you. Now. Please."

He starts to pull away, leaning toward his nightstand. I want to keep him here; to tell him he doesn't have to put anything between us. But I don't want to scare him away, making it seem like we're more serious than we may be. And I certainly don't want any accidents. So, I let my leg fall away from him as he retrieves a condom, tears the wrapper, and slides it over himself.

A moment later, he's kissing me, his hands roaming over my bare skin, calloused fingers and broad palms tracing my curves and angles. Then, he's back on top of me, this time with my wrists caught in one hand over my head, leaving me helpless and exposed. I splay my legs wider, begging him for more. When he pushes my panties aside and slides into me, I can't hold back my moan. It's guttural and animalistic, the craving for him taking over. I'm so slick and ready for him that it doesn't take any time to adjust to his size this time.

"Gods, Lana," he groans into my hair, burrowing his face into my neck as he rocks his hips. His fingers squeeze into my wrists, and I move my hips to his rhythm encouraging him to take more from me.

I'm panting as his thrusts increase, his grip rougher. My climax is coiling tight, my hips meeting his pace and bringing me closer to another release. Neither of us hold back this time. Max releases my wrists, gripping my ass with one hand so tight it would bruise a human and burying the other in my hair as he roughly tilts my head back to kiss me. I grab his ass with both hands, barely containing my claws as I pull him closer with each thrust.

"Fuck, Max. I'm coming. I'm coming," I cry, unable to

control the motion of my hips as I shatter around him. I don't think I've ever felt like this before, ever come so hard —alone or with anyone else.

Max thrusts a few more times, crying out sharply with his face buried in my neck as he finishes. He rolls off me, lying limp next to me on the bed. In the soft light of his lamp we glance over at one another. We're both breathing hard, hair wild and messy, eyes still gold. I can't help but bite my lower lip before I grin at him. He returns the look and we both let out a breathy giggle before leaning across and kissing.

"Holy. Shit." Max breathes against my swollen lips. I'm certain I'm red from the scrape of his beard and the intensity of our kisses.

"Holy. Shit." I agree.

———

I wake to sunlight streaming through half closed blinds, curled amongst Max's sheets. His forearm rests across his eyes, his other hand resting on my lower back as he sleeps. We took a break, stripping me out of the torn fishnets and boots in favor of one of his tees, snacking on microwave popcorn and eating ice cream out of the carton. But before we knew it we were kissing and forgetting the ice cream, left to melt on the counter.

Why am I up?

It can't be past seven in the morning, far too early for me to be awake after such a late night. My phone buzzes. Stupid fucking phone.

I ignore it, rolling on my side and snuggling against Max. He smiles and makes a soft sound in his throat, rolling over and wrapping his arms around me so he can pull me closer.

It buzzes again.

Who is messaging me this fucking early?

"Please make it stop," Max mumbles against my hair.

Groaning, I extract myself from our tangle of limbs and hang partially over the bed to pull my phone from the little clutch I left it in last night. I swat at Max's hand grabbing my ass cheek, laughing as I look at the screen.

Freaking, Shane.

He's sent a few messages, the notifications bar illuminating again with another one while I squint at the glowing screen.

My mom replied to my message last night, too. I'd sent her a picture of me all dressed up before we went out and one of the front of the theater lit up in the dark of the city. But once we entered the theater, I set my phone to vibrate and hadn't thought about it since, too entangled with Max to wonder if she replied. I expect her to have gushed about the city scene, or to comment about the fishnet tights on display under the leather shorts, but when I see her messages, I sit up. My heart begins to hammer quicker as I read through them again.

"You okay?" Max murmurs, kissing my shoulder. He can hear my heartbeat rushing, my quickened breathing, scent the change from relaxation to worry.

MOM

Hey, honey. You look so pretty. I hope you have a wonderful night.

MOM

I don't want to spoil your fun, but can you call me tomorrow? It's about Aubrey.

A pang of guilt thrums through me.

Why did I wait until Shane told me about his trip to check in?

How could I have been so selfish? I knew Aubrey was acting weird when I left.

I should have told Shane the truth instead of trying to protect anyone.

What a shitty second.

What a shitty sister...daughter...pack member...Is *this* why Taryn left?

Max runs a palm down my arm, soothing me, but making me wonder, *am I going to ruin this too?* Can I really have all the things that make me feel whole?

SHANE

Hey, sorry to bother you so early, but Mom called and sounds worried about Aubrey. She seemed cagey though. You know something I don't?

SHANE

Where are you? I came over but you didn't answer.

Nosy fucker.

I send a text to my mom promising to call in a little while, one to Aubrey checking in again—he still hasn't replied to my last messages—and can't resist a snarky reply to Shane telling him to mind his own business. I add that I'll be home in a few hours so we can call Mama together. Then, I turn to Max.

He's laid back on the pillows, his chest and stomach bare, the sheet pooling across his hips. Gods, I want to run my tongue over his abs. To get lost in the feeling of his touch again and again. Longing surges through me. Have I *ever* felt like this for someone before?

He gives me a lazy grin, grey-green eyes flashing gold as he admires me in nothing but his tee shirt.

"*Morning,*" I huff with an exasperated sigh.

"Morning, darlin'. Everything okay?"

"I'm not sure. Shane and my mom are both messaging me about Aubrey. I probably need to get home."

"Home?" His expression falters for a moment, something like panic or pain flickering in the lines of his face. "Like the apartment? Or Woodbine Hollow?"

I can hear his heart stutter momentarily, but I blink and he's back, the same easy going flirt I'm falling... oh shit, that I'm falling in love with?

"Maybe both?" I shrug, scooting closer to him. "But if I have to go to The Hollow, I'm coming back. Okay? I promise."

"You better, we have a standing gig and you've stolen the show."

I want to ask if that's all I've stolen, but the way his heartbeat flutters when I touch him, the way his gaze softens, is all the answer I need. Instead, I just tease, "Oh, you only want me for my fiddle?"

"And your songs." He pokes me in the side, making me giggle involuntarily. "And you."

"Me, huh?" My voice is lower, the laugher fading to want. "Prove it."

He lunges, moving quickly as only a shifter can, pulling me to him and capturing my lips in a searing kiss. I don't think I need to hear him say anything else. I know exactly how he feels as I roll on top of him.

Chapter 34
Lana

Two hours later, I stand in the kitchen of my borrowed apartment, my mother on speakerphone and Shane leaning against the counter with his arms crossed. His expression is solemn and strained.

"Three days, Mama?" I'm incredulous that she's waited to reach out to either of us. That she hasn't said anything about Aubrey acting strange during any of our text check ins. I wasn't surprised he was being distant with Shane, even if I hadn't told my brother that, but the fact that he was also acting that way once Shane left, has me pacing.

"It was right after Shane left and I didn't think anything of it at first. You know he likes to sleep in the woods sometimes," my mother explains with a sigh. "I didn't want to worry anyone."

"Do you think he's been taken? Like they did with Lana?" Shane asks.

I cringe.

"No. I don't. Your father doesn't either. We just didn't

know if either of you knew what's been going on with him. He's not been the same since everything happened with Colton."

My mother sounds tired. Like she's been up searching all night. My father isn't there, likely with the alpha or out in the woods himself.

"It isn't like him to be gone for this long without checking in," she adds.

I should be there. Shane and I both should. I can't bear the idea that one of the wolves who took me might have taken him, too. Especially with Caleb missing and knowing their history.

Kaycia is refilling a coffee mug, bringing it to Shane with a soft smile, while Max perches on the arm of the couch, eyes never leaving me. I can sense him watching me, even when I have my gaze somewhere else.

The high of my night with Max is sufficiently deflated by the news from home. As my mood plummets, guilt settling deep, Max is there. His hand is warm on my lower back, fingers tracing circles up and down my spine, pausing my anxious pacing. It's comforting despite the tightness in my chest.

"One of us will come home to help look, okay?" Shane reassures our mother. "We'll let you know when to expect us as soon as we can."

"Okay, I'll let you know if I hear anything."

"Same here," I say. Shane ends the call with a deep sigh, shaking his head before he sips his coffee.

"Why won't he answer my messages if he's okay?" I wonder aloud.

"Don't worry. It's early in the morning, maybe he's got himself someone he doesn't want to bring home to the parents and he's sleeping off a long night." Max tries to reassure me, but Shane scowls and my worry just roots deeper.

"That's exactly what I'm afraid of," I mutter, biting the inside of my cheek as I look up at Shane.

"Talk to me," Shane presses, something in his tone almost compelling me to explain, unable to resist the command of my alpha. "What do you know that you haven't said?"

"He *did* have someone he didn't want to bring home. He used to make sure he washed the scent off and didn't think any of us knew. Until I caught him."

But I had suspected for a while, long before the trouble with Colton. I had to look out for my little brother, so I kept tabs when he would disappear into the woods. I knew what he was up to for years.

"I figured he'd tell when he was ready," I explain lamely.

Shane's face darkens, his jaw fluttering with irritation. "Who?"

"Caleb."

"Caleb?" Kaycia's brow creases looking between Shane and me, she looks small and painfully human compared to the anger rising in Shane. "Why is that name familiar?"

"Because he's one of the pieces of shit who kidnapped Lana. The one that dragged you out of the woods when you tried to run that night." Shane's voice is a growl now. "*Why* would Aubrey be with Caleb?"

"Because there's no accounting for taste? Because they grew up together in the shadow of you, Ethan, and the rest of your friends? Because you can't help who you fall for?" Max stiffens, fingers halting the soothing circles for a split second. "I have no idea, and I don't know how long ago it started. But he promised me it was over once everything with Colton happened. He didn't give me details, but he said he hadn't spoken to Caleb since I came home. That he wouldn't ever again after what they did to us." I start pacing again. "But now I don't know. I haven't been there for him like I should. I've been selfish."

"*Hey*, don't do that," Max cuts in. "You've been through enough, don't blame yourself for whatever is happening now."

"Max is right," Shane says, shocking me. "You can't blame yourself. Hell, I might have made it worse after announcing the temporary exile. Do you think you could go home for just a bit to help Mom?"

I sigh deeply. I can't tell him no. I have to do what my alpha demands. What my family needs. What my pack expects.

Exactly what I've been worried about while living this little dream of freedom.

"Yeah, all right."

"Lana?" Shane softens. When I meet his gaze, he's the big brother I remember from when I was little. No trace of the alpha wolf. "I'm asking as your brother, not telling you. Can you help them with this? You know Woodbine Hollow better than I do now, and Aubrey trusts you more.

I just can't leave the shop again so quickly or else I would at least go with you."

My relief is staggering, the offer of a choice allowing me to breathe. The chains of duty loosening. "I get it. I can see about booking a flight." I look over at Max, gripping his forearm when I see the sadness in his eyes, and add, "But I have to be back by the weekend. I'm playing with Max again."

Relieved as I may be by Shane letting me know this isn't a permanent return home, guilt still rides me. I was so worked up about Taryn leaving when I moved back in with my family, moping around in my room and only leaving to go to work, then was caught up in the aftermath of my kidnapping, Colton's death, and Shane's return. I didn't stop to think about what Caleb's involvement with every-thing, or the sudden changes in family dynamics, might do to Aubrey. He never flat out told me they were together, or whatever they were doing, but I should have asked.

I don't want to face Woodbine Hollow yet. And even though I'd never admit it to Shane, I don't really have the disposable income necessary for the flights back and forth. But I'll drain what little I have in my account to fly. I can't bear the idea of missing the opportunity to play with Max and the guys again this weekend. I'd never make it back in time if I borrowed a car. So being broke and suffering through shitty flights it is. Maybe the tip jar will be extra full next time.

"You okay?" Max asks once Kaycia and Shane have left us alone.

"Yeah," I reply with a small smile. "Sorry to have to

bail like this. I can think of a lot of other ways I'd prefer to spend the week."

Max chuckles, pushing his hair out of his eyes and giving me a sideways grin that has my heart pounding and stomach flip flopping.

"We have plenty of time for that, darlin'. Assuming you're gonna come back." His voice is even, but a nervous swallow betrays what he's hiding with his casual attitude.

"Oh, believe me. I'll be coming back." I run a palm down his arm, tugging his hand from a pocket and pulling him close. "I'm not done with you, pretty bird."

Max offers a lazy smile, eyes crinkling with amusement before he wraps his other arm around me and pulls me close for a kiss. It's gentle, familiar, like we've done this a hundred times and will have hundreds more ahead of us. "I'm not done with you either," he whispers against my lips when we part, eyes flashing gold as I exhale.

"You wanna talk about it?" Max asks when I'm distracted searching for flights.

"Not really much to talk about at this point. I won't really know anything unless Aubrey answers his damn phone."

"You think Caleb would hurt him?"

I pause, my hand hovering over the keyboard. "He'll regret it if he does."

My voice is cold, my chest burning with anger at the idea of Aubrey being harmed. "Even if he didn't want to go along with Colton, even if he claims he was doing what his alpha demanded, he knew it was wrong. That it could potentially cause a feud that would bloody both

The Hollow and The Ridge. But I think it's even worse that he went along with it *knowing* it would hurt Aubrey." I look over at Max, my heart clenching as I think about the feelings I'm developing for him. "If Shane ordered me to do something that hurt you, I'd tell him to fuck off."

Max looks startled at the admission, hiding a smile by turning on the television. I return to my search, but the memory of the sharp sting of a needle, my legs going weak, and then being bound and tossed into the back of an SUV, come rushing back, raising the hair on my arms and sending a shiver through me.

"Shane may have let Caleb off with an exile after what he did to us, but if he hurts Aubrey, I'll kill him."

"You want me to come with you?" Max asks. Following up with a hesitant, "I mean, not as like your boyfriend or to meet the parents or anything, just—" He stumbles over his words, a flush creeping over his neck. It makes my heart squeeze at how fucking sweet he is, burying my painful memories with amusement.

"You don't have to do that," I reply, sliding off the stool at the island and sitting in his lap on the couch. "I mean, I would love the company, but I know it's short notice and expensive. I can handle it and be back in time for the weekend. But next time..." I pause, worried I'm trying to move things too fast. "Next time, I'd love you to come see where I'm from."

"Next time, then," he agrees, pressing his forehead to mine. "On one condition though."

"What condition?"

"You let me take you to the airport and kiss you goodbye so you don't forget me."

"I don't think that's possible. Forgetting you. But you don't have to do that," I insist. "I can take a cab or something."

"No, you won't. I'll drive you. No sense in dealing with more stress. I insist."

I want to cry knowing he wants to take care of me, without having to ask or even tell him. But instead, I just grab his shirt and pull him into a kiss.

———

Hours later, I stand cramped under the overhead bin, trying to stretch my legs while I wait for the lady in the aisle seat to pull her obviously too full carryon out of the compartment.

"Here, let me help you," I offer, bumping her out of the way with my hip and yanking the suitcase free. She just glares at me, muttering an insincere, "Thank you," before rolling down the aisle.

I pull my duffle free, slinging it over my shoulder and following, anxious to be off the overly crowded plane. The noise and smells on airplanes are always a little over-whelming to my shifter senses, people eating and drinking and playing movies without headphones all making me want to scream.

Thankful I didn't check a bag, I glance down at my phone again. I texted my parents and Max that I'd landed safely, and my dad replied that he'd been circling the terminal for twenty minutes. The joys of flight delays. I had to run through the last airport at my connection due to a mechanical issue on the first plane and barely made my flight to the closest big city to Woodbine Hollow. My last-minute flight consisted of an economy priced, middle seat, with a short connection. Lucky me.

The final leg was spent crammed between the woman with the clearly too large bag and a guy wearing so much cologne I thought my nose would never recover. He tried to strike up a conversation with me, but one harsh stare had him averting his eyes the entire rest of the flight.

When I step into the night air, I'm surprised by how crisp it is, colder than it was even at Shane's cabin. Within a few minutes the rumble of our family truck reaches me, my dad pulling up to the curb in the beat-up farm truck with a grim smile.

"Hey, Daddy," I greet him, shoving my duffle and backpack into the back and climbing in the passenger seat.

"Welcome back, Honeybee," he replies, patting my head like I'm still a pup. His smile is tight, likely over worry for Aubrey, but he still emanates the warmth I'm used to. "How was the flight?"

"Shitty, how was the drive?"

"Shitty." We both laugh as he pulls out into traffic and toward the highway heading north.

My phone pings, a text notification on the screen.

MAX

Glad you made it. How was the flight?

Terrible. Why do you like flying again?

MAX

Because I have wings, darlin'. ;) I hate airplanes.

That makes two of us. I'll call you tomorrow, we are on the road home.

MAX

Sounds good.

The ellipses indicating Max is typing pops up and disappears a couple times before a new message finally comes through.

MAX

I miss you already. Come back soon, okay?

Warmth spreads through my chest reading his words. The idea that he wants me, not just in a casual fling sort of way, weasels it way into my mind. Apparently, it also weasels its way across my face because my dad clears his throat with a chuckle.

"Who's got you smiling like that, girl?" he asks, catching my eyes with a wink.

"No one," I lie, sending a quick: *I miss you, too. I'll be back in no time,* to Max.

"You've never been able to lie, Lana Mae. Tell me true."

Sighing, I give my dad the biggest eye roll possible. But he's right. I know he can read me like a book because I can't lie for shit to him or my mother.

"Just a guy. One of Shane's friends, actually."

Hmph, he snorts. "Your face doesn't look like he's 'just a guy'. Tell me about him."

"He's a musician. He's in the band I've started playing with at the bar. They invited me to join them permanently. That's part of why I flew in, I need to be back for our show this coming weekend."

"Shane showed us the video," he says, taking an exit toward a favorite 24-hour diner on the way home. He puts the truck into park when we reach the parking lot. "The singer, then?"

"Yeah," I answer, unfastening my seatbelt and opening the door. "How'd you know?"

"Call it fatherly intuition." He gives me a warm smile, telling me nothing, but making me wonder what exactly was in that video Kaycia sent Shane. What I couldn't see when I watched it. "Come on, let's eat before we finish the drive. I'll tell you what I know about your little brother."

Chapter 35
Max

My heart sinks watching Lana walk away, strolling through the doors of the airport, even though I know she has to come back, whether for me or all her stuff that's still at Shane's. A shrill honk from the sports car behind me snaps me back to reality. Dragging my gaze from her shrinking silhouette, I slam the gear shift into drive with a grumble.

I'm a little bitter that Shane didn't handle this himself, but I remind myself that this is what it means for a wolf to be part of a pack; responsibility beyond themselves. I answered when Shane was in trouble, but it's not something I've had to deal with since my granny passed. Something no one in my family seemed to understand, aside from my grandmother. It's hard to reconcile that responsibility with the lone wolf I knew Shane to be for so long. I'm happy that he's been reunited with his family, but I can't help but wonder if the years of familial pressure aren't chafing Lana a bit. The planes of her face hardened on the drive to the airport, as though she was rebuilding armor around herself for the task at hand. The same way she looked the first night I saw her.

Instead of stewing, I drown my thoughts on the thirty-minute drive to my place with the windows down and the radio blaring, then start a load of laundry before flopping on the couch and tugging a quilt over me. I inhale deeply, sinking into Lana's scent on the fabric. The quilts I used on our trip still smelled like her when I pulled them from the backseat of the truck, and I ended up draping one over the arm of the couch instead of washing it, ignoring how pathetic that is to admit.

I get a couple of texts from Lana letting me know her flight times, but she has a short connection between them, so with her out of pocket I'm left to my own devices for the rest of the day. I clean up the house a bit, transferring laundry and washing my towels and sheets, then heat a frozen pizza in the oven and crack open a beer.

By the time I've cleaned up the kitchen after dinner and opened a second bottle, my phone chimes. It's Lana letting me know her final flight has landed. I'm relieved that she's on solid ground again, even if it's miles and miles from me.

It's easy to flirt and tease in texts, but I wish I was with her. I know she's worried about her brother, but being back home might bring up memories of her ex and cause her more pain when she's just getting over it all, and figuring out what she really wants. Selfishly, I want to know she's coming back.

I consider what to send next, typing and deleting and

retyping, wondering if I'm being too needy, but I finally give in and send the truth.

> I miss you already. Come back soon, okay?

LANA

> I miss you, too. I'll be back in no time.

My chest squeezes, trying to hold my heart in place as it dances around in my chest at her reply. I consider calling her, to hear that smoky voice whisper through the distance like she did last night, but I keep myself from sending any more messages for now. I've already shown her my hand; I don't need to come off as clingy. Instead, I pull out my notebook, opening to a new page to jot down a few lines I've been mulling over for a new song.

Maybe one for Lana to sing on her own if she wants.

If she wants this to be a permanent thing: the city. The band. Me.

———

The work week comes too quickly, as they always do. Being a freelance designer gives me the autonomy to get up and do my job whenever I feel like it, but Ryan messaged me late Monday evening to tell me he might have secured our final addition to round out the band. His cousin is coming to town to look at apartments and is bringing his guitar with him.

Now, rather than enjoying a slow morning and

working on a brand kit this afternoon like I planned, I've rearranged the day so I can finish this first round of branding and meet Ryan and his cousin. If he's a good fit, we might be able to squeeze in a couple of practices to try him out this weekend. It feels like things are finally falling into place with the band and my personal life, but I hesitate to breathe too easily, always worrying the other shoe will drop.

Pouring a second cup of coffee, I grab the last piece of bacon from the plate and head to my desk to get to work. I check my phone once more before turning it on silent. I can't focus if texts and calls ring through often, but I do send one quick "Good morning" text to Lana before opening my laptop. She's been quiet since she's been gone. It's to be expected, between spotty rural connection and focusing on the pack, but I still think about her constantly and feel like a pimple-faced kid with his first crush, checking my phone to see if I've missed a message from her.

———

Six hours later, I sit around a table with Ryan, Jet, and Ryan's cousin, Alistair. Despite being cousins, Ryan and Alistair could easily be siblings. Same wiry build and coloring, same musical interests and background. A shared set of musically inclined grandparents shelled out for lessons from the time they could reach piano keys, and both took a shine to playing. Ryan transitioned to bass, while Alistair turned to guitar, attracted by

complicated riffs and the attention they could get him—
even if he didn't admit that part out loud— and kept up
with the keys. He'd be a perfect addition to the core of
the band, while Lana's fiddle fleshes out our developing
sound and adds harmony on vocals. Fairweather Creek
might finally get out of our regular dives and onto bigger
stages, maybe even on tour if I have anything to say
about it.

"Let's get Lana on the line and see what she thinks,"
Jet offers, pouring himself another beer from the pitcher on
the table.

"Who's Lana?" Alistair asks around a nacho.

"Max's girl," Ryan jokes, elbowing me like we're
teenage boys.

I don't deign responding to the comment, explaining,
"She's our fiddle player." But I can't hide the smile that
basically confirms Ryan's declaration. "She just started
playing with us and writing some songs."

"She's damn good. And would whoop your ass in a
heartbeat if you did her dirty. You better watch yourself,"
Jet adds with a grin and a wink. "Think you're going to
finally settle down with this one?"

"Sounds like he better if she's as good as you're all
making her sound," Alistair chimes in. "Why isn't she here
tonight?" He looks around as though Lana might pop up,
but the sports bar down the road from my condo is full of
the usual: guys drinking happy hour beers and watching
whatever highlights are on the big screens.

"She had to go take care of some family stuff back
home. I can call her though, give me a minute." I pull out

my phone and swipe through until Lana's name pops up. She answers on the second ring.

"Hey you." Lana's warm voice runs straight down my spine and sends my stomach flipping. "How's my pretty bird faring without me?"

"Aww, well, you know I'd be a lot better with you here instead of these guys, but I can't be choosy with you out of town. I've got Ryan and Jet here. Ryan brought his cousin Alistair out to meet us. He's interested in joining the band."

"Oh, yeah? Am I on speaker?"

"You are now," I answer, clicking the speaker button and holding the phone out so she can be included in the conversation.

"Hey, Lana!" Ryan says.

"Hey, girl. How's the trip?" Jet asks.

"Not bad, just at the little grocery store picking up a few things. What's your story, Alistair?" Lana asks. I can hear the crinkle of bags, maybe chips, the squeak of a shopping cart's wheel. Things the guys would never notice, but my hearing picks up on easily. I also pick up on Lana's distraction. Is it from shopping, or something more serious back home?

"Hi, Lana. It's Alistair. I'm a guitarist and occasionally play the piano. Heard you're new, too?"

"Yeah. Fiddle and vocals, I guess. Still trying to find my place," she says, followed by the sound of cans hitting the metal of the cart.

"When are you back? We can have a couple of sessions if you're home in time before the next show," Jet offers.

"Uh, I'm not sure. Should be—" Her distraction has increased, and now I hear a worried little intake of breath. "*Shit.*"

"Lana? You okay?" I ask. I take her off speaker and furrow my brow as I lift it back to my ear. For a few seconds there's only silence, and I begin to think the connection has failed.

Finally, she exhales and says, "Yeah. I'm okay now. I'll call you back."

The line goes dead before I can reply.

"She'll call back," I tell the guys, hoping the long pull on my beer hides the worry written on my face.

Chapter 36
Lana

I've spent nearly the entire time since my feet hit the ground in Woodbine Hollow in my wolf form, searching for Aubrey alongside my parents and trying to find any evidence that he might have left with Caleb. I found a few places with both their scents, but no trace of either of them. I'm beginning to suspect that this is less of a case of retribution and more of a case of star-crossed lovers being stupid and running off together, but I can't shake the memory of what happened to me only a few months ago.

I've barely slept, my mind churning through worst case scenarios where Aubrey is tied in the back of an SUV in my place. It's impossible to find rest, and I long for Max's arms to comfort me. I've been making do with one of his tee shirts that I refuse to wash. It's the one I'm wearing now as I stand stock still in the dairy section of the small Woodbine Hollow grocery store.

Her scent caught me before the sight. That same familiar smell that I'd finally washed out of my jacket, my sheets, my towels. The scent of the wolf I shared a home and a bed with for nearly three years.

The smell of vetiver and jasmine stole my breath and froze my thoughts just for a moment, that old hurt surfacing and twisting my heart. I couldn't really focus on what Max or the guys were saying, not with my heart pounding with the itch to flee. I left the carton of milk on the cold shelf and let the door close softly, glancing around with the phone pressed to my ear while Ryan or Jet—maybe Alistair?—talked about me coming back to town to practice before the next show.

Glancing down the aisle I wonder if I can slip past the shelves of canned goods and out the front door without being noticed. But before I can abandon my cart, she turns the corner, eyes focused as though she scented me, too. Like she was hunting me.

Taryn.

"*Shit*," I whisper, still holding the phone against my ear.

"Lana? You okay?" Max's voice is deep and close, he's taken me off speaker and the concern in his tone brings me back to the present.

The memory of his shampoo and cologne, wrapped around me in his shirt, drowns out the perfume that haunted me for weeks, months, as I lay curled up in one of the sweatshirts she left behind. I'm reminded that I have someone waiting for me back in Argent. Someone who cares for me just the way I am. Any hold Taryn had on me before, any shards of broken heart that might have been hidden in the corners of my soul, are swept away like dust caught in the flapping of wings by the knowledge that Max is waiting for me.

"Yeah. I'm okay now," I reassure him with a soft smile he can't see. "I'll call you back."

I hang up before Max can ask any other questions. I feel guilty knowing he'll worry until I call, but I'm not going to make a big deal out of running into my ex. I shove my phone into my back pocket and cross my arms, the smile on my face vanishing, while Taryn prowls in my direction.

Her dark hair falls in loose curls around her shoulders, the scent of her expensive shampoo reaching me as she strolls closer, pretending to inspect the eggs between glances at me. I exhale sharply to clear it. Instead of remembering how those strands felt between my fingers, I think of Max and his dark waves—okay, so, I have a type. Her dark eyes are wary as she nears me, but her lips tilt into a smile when she's a couple of feet from the end of my shopping cart.

"I thought that was your family's truck out front." Her voice is just as I remember it. She widens her smile.

I don't.

"Taryn." My reply is flat. Emotionless.

"Don't be like that," she pouts.

"I'm sorry? Like what? Surprised to see you in the local grocery store after you walked out on me and haven't been seen around The Hollow in months?" I remind myself that I don't want to let my emotions take over but can't fight the scowl that wrinkles my brow.

"I've been back a couple of weeks. I just needed to get away for a bit for a change of scenery."

"How nice for you. Not much has changed here."

"Oh, I hear a lot has changed." She tosses her hair, her eyes glittering as she inspects me. That look used to make me melt, but I'm as cool as the refrigerator next to me. "Colton Ross is dead. Your big brother's back. As an *alpha*. And you're his second?"

She's done her digging.

"Didn't realize you were so concerned with pack politics or the rungs of the social ladder."

Finally deterred at my refusal to soften, she cocks her head, smile dropping as she studies me. Her gaze runs down my body, catching on the slightly oversized fit of my tee, and I'm happy that what would have weakened me before just makes me frown. When I remain silent, Taryn scowls. "You've changed."

"*Hmph*," I scoff. "A shitty break up will do that a girl. Look, I gotta get going. Mama needs the truck for an appointment later." I start to push the cart past, but she places a hand on the metal, halting it.

"You look different, Lana..." She glances around, as though she's worried someone is listening. Let them listen.

Taryn steps closer, dragging her fingers along the metal of the cart. For a moment, I think she might touch me. I flex my jaw in irritation, holding in a growl. I will *not* move back. I am a ranked pack member now. No one forces me to do anything. "You look *good*. But—" she pauses, taking a deep inhale and making me grit my teeth. She's about to get a full nose of falcon. "—you *smell* different, too."

"I'm not the only one who's changed apparently. I don't remember you being rude, Taryn. You were always so concerned with appearances, remember? Always reminding me not to lose my temper or cause a scene. Always reading the room. Maybe you should read it now."

My temper flares and my eyes flash gold. Taryn takes a small step back, but still keeps her hand on the cart like she can keep me captive.

"You won't even talk to me?"

"What is there to say? You said your piece before you walked out. I haven't changed. I'm the exact same wolf I was when we were together. It wasn't enough for you then, so don't come sniffing around me now." I realize I'm gripping the handle of the shopping cart so hard my knuckles are white. The hard plastic covering the metal handle is beginning to crack. "I have to go."

"Heard you're playing music with a real band in the big city," Taryn says as I push the cart past her, forcing her to remove her grip or lose a fingernail. I pause, exhaling deeply knowing Shane accidentally did this to me. "Heard you're pretty good."

"The bands I used to play with here were real, too." She scoffs a little, but I don't let her speak. "And if you gave a shit, you would have encouraged my music years ago. Leave me alone. I know you're capable, you did a great job before." I forge on, avoiding her outstretched hand before it can land on my arm.

"I'm glad you're okay!" Taryn calls after me, but I keep walking, pushing the cart with its squeaky wheel to the self-checkout where I pay little attention to which bags I throw my groceries in, or which pack members might be taking in the latest gossip. I pay and rush out before the receipt prints.

When I reach the truck my hands shake, making it hard to get the key in the door. Damn old vehicles without electronic locks. I finally get the door open and fling the groceries across the front seat. Sitting behind the wheel I suck in deep breaths of the clear mountain air, removing the reek of Taryn Rogers from my nose.

———

My mother is in the kitchen when I get back to the house, and the look she gives me lets me know that she's going to ask me what's wrong before I can put the groceries away and escape upstairs.

She drapes the dishtowel over the breakfast dishes drying in the rack and leans against the counter with her arms crossed over her chest. "What happened to you?"

"Nothing," I mutter uselessly as I toss a bag of chips on the shelf. I doubt any of them survived the trip home.

"*Lana*," her voice is a warning, like when she knew I was up to no good as a little kid. If I were in my wolf form my ears would be laid back at the tone. "You saw Taryn, didn't you?"

"How did you know?"

"Because you look wrung out, just like you did until your brother came back."

"I—" I start to deny it but bite my tongue. I *was* "wrung out", as Mama put it.

"Don't let that girl try to worm her way back into your life. Not when things are changing for the better for you."

"I have no intention of letting her back in. It was just unexpected to see her." I *don't* want anything to do with Taryn. I can't really even explain why I got so flustered, my feelings for her are gone at this point. "I don't even know why it upset me."

"Because, honey, she left you and shook up everything you'd gotten used to. But I think that uncertainty has helped you in the long run." My mother smiles, her eyes creasing in the corners as she approaches and wraps me in a hug. "I'm proud of you for getting out of here and doing something for yourself."

"What do you mean?" I never really thought I would leave The Hollow. I certainly never thought it was something my family would think was good for me.

"I know you took it upon yourself to watch out for Aubrey and take on some of Shane's responsibilities once he was exiled, but you were still a kid. I'm sorry if I leaned too hard on you during those years after everything happened." She holds me away from her a little, looking up slightly to meet my eyes from her shorter height. "I've always been proud of you Lana, but nothing made me prouder than seeing that video of you smiling with Daddy's fiddle on that stage." Tears well and catch in her lashes before she can dash them away.

"Mama," I soothe her, hugging her tight again before she can begin crying in earnest. She soon pulls away and shakes her head to clear the emotions.

"I mean it. We love you being here, and Shane may

need you as his second, but you can do what's best for you. If that means traveling back and forth like he's doing, or if it means you need to hand off the duty to someone else, that's your call to make. Don't give up what makes you happy just because you think it's expected of you. I love this pack and this town, but if it isn't what you want or need, then you do something different. Do you understand?"

"But Aubrey," I argue, unable to process the fact that my mother is giving me her blessing to leave if I want to. "He needs me. The pack comes first."

"The pack will always be here, Lana. And your little brother is a grown man, and a capable wolf. I have to remind myself of that sometimes. I know I babied him, partially because he was my last pup and partially because I failed to protect Shane. I'm worried for him, but I have a suspicion he's finally testing his leash. He's been acting secretive for a while, even if you hadn't noticed. I'm his mama, I knew something was wrong, I just didn't know he would run off without telling anyone."

"Do you know something I don't?" I ask, studying my mother's face. She's softer than I am, her features blurred on the edges with age, but tenacity shines fiercely in the hazel eyes she gave to Shane and me. My phone vibrates in my pocket, distracting me from studying her for a moment.

"I've told you and Shane what you need to know. I appreciate that he sent you home, but if you haven't caught a trail or heard from Aubrey by tomorrow, I think you should go on back to Argent. Your daddy and I can keep on hunting. I'm thinking of heading over the hill to visit with Calliope later this week."

"Caleb's mom?"

When the phone vibrates again, she smiles, ignoring my question. "Someone wants to talk to you. Better go take it."

She shoos me out with flapping hands, then heads out the front door, leaving me in a state of confusion and relief as I look down to see who's calling.

Chapter 37
Max

I've given Lana over an hour to call me back and still no word. I left the guys at the sports bar fifteen minutes ago, claiming I forgot to send an email to a client. It was a lame excuse to stop watching games I didn't care about and listening to small talk I wasn't participating in, but no one stopped me. Now, my mind has pivoted back to the only thing that I care about at the moment.

Is she okay? Did something happen? Have I scared her off?

I don't know why I can't stop thinking the worst. I'm usually the first to laugh things off and crack a joke or flirt my way into a good mood. But nothing sounded funny on our call and the only one I want to flirt with is Lana, so none of those things will fix me this time.

Finally, as I round the corner of my street I give in, stepping out of the way of other pedestrians to call her. I breathe a sigh of relief when she answers on the second ring, an unbidden smile across my face when she breath-lessly says, "Hey there, pretty bird."

"You had me worried, darlin'. Where'd you run off to?" I'm trying for nonchalance, leaning against the brick build-ing, but I sound like a worried mess.

"I, ah—I ran into someone I didn't want to see. I needed a minute."

My heart drops. "Are you okay? Can I do anything?" I ask, as though I'm any use to her this far away.

"I'm fine. It was just my ex." My heart sinks even farther, making me wonder if it will even be in my body by the time I get off the call. I guess if she stays in Woodbine Hollow I can get a decent heartbreak song out of it. My stomach twists with misery.

"Oh. Gotcha."

"Max?"

"Yeah?" I croak, clearing my throat.

"I miss you," she whispers. "I think I'll fly home the day after tomorrow."

"Home?" I question, confused.

"Yeah. Back to Argent. We can still have another rehearsal. Maybe I can meet the new guy? You think he's a good fit?"

"Oh, yeah. I think it will be good. That's a good plan. Just send me your flight info and I'll pick you up."

"You don't have to be my chauffeur."

"I know. But I wanna see you as soon as you're back."

"Yeah. Me too. Okay, well, I gotta go help mom with dinner. I'll keep you posted on when I'm back in town."

"Be careful, Lana. I'll see you soon."

"Bye, Max."

"Bye."

———

"Tell me about this Taryn," I demand of Shane, walking into his shop the next morning.

"Don't you have things to do?" Shane asks, leaned over greasy pieces of motorcycle parts.

"Yeah, your sister," Raquel goads. She dodges when I throw a socket at her.

"I brought you both coffee, assholes. Now, tell me what you know."

"Look, man. Taryn and Lana's dealings are her business. If you want to know about them then ask her." Shane goes back to his work, but his attitude pisses me off.

"Fuck you."

I drop the to-go cups on the concrete floor, sending Raquel's macchiato and Shane's drip with cream splashing onto the bike Shane's working on and Raquel's boots.

"*What?*" he looks surprised. As though his happy-go-lucky, man-whore friend doesn't have an angry apex predator side just like he does.

"What the fuck, Max?" Raquel bristles, looking between me, Shane, and the spill.

"Yeah, what the fuck?" Shane stands, wiping his greasy fingers on his work jeans. I expect him to push me, or deck me, or toss me out on my ass for crashing into his work like some tidal wave of jealousy.

"I—" I'm breathing hard, trying to fight the warring

emotions within me. The fear and sadness from when I was a little kid who didn't understand why no one wanted him, the deep aching need I feel for Lana, all of it pushing and pulling within me, threatening to break me.

"I think I'm fucking in love with her, man. And she told me she ran into her ex yesterday and I need to know, Shane. I need to know if she's going to go running back and leave me here alone. I need you to tell me what you know. I need—" I'm panting, and I run my hands through my hair and press them against my eyes to try to keep from completely breaking down. "I need to know if she's just having a good time with me until she goes back to her."

"Whoa. Max." I've never heard Raquel sound so soft. "Take a deep breath."

Before I can do anything, strong arms are circling me, holding me against a hard chest. Shane. He smells similar to Lana, wolf but darker, the scent of the shop an integral part of him. The metal and grease and soap. He's not throwing me out. He's just holding me.

"Calm down, man. Calm down." Shane's voice rumbles, and even though I'm not a wolf, not part of his pack, I do as he says. "I didn't know. I didn't know it was that serious for you. I'll tell you what I know about it. Okay?"

"Okay." I try to breathe deeper, to calm my heartbeat. A few rough pats to the back follow before Shane releases me and Raquel pulls up a rolling mechanic's stool to listen, keeping her mouth shut for once.

———

"What a cunt," Raquel pulls no punches when Shane finishes sharing what he knows about Lana and Taryn's break up. I mentally echo the sentiment. "Poor Lana."

"Don't let her hear you say that," Shane says, taking a deep breath. He turns to me, lips in a small frown. "So, now that you know, can you relax? I'm sure she was shaken up over seeing Taryn for the first time since their split, but I don't think she would even consider giving her another chance. Not after everything that's happened."

"Yeah. Okay. You're right." I feel better about our prospects, but worse about the pain Lana's been hiding. She's mentioned the break-up, but not how sudden it seemed. Not how her ex seemed to snuff out everything she was and that she's building it all back now.

She's been through so much over the last few months that I feel selfish panicking. If she wanted to fly to the moon for a break, I wouldn't stop her. Not when she deserves time to figure shit out.

"You've been good for her, Max. It's been a long time since I've seen her, but she's so much better than she was even when she moved here. I haven't heard her having nightmares anymore. She's happy. If you're the reason, I'm glad." Shane pats me roughly on the shoulder, then stands. "Now, I have to get back to work so get the hell out of here, okay?" His smile tells me he's joking. Mostly.

I'm on my way out the bay door when Raquel grabs my arm and pulls me around the corner of the garage.

"Are you going to be okay?" Raquel asks, serious for once.

"Yeah, I just have some of my own shit to work on. Don't tell Lana."

She scowls, and I know she's going to call and tell Jamila as soon as I'm out of earshot, but I also know Jamila can keep a secret.

"Are you...?" She doesn't have to finish the sentence. I know what she means. What Lana means to me.

"I think so."

"Okay, I'll won't say anything until she figures it out. But I'm sick of having these conversations with you dense men. You need to talk to her. For both of your sakes."

"Yeah. I will."

I walk down the sidewalk ignoring the crush of the pedestrians milling through a touristy section of the city, dodging people when they stop to take pictures of buildings and statues I walk by every day, considering whether I want to trash what I'm wearing in an alley so I can shift and fly over the buildings to clear my mind. I don't think I can afford to lose another pair of jeans and boots. Looks like I'm stuck as a human.

It doesn't matter which form I'm in anyway. I can't escape the truth running through my mind.

Raquel knows. Which means Shane knows.

And if they know, then Jamila and Kaycia do, too.

I've bonded to Lana.

Even if she doesn't return the attachment, I can't help what I feel. I've got to talk to her about it, and about what she wants from this sooner than I planned. At least I know she'll be home tomorrow.

Pulling out my phone I check again for nonexistent

text messages. I remind myself that she's dealing with shit with her pack, her family. And she's an hour behind me with the time zone difference. I text Ryan and Jet instead, setting up a rehearsal and making sure Ryan gets Alistair there. Anything to keep my mind steady.

Chapter 38
Lana

Speaking to Max helps me settle after seeing Taryn. Once we hang up, I go sit on Aubrey's empty bed and look around at the room. I've already searched under the mattress, riffling through the drawers and shaking out notebooks, but nothing tells me more than I knew before I got here. I lay back against the pillow and stare at the ceiling, dialing Aubrey's number for the hundredth time and letting it ring until it goes to voicemail. Again.

I feel like a failure. I can't wrap my head around how Aubrey would just leave without telling anyone. Unless *I* made him feel like he couldn't tell me. After I came home with Shane and told Aubrey who had lured me into being captured, I made it clear that if Aubrey supported me and our family, he couldn't possibly still involve himself with Caleb.

But after seeing Taryn today, having that tangle of feelings surface, I realize how unfair that ultimatum was to Aubrey. Even if he hated what Caleb did, I guarantee his feelings for him were still there under the anger. They had already hidden what was going on between them for fear of being forced apart by the packs. Now, with Shane's declaration that Caleb would be exiled, I have no doubt his emotions were tangled even further.

The longer we search, the more certain I am that Aubrey is with Caleb. That Shane and I forced his hand in making this decision. I don't agree with his choice. I don't think I can ever forgive Caleb for his part in what happened to me and what it forced Shane to do. In fact, I just might rip his head off his shoulders if I ever see him again, but at this point I just want to know Aubrey's safe.

With a deep sign, I dial the familiar number again, prepared to leave a voicemail. When the recording beeps, I say, "Hi, Aubs. It's Lana. Again. Listen, if you could just call me back and let me know you're okay, then I can call Mom and Dad off the search. I think I finally understand what's going on, and I get it. Sort of. We won't come find you. We won't punish anyone. Can you just call and let me know you're safe? I love you, Aubrey. I mean it. No matter what."

———

"Lana! *Lana!*" My mother's voice is panicked, her fear and pain causing my adrenaline to surge and my wolf to snarl, tearing through my human form as teeth and claws come to the surface to protect her. To protect my family. Protect myself.

"Lana Mae McKinley, stand down." My father's voice

is harsh, a deep growl that feels like a chain dragging me back to a calmer state. I may be Shane's second, the same rank as my father, but he's still my elder. My blood. His word will stop me in my tracks unless there's a good reason for me to fight it.

I blink. My breathing is ragged. The taste of fear is bitter across my tongue as I suck in the scents that surround me, registering the familiar: Mama. Daddy. My room. Home.

When I blink again, I realize I'm on my bed in my childhood bedroom. The soft, cotton sheets are torn and the down comforter leaks feathers across the floor. A low whine breaks free of my throat. I'm in my wolf form, hunkered on my bed like a scolded puppy. I hadn't shifted to sleep tonight, thinking I had gotten over everything in the last few months. I've been sleeping regularly as a human, but tonight my dreams got the best of me.

My mom wears a robe over her pajamas and sits on the edge of the bed, as though she was comforting me while my father waited in the doorway in pajama pants.

"Lana? Are you okay? Is it getting worse?" my mother asks. Her eyes are so sad it hurts. I scoot closer, moving my paws near her leg as I nuzzle my snout against her thigh with another whine.

"I'll give you two some privacy," Daddy says, closing the door behind him. When it clicks shut, after my mother strokes her fingers through my fur a time or two, I shift, pulling on loose pajama pants and the same tee shirt of Max's that I wore to the store that afternoon.

"Still having nightmares?" Mama asks. I didn't even

realize she knew. But I should have. How could anyone living in this house, especially with shifter hearing, *not* know I was waking up terrified almost every night.

"I hadn't been. Not for a little while now," I confess.

I feel like a little kid as I lay my head on her lap for her to play with my hair. Her touch is soothing and for the first time in a while I let myself be vulnerable with her, let the tears come, let my shoulders shake with a sob as I wrap my arms around myself.

"You were screaming, honey. It scared me. I thought someone had come for you again. I thought your daddy was going to rip the door off the hinges."

"It was just a dream. I'm okay." Was it exhaustion or panic that brought on the shift in my sleep?

"What was it about?" My mother strokes my hair again.

"Colton. What I did." I curl into her, hiding my face. "It's just..." I sigh, sitting up and wiping my eyes. "I thought I was better. I hadn't had a nightmare in a while. I don't know if it's being back here or what. I feel so weak."

"It's not weak to mourn or to regret. Even if the death was warranted, taking a life should never be easy, Lana."

"I know. I talked to Shane about it. He said the same thing."

"My poor babies." Mama wraps me in a tight hug, holding me until I pull away.

"I think I need to go back to Argent. It's too hard for me here right now and I can't help if I'm a mess. I'm sorry I failed you."

"You've never failed us, Lana," Daddy says, standing in

the doorway again, having moved so silently I didn't hear the door reopening. "Never once. If anything, we failed you if you'd think such a thing."

To keep him from seeing the emotion on my face, I snag my phone from the nightstand to check the time. The missed call and voicemail symbol have me gasping before I can reply to him.

"Aubrey called!" I cry, tapping the voicemail to listen on speaker.

"Hey, sis," Aubrey says. He sounds...fine. "Got your messages. All of them. I'm good. I promise. I just needed some time away from The Hollow. I'd think *you* of all wolves might understand that. I promise that I'll keep in touch and I'll call Mom soon. I just needed some space to figure things out. Stop worrying about me, okay? I love you."

A tear falls, running down my cheek as I stare at the phone. "What a little shit," I exhale, shaking my head and looking at my parents. "Did he think we wouldn't all freak out?"

I'm relieved that Aubrey has finally let us know he's okay, but a flicker of rage shimmers in my chest at his selfish lack of concern. Like I hadn't upended my schedule to fly back here and run all over the place looking for him. Like my parents needed another child to go missing. I grit my teeth.

"Finally," Mama breathes, the relief palpable in her tone.

"I'm going to skin that boy when he gets back," Daddy

grumbles, but then he focuses on me again, as though sensing the anger rising in me.

"I just might help you," I reply, narrowing my eyes at the phone.

"You can go back to the city, be with your alpha and your band. I'll keep you posted on whether anything comes up here that we need you for. It's time you followed your heart." He pats me on the top of the head before retreating to the hallway. Turning back, he adds, "Just let me know when your flight is and I'll take you to the airport."

———

I told Max I would tell him when I was coming home so he could pick me up, but I didn't want to worry him by coming home a day early. So instead, I booked the earliest, cheapest flight I could find and got a cab from the airport to Shane's—*my*—apartment. The sun had long set by the time I fit my key in the lock, the low sounds of Shane and Kaycia's music greeting me from the neighboring door. Their voices rose and fell as I stood in the hall, the tones light and relaxed, and I was happy for my brother. For the life he's built.

I'm ready to build one for myself, too.

Once I'd dumped my suitcase into the dirty laundry hamper and showered, I pulled out my phone to text Max.

Hey pretty bird, what are you up to?

MAX

Trying out a couple new things with the guys. How's it going?

Anything good? How's Alistair fitting in?

MAX

Really well, I'll send you a video of what we were working on.

Why don't you show it to me in person?

MAX

Okay, sure. Reception still bad in Woodbine?

No.

MAX

?

Come see me.

MAX

Like fly out?

Yeah. Take off your clothes. Take flight. And come see me. At my apartment. Right now.

No answer.

Either I've hurt his feelings that I didn't tell him I was coming home, or I will have a very naked falcon shifter on my balcony in a short time. I open the slider, letting the sounds of the city infiltrate the silence of my apartment. Tonight, they're familiar instead of a nuisance—*when did that happen?* With my hair damp around my shoulders, I take out my fiddle and draw the bow across the strings. Then, I lose myself in an old mountain song.

Fifteen minutes later, the cry of a falcon interrupts the song I'm working on. Max flies in, talons clutching his phone. He drops it on the bed before shifting, his feet gracefully hitting the floor as he does so.

"Hey." I whisper, smiling at his naked form outlined by the streetlamp shining through the slider.

"Hey," he replies, grinning at me, eyes flashing in the dim light.

It only takes seconds before he's kissing me, holding my face in his hands as he claims my lips. I kiss him back, wrapping one arm behind him to hold him close while I hold my fiddle and bow in the other.

Relief floods me from his touch, being near him soothes me more than anything else I've found, and I relax into his embrace as he walks me farther into the apartment. He breaks our kiss, pressing his forehead against mine while he takes my fiddle and bow, placing them reverently in the case. When he returns to me, he runs his hands under my shirt, exploring the bare skin beneath.

"I missed you," I confess, tucking my cheek against his shoulder and breathing in his scent.

He groans, "Gods, I missed you, too."

Our kisses begin softly, like we're relearning one another after our brief separation, but soon become frenzied. Max backs me up so I'm standing with my lower back pressed against the kitchen island. He chuckles against my lips when I surprise him by pushing back abruptly so his naked skin pebbles against the bite of the cold granite near the stove. I return his kisses, deepening them before dragging my tongue up the side of his throat.

"I'm sure Shane would love to know my bare ass is almost on his countertop," Max jokes between kisses. His hands roam under my shirt, stroking down my sides.

"You really thinking about my brother right now? Should I be worried about who caused this?" I tease in a whisper, wrapping my hand around his hard cock.

"Watch your mouth," he growls back, slanting his mouth over mine and biting my lip as I stroke up and down his length. "Maybe I need to bend you over this counter to show you exactly who I'm thinking about."

His growl turns to a moan when I drop to my knees with a smile, looking up into his eyes as I take him into my mouth. "That works, too," he sighs, gripping my hair and guiding my movements.

After teasing him to the brink, I pull away and I kiss up his stomach until I'm back on my feet, arms wrapped around his shoulders. "How do you want me?" I whisper against the shell of his ear.

"Take your clothes off," he commands, eyes molten gold as he strokes himself.

I swallow shakily, biting my lip as I pull off my tank top and loose pajama shorts to stand bared before him.

"Go get on your hands and knees on the bed. *Now*." Max pushes off the counter and lands one hearty smack to my right ass cheek when I turn to do as I'm told.

I chuckle when through the wall I hear, "Oh, for fuck's sake," followed by Kaycia's giggle and then the door opening and closing and two sets of footsteps heading down the stairs. But my humor is replaced by desire as I crawl onto the bed, waiting for Max to join me. I'm vulnerable, facing away from him, but soft footsteps approach, and I shiver with anticipation when he runs a hand down my back and over my ass.

"Sounds like you don't have to worry about being quiet tonight, darlin'," Max whispers against my ear. A little moan escapes my lips and I arch my back for him, the movement earning a sound of approval low in his throat. "Fuck, I missed you."

Kissing down my spine, Max works his fingers between my thighs, sliding one, then two inside me. He curls them toward the front of my body and hits just the right spot to have me seeing stars, moving quicker as my breathing hitches. When I cry out with my release, he smiles against my shoulder.

"Do you have any protection? I don't really have pockets when I'm flying."

"Uh," I mumble. "Maybe in the drawer? I'm sorry, I didn't think about it." I flush with embarrassment for not thinking ahead, my head clearing as I start to roll on to my side to check.

"Stay just like that. I like this view." Max chuckles and slides off the bed to check the nightstand, finding a box of condoms.

"Oh, thank the gods."

"Eager, are we?" he teases me.

"Fuck yes, I am. Now come on."

I watch as Max sheaths himself and then kneels on the bed near my hips. Within a few moments, he's behind me pressing against my entrance, then sliding into me as I groan into the pillow. He starts with a slow rhythm, coaxing moans from me with each thrust, but soon gives in and increases the speed.

I reach between my legs, stroking my clit as he grips my hips. When I plummet over the edge a second time, I nearly collapse onto my stomach, but Max holds me tight, his fingers surely marking my skin, even if only for a short time before the bruising fades. He comes with a hoarse shout, leaning over my back and kissing my neck and shoulder before pulling out and letting me lay splayed on the covers as he tosses the condom in the trash.

After, I lay with my cheek on Max's chest, the dusting of dark hair tickling my skin. He aimlessly strokes my hair, his breathing growing deeper as he relaxes further. I want to tell him that I didn't just miss him. I needed him. That when I saw Taryn, all that kept me from falling apart was the thought of him and the life I'm building here. I wanted to run to the truck and drive all the way to Argent to wrap my arms around him and remind myself of what it feels like to be cared for unconditionally. But instead, I just say, "The nightmares came back."

He perks up, arm tightening around me as he looks down. "What do you mean?"

"I haven't had them since we started spending time together. But they came back. I woke up screaming. Woke up thinking they'd taken me again. That they'd hurt you and Shane and Kaycia. Colton was there, in my dream."

"I've got you now, Lana. No one's going to hurt you again." He presses a kiss on the top of my head, then within another few moments his breathing changes and I know he's fallen asleep.

"I know," I whisper to his sleeping form. I hope. Because I don't think he would ever mean to hurt me, but after everything with Taryn I have a kernel of fear. An urge to fight what I'm finally admitting to myself about the two of us. A constant doubt that the next person I give myself to completely will be the one to destroy everything that I have left.

I hope he doesn't prove me right.

Chapter 39
Max

When I wake, I'm naked in Lana's bed alone. She's sitting on the balcony with a mug of coffee in her hand and a blanket wrapped around her shoulders. The breeze sneaking through the crack in the slider is chilly. Autumn has settled over the city.

I look around, deciding to raid one of the dresser drawers for a pair of Shane's athletic shorts before I join her. I know Kaycia realizes shifters aren't as modest as humans, but the last thing I need is to give her a start by wandering around naked on the balcony next door at eight in the morning. Shane has mentioned she likes to sit out there with her coffee, so I don't want to risk it. Plus, the cold really doesn't do flattering things to a guy.

"There's coffee for you!" Lana calls through the door, her wolf hearing picking up on my rustling around.

"Thanks." I stir a spoonful of sugar into the black coffee, watching the dark liquid swirl around the mug. I should use this quiet morning to tell her how I feel. I can wrap her in the blanket and confess that I think I've bonded with her. Ask if she feels it, too. The worry that she might shun me seems nearly impossible after the nights we've spent together, but it still rears its ugly head and causes me to wince with the near physical pain the idea of rejection causes.

Stepping out on the cold wrought iron I find Lana holding my phone, watching something intently.

"This guy is *good*," she announces, holding it out for me to see that she's watching the video I recorded at the practice with Alistair playing a few riffs and generally jamming with the guys. "I hope you don't mind that I started watching without you. I didn't scroll back very far. Any other homemade videos are your little secrets." She winks, but her heart isn't in it.

"You won't find anything exciting, don't worry. But yeah, he is. I think he'll be a good fit. He's chill like Ryan and already knew Jet from when they were all growing up. We can get a couple of nights in for practice before the weekend since you're back in town early."

I lean down, tilting her chin up so I can kiss her forehead. "Good morning," I say as I pull away, dragging one of the chairs closer so I can sit next to her.

"Morning, pretty bird," she replies. As she hands me the phone she glances at my bare chest, then the shorts I snagged from the drawer. Lana bites her lip, fighting laughter for only a moment.

"What's so funny?" I ask, sipping my coffee as though I don't know Shane's shorts are entirely too long for me.

"You look like you're playing dress up, how are those even staying on?" I love to see her smile like this, wide and unburdened. Her eyes are bright and any thought of nightmares or the past are forgotten in these moments.

"The drawstring is doing all the work."

"Those look like shorts he's had since high school, so you better hope the drawstring doesn't decide today's the day to give up the ghost."

"Oh, like you don't want to see me naked again," I tease.

"I wouldn't mind," her voice drops low, eyes drifting over my chest.

I lean over and wrap a hand behind her head, pulling her close for a kiss, then two. We settle on the balcony, comfortably discussing plans for the band and practice and the upcoming show at Lucy's. The conversation and subsequent shared shower steal my momentum, and by the time I'm getting ready to shift and head home, I've failed to express my feelings to her or to ask her about what happened with Taryn.

As though she's trying to avoid the same topic she begins to get dressed, telling me that she has to work a lunch shift she traded with another bartender to make up for the ones she's missed this week. "I'll be at practice after though," she says. She kisses me deeply, running her palms down my chest and drawing a low moan from me before she smacks my ass in payback from last night. We both chuckle before she tells me to fly home.

———

I wait in my condo with the guys that evening. I spent most of the day working on some new logo ideas for merch, something I always toy with, but think I might have finally gotten right. Ryan and Jet seem excited, Alistair is open to anything being the new guy, but I want Lana's approval before making any decisions.

I hear her on the steps out front long before she knocks, but with humans around I can't rush to open the door for her until her taps echo on the wood of the door. As I'm walking toward the door, she opens it and steps inside.

"Hey, darlin'."

"Hey, pretty bird," she whispers, too low for the guys to hear. I have to hold myself back from pulling her close and kissing her.

"Hey, Lana!" Jet calls, blowing smoke from a joint out the window. She wrinkles her nose at the pungent scent, but just smiles and waves, brushing past me with a knowing glance.

Tease.

"Hey everyone," she says, shedding her jacket and opening her case. "Sorry, I'm late." She extends her hand to Alistair, shaking his when he reaches out. "Hi, I'm Lana."

"Nice to meet you," he replies. He looks between us and smiles at Ryan, as if to say 'yeah, they're definitely fucking.' It's not a secret, but it's also not something I've bragged about to them. Not like some of my casual flings or recurring fuck buddies. I don't need them thinking about her like that.

"Let's play some music," I announce, glaring at Ryan. He just shakes his head and picks up his bass.

Lana gives me a wry smile but just takes up a place near Ryan and tests the bow against the strings.

We spend the rest of the night, and the next two, practicing. Lana has written a new song, and I've been toying with two more, so we work on learning those and getting Alistair and Lana up to speed on our usual covers and originals, adding parts for Lana, and discovering our new sound. By the time Saturday rolls around I'm feeling confident and more excited about the show than I have in a long time.

We do all right at Lucy's, but with a full band and more original music, I think we have a chance to stand out and get noticed. It feels like tonight could be the night things really start changing for us. The crowd is packed in, whether because it's a holiday weekend and everyone wants to get an early start on celebrating, or whether it's because they liked what they saw last time, I don't know. But it's good news for us and our tip jar.

Even though we have the show later, Lana's working behind the bar for the happy hour shift. The rest of us have our instruments set up and gather around one of the high tops near the bar. I can barely drag my eyes from her tonight. We've spent nearly every night together since she got home, but we've been so exhausted from rehearsals and working that I haven't brought up what that means for our relationship. I'm a chicken shit, but I've been soaking in the comfort of just being with her without having to have the discussion.

Jamila laughs at something the barback says and Lana throws a towel at the college kid, joining Jamila with her head thrown back. She's visibly different than when she first arrived in Argent. Relaxed, smiling, comfortable in the crowd rather than wary and ready to snarl. She's got her golden hair messy under a mesh back cap and wears a cropped band tee with her ripped jeans and boots tonight, ready to make the crowd swoon when she plays, just like she makes me.

"Dude, we need to talk about that." Ryan nudges my shoulder, bringing my attention back to the guys and the drained pitcher on the table.

"Yeah," Alistair agrees, tapping a new pack of cigarettes against his palm before unwrapping them and flipping one upside down. He pulls another free and lets it dangle from his lips, playing with his lighter while he waits to go outside for a smoke.

"Why do I feel like I'm being ganged up on in my own band?" I bristle. Alistair may be Ryan's cousin, but he barely knows me or Lana.

"Look, Max," Jet starts, fidgeting with his pint glass, then running a hand over his chin. "We all love Lana, she's fucking smoking on the fiddle and we need her. But—" Jet looks over at the other guys.

"But, what?" I throw back the rest of my beer, swallowing it in one gulp. I'm not feeling warm and fuzzy about the evening anymore.

"What happens when you two break up? Or she goes back to whatever backwoods she came from?" Ryan has the decency to look like he feels bad asking, but the dickhead asks anyway. Jet grimaces and finishes his beer, not meeting my eyes.

"Fuck you, man," I snarl. I must have been louder than I thought because Lana looks over sharply and Raquel lightly hops from the edge of the stool she was perched on, ready for trouble.

I wave them both off, pretending like I'm fine, but I'm having to fight to keep my eyes from glowing.

"I'm just trying to protect you. And us." Ryan drains the rest of his beer. "Have you talked to her about it? Mixing business and pleasure? Bands have imploded for stupider reasons than a couple breaking up."

"We—" I can't defend anything, because we *haven't* talked about it. I hate to admit they might be right. "We aren't even officially together."

"I'm only adding my two cents because I don't want to move up here if this is a temporary thing," Alistair says, flicking his lighter a couple of times before placing his hand on my shoulder. I want to jerk away from him, but I don't. He has a right to be concerned for his future.

When I look back over, Lana is still standing at attention, eyes flitting between all of us. I smile at her, easing her mind, even if mine is racing through all the potential heartbreak that might ensue if she does decide to leave us.

"Let's play tonight and see how it goes. I'm not saying you two aren't going to end up together with a house full of babies and a wall of platinum albums, but I also gotta look out for me and the guys. And for you. You're my friend, Max. We good?" Ryan studies my face, his mouth tight as he waits for my reaction. "Next round on me?"

"Yeah, all right. I get it." I shrug it off, pretending like I'm back to my normal self. The one that doesn't worry about how a relationship is going to go because none of them matter anyway. But my chest squeezes when I catch Lana staring again. Because it does matter this time.

Chapter 40
Lana

I don't like the way the guys are watching me, or the way Max's body tenses as he speaks with them. His muscles coil in a way I haven't seen before. I'm usually the one holding back my anger. But in the end, he smiles and waves at me like nothing is amiss. He lets Ryan pat his shoulder and when the bassist brings the pitcher back for a refill nothing seems out of the ordinary. Even so, a little pit of doubt opens in my chest as I wipe a spill from the bar and hand out a cocktail napkin to one of the ladies who just sat down.

It's busy tonight, noisy with people's laughter and chatter. Spirits are high in anticipation for live music on a long weekend. Upbeat old songs are on repeat on the jukebox and they harmonize with the clink of glasses and clack of billiards balls. Happy hour appetizers and drink specials keep Jamila and me busy, barely speaking for most of our shift as we pass each other and pour drinks.

"You ready for tonight?" Jamila asks me when we have a small break in the rush.

"I think so. I'm really excited, but I also feel like I could throw up." I stack pint glasses, letting them clink together more than normal. Stupid nerves.

Jamila gives me a sideways look that has me explaining, "Last time if I was awful, it was a one-time thing, ya know? 'Oh, look, the new bartender doing them a solid.' *Now* they see me as part of the band. What if I forget everything?" I toss the bar rag over my shoulder and run my palm over my face.

"Girl—" Jamila stands with her hands on her hips, glaring at me. "You play that fiddle like it's a part of your soul. You know the music by heart. Do you think that new guy is worried about how he's going to do?" She nods toward Alistair, leaning back on his stool checking out one of the women who just came in the door with an unlit cigarette dangling from his lips.

"No. He looks like he's more worried about getting laid." I admit, pulling a ticket to mix a cocktail.

"Exactly. And you already have that locked down, so you don't have anything to worry about." She laughs, bumping me with her hip when I pretend to look scandalized. She plucks the glass and ticket from my fingers and points to the kitchen. "Now go eat something so you don't get all snarly and get your head in the game."

I balance a pizza and basket of wings in one hand as I walk to the table where the band sits, depositing it between the guys and plopping down on a vacant stool. Before they can grab a piece I've already bitten into a slice, wincing when the cheese burns the roof of my mouth.

Jamila was right, as usual. I was getting hungry and bitchy. That explains the nerves and why I think the guys are all watching me warily.

Except, maybe they are.

"What the fuck?" I ask around my bite. "What's y'all's problem?"

"Pre-show jitters." Max murmurs, eyeing the guys like he's daring them to say something. He throws back his beer like he's trying to drown some demons but gives me his usual grin when he catches me watching.

"Well, suck it up and eat. And stop making me nervous." I lean my head over to bump Max affectionately.

He smiles again and rubs circles on my back, but something still feels wrong. I shake it off, sipping water and finishing my greasy meal before getting back behind the bar for another hour.

It seems like the final hour of my shift passes in a blink because now I'm standing on the stage with lights doing their damnedest to blind me while Max charms the audience.

He drawls his welcome and the people standing near the stage cheer and clap. When did so many people get here?

"How y'all doing this evening, Lucy's?" Max asks to

cheers and "woos" from the audience. "We've got something special for you tonight. Not only is Lana McKinley back on fiddle, but we've got Alistair Simonetti with us on lead guitar. Give 'em a warm welcome and let's see what you think!" Everyone cheers and claps again, bottles and glasses held up to show their approval.

The song begins, the beat from Jet's drums and Ryan's steady bass line merging with my heartbeat. Jamila was right, I know this. I know every song. I close my eyes and tap my toe until it's my turn to shine, then I draw my bow across the strings and let my soul sing.

Carson has us playing two sets tonight since Max assured him we have enough music prepared. We'll play at our normal time, then have a short break before the second. We decided to close the first set on a slower, more intimate note, with our duet. It's the first song we wrote together, but hopefully not the last.

Couples pair up and hold one another close, swaying to the lyrics. Max and my voices ebb and flow like a rushing river, comforting like the harmony of my packs' howls when I was back home. My fiddle and his acoustic guitar are the only accompaniment and it feels like we're the only two people in the room as we share breath at the microphone. When the song ends, I'm certain that what I've suspected is true.

He's mine.

A bond has forged between us, strong and steady. I ignored it, told myself he wouldn't feel the same way. I kept insisting that he's a falcon and flirt, just Shane's buddy out to show me a good time while I healed from everything.

He was supposed to be a distraction that I could enjoy for a little while, but couldn't have permanently because of my commitment to Shane and the pack. But I feel it now as I smile at him under the bright spotlight, our hearts beating in a matching rhythm with each other, confirming that I couldn't fight this even if I wanted to. I wish I wasn't wearing a stupid cap so I could press my forehead to his, to try to tell him everything with a gentle touch.

He's mine and I'm his and I have to figure out how to balance my loyalty to the pack and my ties to him because I can't bear to give him up. I won't.

The crowd cheers and from behind us I hear Ryan whisper to one of the guys. "Maybe we don't have to worry. Look at them."

I don't know what he's talking about, and I don't ask, my eyes affixed to Max as he takes his guitar off and smiles at me. We all hop off stage, making our way to a table set aside by the bar for our break. Max and I bring up the rear, his fingers brushing against mine and sending a spark through me.

I nearly squeeze my thighs together at the touch, wondering if we could borrow Carson's office for the break. I bet we could make it quick. I grin, opening my mouth to say as much, when a man catches Max's arm and brings us to a halt. My eyes nearly glow gold at the uninvited intrusion, but I keep my mouth shut as the middle aged man introduces himself.

"Max Acheson? I'm Zach Harrington. I'm a band manager with 85E and have been following you guys for a while now." Max cocks his head, just like he would in falcon form as he listens. "I love your growth and the sound you're creating. It could really take off. Would you be interested in talking about additional bookings?" He hands Max a business card, continuing to speak rapidly as my eyes scan the crowd.

Chapter 41
Max

The first set was on fire. Lana and Alistair did exactly what I knew they would, they took our sound to the next level and the duet between Lana and me almost had me coming undone on stage.

My emotions are so raw and open after performing together. I have to tell her how I feel tonight; I can't keep it in any longer. Not just because of what the guys said, but because I have to know. I need to hear her say it—that she feels the same way.

If we need to figure out some way to spend time in two places while we make music, I'm willing to do it. I can do my design work anywhere if she needs to go back to Woodbine Hollow. We can work it out.

When our duet ends and she gives me that soft look, I almost pull her in for a kiss in front of everyone. But I don't. I'm afraid if I get started, I won't be able to stop, and we still have a second set to perform.

The guys are already on the way to the table for

refreshments, people patting their backs and offering to buy them drinks later. I love this crowd. These people are like family. Some of them have come out to support us week after week for years. And now they're embracing Lana and Alistair, too. For the first time in a while, I love my life. I feel whole and loved in every way.

Lana's hand tightens on mine when a guy grabs my arm to get my attention as we pass. I can imagine her wolf's hackles rising with hostility. But she relaxes when he introduces himself. Her eyes scan the crowd while I let him talk, turning the business card over and over in my fingers. They're nearly trembling with disbelief.

I've heard of Zach Harrington before. He and 85E Management have helped several other bands get gigs around town, and most recently got one local band booked as the opener on a multi-state tour with a couple big headliners. If he's serious this might mean everything is truly coming together for us. This type of representation might open the doors to cut an album, or more.

"Well, I'll have to talk to the band," I answer, hoping I'm playing it cool.

"Of course," he replies. He shakes my hand and Lana's. "I'm looking forward to the second set, but I wanted to catch up before the end of the night. I'm looking forward to hearing from you."

"Sounds good. Thanks for coming out."

Lana gives a tight smile and watches him melt back into the crowd. She's relaxed now and meets my excitement with a soft brush of her lips against mine.

"Can you believe that?" I ask breathlessly.

"It's great, Max. I don't know what the hell any of it means really, but it sure sounds exciting." I forget she hasn't been doing this long and doesn't understand all the ins and outs.

Shit, *I* don't even know everything. I wonder if I should ask someone what to do next as we make our way over to the table where the guys have been watching attentively.

Lana lets me explain, drinking from a bottle of water and wiping her brow under her cap. Suddenly, the bottle crunches in her hand, some overflowing and running down her forearm before splattering onto the concrete floor. I stop in mid-sentence, eyes following hers as they track Shane. He and Kaycia were sitting with Raquel in their usual spots for the show, but now he pushes through the crowd with a grim expression. Kaycia hangs back, eyes worried, while Raquel stands at attention next to her. All of us watch as Shane approaches a petite brunette making her way through the crowd.

She's heading toward us. It's clear Shane is doing his best to head her off without actually picking anyone up and moving them out of the way. Lana places the crumpled plastic bottle on the table and whispers, "I'll be right back," heading straight for the woman and her brother without another word.

I watch, my heart sinking and stomach souring as Lana grabs the smiling woman—no, wolf—and all but drags her to the front door and outside. Shane follows closely behind. Neither look happy.

"What's going on with the McKinley siblings?" Ryan

asks. "They both look like they'd like to tear that chick apart."

"That's Taryn," I answer. I shouldn't know for sure. But deep down I do.

"Who?" Jet asks.

"Her ex."

"Gods damn it," Ryan sighs.

Chapter 42
Lana

"I've got this Shane." I grind the words through my teeth, forcing my wolf to stay hidden so my eyes don't glow and claws don't sprout to dig through Taryn's arm in front of Rodrigo, who's sitting on his stool by the front door checking IDs.

"Are you sure?" Shane asks. He's glaring at Taryn so menacingly that she practically cowers behind me. As if I would stop him from attacking her right now.

I'm so angry that I'm shaking, tears threatening to fall from my fury. Something that pisses me off because I'm in no way sad over Taryn anymore. I'm shocked she would come to Argent, and I'm nauseated that she's shown up and potentially ruined one of the best nights I've had and spoiled Max's excitement.

Max. Oh, shit. I hadn't even thought about what this might look like. I'm torn between running back in to explain and staying here to find out what the fuck she thinks she's doing.

"Yeah, I'm fine. Please go tell Max it's okay. I'll be back in for the second half."

Shane grumbles his response but is reluctant to leave. I look over my shoulder and glare at him before he finally holds his hands up and heads back. He whispers something to Rodrigo, then disappears back in the front door.

"What the fuck, Taryn?" I shout, drawing attention from people walking by.

"I'm sorry." She holds her hands up in surrender, dark eyes remorseful, but I don't care. "I get it now."

"You get *what*? What the fuck were you thinking? Did I not make it clear enough when I saw you in Woodbine Hollow? I don't want you!" I'm shaking, my claws and fangs aching for me to shift. "I don't want to see you or speak to you or breathe the same air as you. *Why* would you think it was a good idea to come all the way here to surprise me like this?"

"I don't know. I missed you. When I saw you in the grocery I thought 'my gods, she's a different person. I want to know *that* Lana.' I didn't *think*. I saw your name listed on a concert newsletter I follow. I had a long weekend and just booked a flight." She looks sheepish as she adds, "I thought a grand gesture might make it better."

I scoff and throw my hands in the air at her arrogance, that I would just take her back because she bought a plane ticket.

"I'm the same fucking person you left sobbing on our front porch, you asshole! You didn't *like* me like this. You never cared when I played, or wrote, or sang. You wanted me to watch your back and not embarrass you and be polite and get along with the rest of the people you wanted to impress. Now that I'm playing and people want to see me, *now* you think I'm worth it? Now that my brother isn't an exiled embarrassment and has some power you want me again? That makes me worthy? Fuck you, Taryn."

"It's because of *him*. You're different because he loves you. The *real* you. And because you truly love him. I get it now."

"*What?* Who?" I'm confused now, my anger fading slightly.

"That singer. It was him I smelled on you at the store, wasn't it? He's not a wolf, but he looks at you the way you deserve. To be admired." She hangs her head, the dark waves hiding her face. "I realize how fucked up I was to you and I'm sorry, Lana. The way you two sang together. The way you looked at each other. I get it. I'm sorry."

When she looks back up at me, she seems sincere, but I'm still so angry that my hands continue to tremble. The fact that she thinks I'm only worthy because of who I'm dating riles me. Max helped by letting me shine, but I'm not a reflection of him. I create my own light and Taryn won't dim it ever again.

"I'm different because of *me*. Because I allowed myself to feel something and take what I wanted." I pause for a moment to calm myself. "But he helped. He's mine and I won't have you ruining this for me."

"I know. Can you forgive me?"

"I don't know. But I sure as shit won't be doing it tonight."

"I accept that. And I *am* sorry, Lana. I realize now I can't be what you need."

Taryn opens her arms and for a moment she's the lone wolf who was new in town, looking for a pack and a place within it. I can almost see the young woman that I fell in love with over pancakes at the diner all those years ago. The one that grew and changed, the same as me. We just grew apart and changed into different people.

I can forgive her. Shit, I should probably *thank* her. Without her breaking my heart, I might have never figured out what really made it beat. What love really feels like.

Sighing at the glassy shimmer of tears on her lashes, I return her embrace. I'm giving her the closure I needed so badly. Even if she doesn't deserve it. Wrapped in her arms I feel nothing, though. Nothing like what I have waiting for me inside. I tense, ready to pull away, but let her hold on a little longer than I should.

I only realize my error when I hear a broken sound behind me.

Spinning, I catch sight of Max's back, rushing back into the bar. I push Taryn away and sprint after him.

I don't give a shit that Rodrigo looks surprised at my speed as I push past the broad-shouldered bouncer and into the neon glow of Lucy's. I spot Shane over the crowd, when he sees me, he points toward the back hallway where Carson's office and the emergency exit is. I shoulder my way through the people on the dance floor, some of them pissed at my rudeness.

None of them matter. I have to catch up to Max.

If he were a human, I wouldn't be so frantic, but he has

a much easier out than a regular guy. I can't let him ruin his chance with that manager or wreck what he's built with this band because of some shitty misunderstanding. I can't let the band down. Even if he doesn't want to stay for me.

The hallway is just past where the guys are sitting at the table. The next set starts soon. They're finishing their drinks and look annoyed with me as I rush past.

"What did I say? If they're already fighting, we're fucked," Alistair whispers, thinking I can't hear him.

"Fuck you, Alistair," I snarl. They all look alarmed at my reaction. "We'll be back soon."

I hope, I don't add.

I skid into Carson's office, finding it empty, as expected. I didn't really think Max would just hide out. If I know him, he's getting some air. I just hope it's only filling his lungs, not his wings.

The emergency door says it's alarmed, but I know after months of shifts that that's just a sign to keep drunks from running out on their tabs. I push through the door and look around the alley, my night vision allowing me to see everything with ease.

"Max?" I call, frantic when he's not on the ground. The fire escape ladder is down, and I clatter up the rungs, reaching the roof in moments. "Max!"

He stands on the backside of the building, the waxing moon casting white light on half of his face. His tee is in his hand, boots kicked off. A hint of liquid shows on his cheek bones, disappearing into the dark shadow of his stubble.

"Don't do it. It isn't what you think. I don't want her. Don't you dare fly off," I command, angry that he's assuming the worst. That he thinks the best option is to run instead of talk to me. His jaw muscles tense, grinding as he chews on his cheek. He sighs deeply as he drops his shirt and closes his eyes, preparing to shift.

"Was it all in my head?" he whispers. Anyone without shifter senses wouldn't have heard him over the city surrounding us.

"What?" I reply, my voice shaking.

"Was it just the songs? Just creative chemistry?" He won't look at me, but he doesn't need to for me to see him trembling. "If so, I won't make you stay."

Before I can answer, he's stepped closer to the edge, like he'll take flight any moment. A sob breaks from me as I call out, "You know damn well it's never just been the songs. If you leave me and the guys like this, you're no better than any of them." My voice cracks. We haven't confessed our emotions, but I thought he knew how I felt. "Please, don't. Don't abandon me."

Tears stream freely now, and I fall to my knees on the roof. It's just like when Taryn left, me crying and holding myself together all alone.

But not for long.

Max's scent wraps around me as he pulls me to my feet and wraps his arms around me. "I'll never abandon you, Lana." He presses soft kisses to the top of my head through the sweaty cap I'm still wearing. "I'm sorry. I panicked. I don't know how to do this."

"To do what?"

"To love someone."

But he does. In all his actions he's shown how deeply

he knows how to love. When he risked himself to help Shane and me against Colton. How he cares for his friends and his bandmates, giving freely of his time and resources. And how he's shown me over and over with his actions.

I hold him close. "Yes, you do. I love you, too. You're mine, Max. No one else matters."

Chapter 43
Max

Holding Lana close to me, I bury my face in the crook of her neck, breathing her in.

She loves me.

She feels the bond between us as deeply as I do.

Drunk on her scent, I whisper, "I do, Lana. I do love you."

When she kisses me, I can't believe I'd ever doubted it. I was a fool to not know already, to have allowed my doubt to make me even consider running.

I should have listened to Shane when he told me she was fine. I don't know what I expected to see when I walked out front like a knight marching to save his queen, but I knew how hard Lana had worked to get over their breakup. I couldn't stand to think about her facing the shock of Taryn turning up in Argent with no one to support her. It was a punch in the gut when I walked out of Lucy's to find Lana tenderly hugging her ex-girlfriend.

So, I panicked.

The rage that fueled Lana as she dragged Taryn through the bar was all but gone, as though it has been a figment of my imagination. I didn't want to interrupt. I didn't want her to see the pain I knew I wouldn't be able to hide. I didn't think I could speak if she tried to explain or, gods forbid, told me 'It's been fun, but I've got to go back home'.

So, I did exactly what I expected everyone else to do. I ran.

Plowing through the crowded bar, I barely heard when Shane and Raquel called my name. Thankfully, neither of them could catch me with all the people lined up for drinks. The guys in the band tried to stop me, but I shoved Ryan so hard he nearly knocked over his stool when I passed. No one else followed. No one else mattered.

My heart broke and crumbled as I pushed through the emergency exit and climbed the fire escape. I didn't how to stand there and meet her ex and pretend I was just a bandmate. I had immediately assumed the worst, that I wasn't worthy or wanted, just like I'd felt when I was five wondering what I'd done wrong.

Guilt surged through me when I heard Lana's voice in the alley a few minutes after I'd reached the roof, debating whether I should shift or not. When she sank to her knees crying, I couldn't believe what I was considering.

With her in my arms, I wonder how I could have been so fucking stupid. How could I have turned into someone who would leave the person they love behind without saying a word?

It would make me no better than my mother.

When she lays her cheek on my shoulder, I squeeze her tighter, hoping she doesn't think I'm a coward for not begging her there in front of everyone to stay. That she doesn't resent the fact that she had to come find me.

All those worries are wiped away when she looks at me, lips turning up in a smile though her eyes are still glassy with tears, her mascara smudged on her cheekbones. I wipe the streaks away with my thumbs. I'll never be the one to make her cry like that again. Not after everything we've shared with each other.

She's mine.

When she told me that she loved me, called me hers, my heart knitted itself back together stronger than ever before. I don't care who I have to fight for her, or if we don't work out in the end. I can't hide from a love like this anymore because I'm afraid the worst might happen.

Because not everyone leaves. I know that now.

I sure won't.

Lana's cap falls off when I brush my lips against hers, tasting our remaining tears mixed together as she pulls me closer and deepens the kiss with a soft moan. We tremble from our shared emotions, and when she finally pulls away, she buries her face in my neck, breathing deeply as she rubs her body against my bare chest.

"You smell like her," I murmur, a surge of possessiveness flaring at the unfamiliar wolf scent.

"Not for long," she answers, holding me tight, as though she's masking Taryn's signature with mine. There will be no confusion to any other shifter who we belong to when we leave this roof.

"Oh, shit." I reluctantly pull away before I let myself get too distracted by the pleasant friction of her body against my bare chest. "We still have another set to do in —" I look at my watch "—less than five minutes." I gently kiss her once more, holding her face in my hands for a moment. "We'll talk about this after, yeah?"

"Yeah. Get dressed." She tucks her messy hair under her cap, rubbing the smeared mascara from under her eyes, and smiling at me as I walk back over to pick up my shirt and pull on my boots.

We're climbing back down the fire escape when the exit door opens. Jet hesitantly sticks his head out. "Uh— Max? Lana?"

"Yeah, we're coming. Sorry!" Lana calls back, pretending there's nothing at all strange about us being on the roof.

"Everything okay?" Jet asks. "I hope what the guys said earlier didn't cause this."

"What did the guys say earlier?" Lana bristles, looking between Jet and me.

"Oh. Shit." Jet scoots down the hall quickly as Lana rounds on me.

Sighing, I run my fingers through my hair, then urge her to keep walking with a hand on her lower back. "They were worried that if we split up it would kill the band."

"Oh." She scowls, then pushes me against the wall near Carson's office. "Well, I don't think they have to worry about that," she whispers against my lips before kissing me.

"Nah, I don't either." I reply against her mouth, squeezing her ass. "Let's go finish this." Before I take her hand and lead her down the hallway, she pulls me close, wrapping her arms around my neck.

"I love you, pretty bird."

"I love you, darlin'."

She presses one last kiss to my lips before we head to the stage, brushing off curious looks from our friends and the band.

The rest of the set goes off without a hitch. The crowd is vibing with the music, Lana and Alistair fit in like a dream, and our original songs and new duets bring more cheers than anything else. I spot Zach Harrington chatting with Raquel and Jamila at the bar as he pays his tab, but don't think too hard about what Raquel might be telling him.

For the entire second set I can barely pull my eyes away from Lana, as though the strength of our bond has been solidified and keeps me in her orbit. She smiles and sways with her fiddle, playing off Alistair and his riffs and casting sultry looks my way when I sing directly to her.

When the final song ends, Lana takes her cap off and kisses me under the spotlight for everyone to see. The bar cheers and my heart soars higher than I've ever flown before.

Epilogue
Lana

"Why does this sound like some weird family reunion crossed with corporate team building? Are you sure it's a good idea?" I ask Shane, holding the phone between my ear and shoulder as I fold clothing and place it inside my open duffle bag.

"Yes. And I'd appreciate it if you act more excited because I'm not looking forward to it any more than you are." He sounds fuzzy, the reception spotty wherever he's at in Woodbine Hollow.

He and Kaycia took a flight out earlier in the week to meet again with Jon Cameron to discuss arrangements for the trial merger of the packs. Shane isn't quite ready to commit to moving home, and Cameron and our father are comfortable acting as middlemen for a while. It gives me a little reprieve as his second, too.

They thought a merging of the packs would work best with some kind of symbolic event to keep everyone in good spirits. So now we're all prepping for a weekend of potlucks and games in the hills and valleys we grew up in. Both packs together. Minus the ones who attacked me.

"Okay, I'll be sure to pick out matching shirts or some shit so we all look like we're having fun. Deal?"

Shane groans. "When are you coming to town again?"

"I'm flying down to Reedsville to meet Max tomorrow morning. We think the album will be done within a week and he'll drive us both up as soon as we're done. He's been prepping everything, so I just need to show up and play."

After meeting Zach Harrington at our show a few weeks ago, we ended up signing on with him for a trial period. We're supposed to record five songs with the guys for our first EP so we have copies to sell when we open for a couple shows coming up over the next few months. Things are moving quickly, and Max and I are both excited and nervous about what that means for our living situation and my rank in the pack. I haven't officially resigned as Shane's second. But if this merger works, neither Shane nor I will have to make huge changes to our lives, yet.

I hung back in Argent longer to work as many shifts as I could to pad my bank account since I'm going to be off for a few weeks. Who knows, maybe soon I'll make enough money from music so I don't have to sling drinks anymore.

The only thing dampening my excitement is the fact that no one knows exactly where Aubrey is. Despite reassurances that he's fine, he continues to avoid telling me where he is or confirm who he's with, only reiterating he needs some time away from pack drama to sort some things.

"You're not living in The Hollow either, Lana. Stop being a hypocrite," he said in our last call.

Ouch—that one stung.

He promised he'll come home when the time is right, but it still feels wrong for a part of our family to be missing when we just felt whole again. Especially when we're supposed to be showing a united front.

"Okay, keep me posted."

"Will do! And tell Kaycia that I watered the plants today and that Ms. Sandoval from downstairs said she'll check them for her while we're all gone. You don't have anything weird laying around that you want me to hide from her, right?" I laugh, holding up a new leather harness with a grin. Max will have a surprise when I get there. Guess we will see if he really is down to try anything once. I shove it in the bottom of my bag, hoping no one blinks at it passing through the airport baggage check.

Shane murmurs something unintelligible to Kaycia as I zip up the bag, pausing when a knock sounds at the door.

"That's weird," I tell him. "Raquel and Jamila told me they're on a date tonight, and anyone else who would stop by is out of town."

"Maybe Ms. Sandoval has questions," he offers, but his voice is wary. "Use the peephole."

My nerves tingle and my adrenaline spikes. Even though I'm strong, I still have flashbacks of when Colton's guys ambushed me. Being completely alone with a stranger at the door makes that memory flicker to the surface.

No shit, Shane.

"Stay on the phone with me, okay?" I mutter, trying to sound nonchalant.

Crossing the studio, I peer through the peephole, then yank the door open with a gasp.

"Lana? You okay?" Shane growls.

"Holy shit! Aubrey!" I hold the phone in one hand and wrap my little brother in a tight embrace. My cheeks burn from how wide my smile stretches when I see him.

"What?" I can hear Shane calling through the phone.

"Shane! It's—" My smile fades as I track the other scent in the stairwell behind Aubrey, finding the last wolf I expected to see waiting to flee down to the lobby.

"What is it?" Shane demands, voice raising when I haven't answered. "*Lana?*"

My eyes glow with fury as I glare at Caleb Davidson, head bowed with eyes downcast in submission. A growl starts deep in my chest when Aubrey steps back and takes Caleb's hand in his.

"We may have a problem," I whisper into the phone, my eyes locked on the matching rings on Aubrey and Caleb's fingers.

Continue *The Wolves of Woodbine Hollow* in Book 3.

Afterword

Thank you so much for reading Lana and Max's story.

If you enjoyed this book please consider leaving a review on Amazon or Goodreads (or any of your other favorite review spots).

Reviews and word of mouth are the best ways you can support your favorite indie authors, and I appreciate every review! The more people who read my stories, the more I can continue to write and share them with the world!

xo,
LB

Acknowledgments

These never get any easier, even six books in! I always have to thank my family for dealing with the panic and doubt that sets in throughout the writing/editing/publishing process. Who knew I would be a mess every single time?:)

To Kelly, Krystal, Kristen, and Sarah: You listen to my daily "podcasts" about anything and everything under the sun and let me bounce ideas off you (good and bad). I'm go glad we've all found each other and we HAVE to find a way to meet in person soon.

Hayley Turner, it was such a pleasure to work with you to bring Max and Lana's duet to life. I was so lucky that you love the same kind of music I do and can't believe someone is singing words I wrote.

To my alphas, betas, ARC readers, fellow authors, and other readers/supporters: Whether you've been here since 2022 or you just stumbled upon my work, THANK YOU. Your support, reactions, voice memos, and reviews really make my world go round. I couldn't do it without you!

About the Author

L.B. Benson is a native Texan and a lifelong reader. She formally immortalized her love of books by earning a Bachelor of Arts in English from the University of Texas. While she primarily writes romance, you can find her engrossed in almost any genre.

L.B. spends her spare time dreaming up stories in the Texas countryside where she lives with her family.

———

Stay up to date by following along at https://lbtheauthor.com or on social media (@lb_the_author).

 instagram.com/lb_the_author